A Dangerous Love 2
Can't Let Go

**Lock Down Publications
Presents
A Dangerous Love 2
Can't Let Go
A Novel by *J Peach***

A Dangerous Love 2
Can't Let Go

First Edition November 2014
Printed in the United States of America

This is a work of fiction. Names, characters, places, and incidents either are products of the author's imagination or are used fictitiously. Any similarity to actual events or locales or persons, living or dead, is entirely coincidental.

Lock Down Publications
Email: j.peach0509@hotmail.com
Facebook: JPeach JPeach
Cover design and layout by: Dynasty's Cover Me
Book interior design by: Shawn Walker
Edited by: Epic Kreationz

Acknowledgements

Da'Jah and Da'Vion, my babies, if it wasn't for you two, the drive to continue on this journey would be nonexistent! You two are my heart and soul, for that alone I push myself to be better every single day! I love y'all so so much!

My mommy, my best friend, thanks so much for your continuous support of my writing. I will always love and appreciate you for that!

Coffee, I truly appreciate you for being my ear whenever I needed to vent or had a question about something. For dealing with my whining self, although you'll never admit it I know I am! So thank you!

Cash, I know I can be irritating at times, thank you for putting up with me. Thank for being the mean, hard publisher you are. I swear if you were nice I won't get anything done, I promise I wouldn't! Lol so don't ever change.

To my readers, I FREAKIN' LOVE each and every one of you, I swear! You guys will never truly know or understand this feeling I have for you all! THANKS for the CONSTANT LOVE and SUPPORT you continue to show me. Thank You, Thank You, Thank You!

THANKS to EVERYONE that had anything to do with the PUBLICATION of my novel. I Truly APPRECIATE You All!!!

J Peach

A Dangerous Love 2
Can't Let Go

Chapter 1

Peaches

My heart dropped as the gun went off. I watched Blaze stumble
back as King's arm jerked. The scream that left my mouth
stopped short as it got caught in my throat from the loud bang.

"What the fuck is wrong with you niggas?" Mike finally
snapped as he pushed Blaze back then snatched King's piece,
which made it to go off.

Relieved my brother wasn't shot, a heavy breath left my
mouth as I quickly went to him. Just too be sure, I did a double
check of his body, not finding any major bleeding. I practically
tucked myself against him. No matter what we went through, at
the end of the day he was all I had.

"King, are you fuckin' serious, my nigga? You 'bout to
shoot yo boy?" The disapproving look on Mike's face seemed to
piss King off.

King snatched his Desert Eagle, then pushed Mike back.

"Fuck you mean? Yo ass just saw what the fuck he did,"
King went off. He pushed me behind him, ready to go for Blaze,
who didn't seem bothered at all.

Mike stepped in front of King and pushed him back
again.

"N'all, let 'em go. Come on, baby." Blaze taunted as he
spit blood from his mouth and then pulled up his jeans.

Mike turned toward Blaze, throwing him a harassing
glare.

"Nigga, chill the fuck out," he spat, then turned his
sights back on King but pointed toward me. "Yo ass ain't say
shit when she clocked that mothafucka over the head with that
strap. I would've choked her mothafuckin' ass too, same shit you
would've done. Fuck outda here with that stupid shit. Peaches
started that fuckin' fight, she could've handled that shit herself,"
Mike fussed, pissed off.

7

I hummed my agreement to his ending statement. If King hadn't kicked Blaze off me, I would have managed to get the taser I knew fell under the broken table and shocked the shit outda his black ass.

"Peaches, shut yo ass up," he snapped at me.

My brows rose at that, *this nigga got me fuck'd up!*

"Mike, who the fuck you think you're talkin' too?" I moved around King to step to him, but my brother grabbed me.

"Peaches, sit the fuck down somewhere. And I dare yo ass to say some shit smart." King eyed me hard, daring me to say something.

I didn't want to fight with him. My body ached from Blaze slamming me into that table. With a smack of my lips, I looked away from King.

"B, put yo hands on her again, my nigga." King harshly spat out.

"Baby girl can handle herself. She pull another gun on me, I'ma fuck her ass up. Boss that shit." Blaze stared directly at me as he talked.

I felt like being childish and talking shit, hell sticking up my middle finger. But the seriousness his voice held had me swallowing my smart remark. Plus, I knew King's ass was going to jump in it. Oh, but once he was gone, Blaze and I were going to have words with no interruptions.

"Look, now ain't the time for this bullshit," Mike emphasized as he pointed to Sly. "Twins should be here in a minute. King, Peaches need to go before they pull up," Mike insisted.

King gazed down at me with furrowed brows.

"Peaches, get yo shit and go, I'll call when you can come back." King informed me. The look he gave set confusion in my body.

"Who is Twins?" The slant to King's eyes had me raising my hands and moving away from him. "Fine, but just in case you stupid son of bitches forgot I do live in an apartment, somebody 'bout heard all this bullshit."

"Shut the fuck up and get out." King yelled, then pushed me toward the door. Not saying another word to him, I snatched my stuff up off the floor and walked out my apartment. Pissed, I purposely slammed the door, my chested rose and fell hard from my heavy breathing.

"Stupid bitch!" I fumed as I bounced down the stairs and out my building.

Once in my car, I started it and quickly pulled off.

***

Two-thirty rolled around I was still at the gun range. I had been there for hours and I still wasn't ready to go. I needed to be by myself. With the stress of the morning weighing heavily on me, Sly being shot, and me not knowing how he was doing, I was on edge. Then add King and Blaze's bullshit on top of that and my nerves were literally out of whack. So much so that my body jittered and my hands shook uncontrollably, which caused my mind to race.

I was wondering whether or not King would ever back off and let me breathe. I was trying to figure out what the fuck Blaze's problem was, even though his possessive ways were kind of sexy. As all that ran through my head, one question remained, *am I willing to throw away my wants to indulge what Blaze could bring?*

The fact that I was even thinking that pissed me off. To be with a hood... A sigh left my mouth and my head shook as I tried to rid myself of those thoughts.

I ejected the clip from my gun and laid it on the wooden stand. Then I grabbed the fifteen round magazine, slammed it inside the Glock, loaded the chamber, then squeezed the trigger. I didn't stopping until every bullet left the clip and it clacked empty. After the third pull, I sat the gun on the stand, then took the ear plugs from my ears as a sigh slipped through my lips.

"Peaches, you have ten minutes," the owner informed me.

"Alright," my head nodded in his direction and I noticed I was the only one still there. As I bent over to pick up the case for my Glock, my phone vibrated.

Jerron's name flashed across the screen. The relationship between me and Ron was complicated, had been since I was fourteen. I debated whether or not I should answer, but thought better of it. With my stress level being so high, just hearing Ron's voice would make me tell him everything that happened. He knew how King was, but to find out about Blaze would only cause problems. Hell, to find comfort in him alone wasn't what I needed.

It just made things easier to not think about him at all. The feelings Blaze brought, the only other person who could cause that giddy ache in the pit of my stomach was Ron, so talking to him would only complicate shit more.

My finger slid across the screen and I rejected his call, but sent him a message that said I was handling business and would call him once I got home. After I pocketed my phone and packed my stuff up, I left the range. Still feeling stressed and not wanting to deal with anyone, I went to mall with the hope that shopping would ease my tensed posture.

***

For the next three hours, I walked around the mall, going into different stores. I had six different bags filled with clothes I'd probably never wear. Even so, I felt a lot better with the binge shopping I'd done. Once I left Rue 21, I went to the T-Mobile stand and bought me another phone. After they put my sim card inside, I headed to the food court. My bags had just left my hands, butt barely touched the chair, and my phone was going off.

Kim's name flashed on the screen and I quickly answered.

"Hey babe, what's up?"

"Bitch, where you at?" Kimmy whispered into the phone.

My brows furrowed and I didn't reply back at first. *Why is she whispering?*

"Peach, King's here," she hurriedly whispered once more. So that's why she was whispering. After the altercation that morning, I had called all of my girls, filled them in on everything, and told them I didn't want to talk to King or Blaze.

My lips smacked in a frustrated matter. "Tell King's ass I'm grown, I don't need his worrisome ass to check up on me. Tell 'em I'm good and to keep his psychotic ass friend the fuck away from me," I snapped, about to hang up.

"Who the fuck you talkin' to, Peaches? I been calling yo ass all fuckin' day." King spoke loud and irritably into the line.

"Well, that's yo boy's fault. His crazy ass threw my phone against the wall and broke it. Look, I'm trying to find a hotel for the night, so I'll call you when I'm settled—" My lie was cut off as King started to talk again.

"Peaches, take yo ass home. I'll be there in a minute. I'ight?" He ordered.

A snort left my mouth, I was done letting King control my every move. "I'm not going home, probably ain't shit there to go to." The attitude in my voice could be heard.

He quickly detected it because a sigh left his mouth. "Look, man, I'm sorry for putting my hands on you. I was wrong, okay." King apologized. He sounded sincere, but I could never be sure with him. I didn't reply back at first. "I got you something," he announced.

I couldn't help the smile that came to my face. "What you get me?" I asked.

"Take ya ass home and see. I'm on my way there now," he laughed.

"Okay, here I come. Bye." Never, would I ever beg for anything or claim to be spoiled, but I would never decline a gift from my brother.

If he messed up, then it was only natural for him to do it. That's probably why he thought doing the shit he did was cool. Once he bought me something, we were right back on good terms. But not this time. Even so, I was taking what he got me.

***

King met me at the door once I walked into my building.

"Hey baby sis—"

"What you do want, King? If you lied about getting me something I'ma be pissed." Straight to the point, I wasn't about to play with him.

King gave me a slight glare as he stared down at me.

"Peaches, shut up, damn, ain't nobody lie to you. Now come on," he said, then snatched my hand into his and pulled me up the stairs to follow.

Once inside, I punched him in the back, making him laugh. We stopped in the entrance of my living room. He moved from in front of me.

I swear my face lite up.

"You got Mommy's table fixed?" After our mom and dad died, I couldn't stand to live in the house no more without them so I moved in with King and was staying with him until I turned eighteen and found my apartment. We kept our parents' place because we didn't have the heart to sell it or get rid of anything.

When I moved, I wanted something of my mom's. I remember she loved this table, apparently she'd found it at the same time my dad found her. Long story short, they both wanted the table, but my mother being a '*don't take shit*' type of woman, she got it and my dad's number. Crazy, but it was special to her, so I wanted it. There wasn't anything special about the table itself beside the story of how she got it. It was a simple mahogany cocktail table with a shelf.

"No, they couldn't fix it, but I got one just like it. I know it don't mean the same and I'm sorry but I also got—" He walked out of the room then returned a short while later with a white and light brown ball of fur. "Here…"

"King, you got me kitten? Seriously," I couldn't help but laugh. How was I gon' take care of a cat? But he was trying to make it up to me. "Thanks, King." I kissed his cheek before a loud squeak left my mouth.

"Damn, Peaches, shit! What the fuck you scream fah? Tryna bust a niggas eardrum," King snapped, covering his ears.

"You got me a TV—"

"I didn't get that, it was here when I got here this morning." My brows furrowed at that and shook my head.

"No, it wasn't." My eyes looked from the TV to King then back again. "That TV wasn't here."

"It was. How the fuck you ain't gon' notice that big ass sixty-five inch sitting there? I swear I wonder about yo ass sometimes." With the shake of his head, he flopped down on the couch before he placed his feet on my table.

"King, I love you, but if you don't get yo feet off my table I swear," his feet quickly came down. "Thank you. We need to get Cherry here some food." I laughed, handing the cat to King. "I'm going to shower, then I'll make us dinner." Before I left the living room I turned back to him. With only one question in mind. "Hey, King, how is Sly?"

"Don't ask questions. Gon'." He quickly dismissed the subject.

I hated the *don't ask questions* rule he had. It only made me want to know more. Even so, I never did.

***

"Peaches, somebody at the door!" King yelled from the living room fifteen minutes later. *I swear that's a lazy nigga, he sitting right there.* "Peaches!"

Hurriedly, I put my hair in a messy bun, then left out of my room.

"I'm coming." Upon entering the living room I noticed my clean carpet. "Why you couldn't answer the door?" As I bypassed him, my hand slapped hard against his head.

"Bitch!" King yelled after me.

"I'm coming, damn!" I called out. "Coming, coming..." Once the door opened, it slammed right back closed and I locked.

Chapter 2

Peaches

"King come get yo friend from my door. I don't want his disrespectful ass here." I walked into the living room, picked up Cherry, my little kitten, then sat on the love seat.

"You want me to fall back and let you be grown. I'm doing that, you got this," was King's nonchalant response.

I didn't get a chance to say nothing back because as soon as my butt hit the couch this mothafucka walks his ass in the room. *Didn't I lock that door?*" I know I locked that damn door—"

"I was being nice, but yo rude ass slammed it in my face so I used my key." This mothafucka had a key to my apartment.

My eyes snapped to King. Only to find his teeth had sunk into his bottom lip. *He thought this shit was funny?*

I sat Cherry down, that dude must have seriously thought he could straight hoe me. Not this one, he don't.

"Blaze, I'm not about to play these little childish ass games with you. Give me my key and leave. Like I don't do this at all and I'm not about to start now. This ain't King's spot nor does he sleep in this bitch or pay a bill. You *his* friend, so don't come over here no more, real talk. Like, I'm so fuckin' done being nice to you. I don't do crazy mothafuckas and yo ass is just that. A rude, crazy, disrespectful ass nigga. I don't deal with yo type, so you gotda go."

I walked past him and Sam, who had shown up with Blaze, then opened my front door with my hand held out, waiting for my key. "Sam, I ain't got a problem with you, we had our problems, but we let it go. King, come get yo friend before I put my hands on him. I don't want an altercation, but I'd get it in with this nigga. Come on, daddy, you got to go."

"I ain't got shit to do with it. Shid, throw yo knuckles on and handle that nigga," King boosted. "I don't get in grown folks shit no more." He pissed me off not taking it seriously.

"King, I'm fo'real right now. Blaze get yo ass out."

Blaze looked at me with amusement clearly in his eyes. He licked his lips—*damn that was sexy*—threw me my key and then walked into the living room. *This bitch.*

Before I could throw a punch, Sam pushed me into the hallway. He closed the door behind him. "Calm yo little violent ass down, man. He had intended to come and apologize for earlier. That man never apologizes and all he been talking about was how he fuck'd up with you and you turn around snap at him."

"The fuck you mean? He's fuckin' crazy and disrespectful. I'm not about to deal with that shit, Sam. You can stay if you want, but he gotda go." My chest rose and fell hard as my breathing picked up. My nerves once again on edge. I wanted to hit him.

"Man, just chill with that, let him apologize at least. He gave you your key, so cool it with all that rowdy shit," suggested Sam.

My eyes rolled and I pushed him back, or tried to anyway.

"Come on, Peaches. If he do anything I'll throw him out," Sam insisted, grabbing my arm.

I pulled away and my shoulder bumped against his arm hard as I walked pasted him into my apartment. "Whatever." With an attitude, I flopped down on the couch. Those two were being the new, irritating Mike and Leon.

"What's up?" Sam spoke to King with a fist bump.

Lifting off the couch, I snatched the remote from King. "You on your own tonight for dinner, I don't feel like cooking nothing," I told him as I put my feet on him.

"What the hell is that on your legs?" Sam asked with a laugh.

"My leg warmers, you like?" I asked, stretching my leg out with a shake which caused the colorful fur to move from one side to the other.

"Hell no, take that shit off."

"Fuck you, bitch!" I laughed at the meaningful look he gave me when the words 'fuck you' left my mouth.

Sam was simply a flirt who couldn't help himself.

"Thirsty? I got some tropical—" Without finishing my sentence, he was leaning against the couch laughing.

"When this happen?" King pointed between Sam and I.

"What?" I asked confused as to what he was referring to.

"Y'all mothafuckas laughing and joking, when that shit happen?"

With a shrug I continued to chuckle until I got myself together.

"That day... No, yesterday. Damn why does it seem like it's been longer? I'm see you too much," I said to Sam as I answered King's question.

"I don't like that shit—" King started, but I cut him off as I glared hard at him.

"Remember, you don't get in grown folks business. And to be honest, I don't care anymore, King. When I decide to start giving a fuck about your feelings when it comes to the dudes I kick it with, then I'd let you know. Until that happens, keep it to yo damn self and don't step to no nigga I chill with. Whether we fuckin' or not isn't your business. I'm done lying and hiding it from you. I'm tired of all this bullshit with you, okay." I wasn't going to have a repeat of last night.

"Whatever, Peaches, you grown," he spoke in that nonchalant tone.

I ignored him while looking at the TV. I tried my hardest to ignore Blaze, but my damn eyes just couldn't help but glance his way.

"Where you get this big ass TV from?" Sam asked.

"I don't know, King bought it." I answered Sam's question.

"No, I didn't. It was here when I got here earlier..." King trailed off as Blaze said something. "What?"

"I got it from Rock, he sold it to me. I called after little mama went to sleep, he took the TV we broke." Blaze replied.

"You bought me a TV?" Yes, I was shocked to say the least because I knew for a fact that the TV wasn't cheap. Hell, my forty-six inch cost almost eight hundred so a sixty-five inch was beyond that.

"I did break yours, right?" He shrugged. "Let me talk to you for a minute," Blaze said, already standing with his hand out for me to take. "Come on man, don't make me have to beg yo ass."

"That'll be some shit to actually see Blaze's ass begging." King laughed making me roll my eyes.

"Peaches, can I please talk to you for a minute?" Blaze asked.

"He's serious—" King started saying, but Blaze cut him.

"Shut the fuck up, King, damn," Blaze snapped at him, making King laugh before his gaze fell back on me. "Peaches, come on man. I promise I ain't on that bullshit right now."

I let out a sigh and stood. Blaze took my hand, then led me to my room. Once inside, he closed the door behind me and walked over to my bed and sat down.

"Look, Peaches, man, I usually don't act like this when it comes to females. It's yo ass, you different as fuck and I like that, real talk. I'm not the jealous type, especially not with a chick I just met, but I am with you. I don't like that shit, but that's something I can't help," Blaze admitted. His hand ran over his head and then down his face in a frustrated manner.

"I don't see why, we're not together or cool. Blaze, I can't be friends with drama and that's exactly what you bring. Shooting Sly was fuck'd up, he didn't do shit to you." I still couldn't believe he did that.

"That's his fault he got shot. I told his ass to stop fuckin' with you and he was tryna be slick," was Blaze's defense. To make matters worse, he was serious.

"What right do you have to make that decision? You don't! You have none at all to be telling someone to stop fucking with me! That's shit King does and I can't have two of him in my life. I said from jump if you were gonna be like this then it's

18

best you stay away from me," I explained seriously. I wasn't up for that extra back and forth thing he wanted to do

"I can't do that. I was serious about you getting to know me on some real shit. As for Sly, I'll leave his ass alone as long as you ain't fuckin' with him like you were," a low, devious laugh left his mouth before he shrugged.

My head shook, this was crazy. What right did he have to come into my life and make choices like that for me?

Not able to believe what he was saying, my arms uncrossed from my chest, "Do you hear what you're saying? Did anything I just say not reach that brain of yours?" I emphasized with a poke to his head.

"Keep yo fuckin' hands off me." Blaze snapped as he slapped my hand away from him. "Why the fuck you gotda make shit difficult, damn! I'm tryin' to be reasonable, but you don't want hear it." His voice rose, the seriousness thick with frustration.

"You're trying to be reasonable about who I can see and who I can't when you have no right to. Blaze, we're not dating. I'm not fucking you or anyone else for that matter. Just like I told King, I get head nothing more nothing less. It's fuck'd up I have to explain this to you when you not my dude or my friend. Hell, you ain't even one of my head buddies–." I felt as if I was really telling him off. Until he waved his hand in front of my face. My mouth snapped shut at the action.

"Yeah, you need to let them go too," he informed me.

With those words I turned away from him.

"Where you going?" He grabbed my forearm to stop me from leaving the room.

I threw my hands up and turned once more to walk away from him because he wasn't even listening. What part of he couldn't tell me what to do didn't Blaze understand?

Apparently none of it.

"Peaches, get yo black ass back over here," Blaze said, getting off the bed.

"Who the fuck do you think you're talking to? You know what? Come on, I'm sick of yo ass," I grunted out while locking the door. I went to my dresser, grabbing my purple brass knuckles and slipped them on.

"The fuck you doing? Gon', Peaches, ain't nobody bout to fight yo little ass," Blaze said with a laugh.

Oh, he thinks I'm playing? Without a second thought, I punched him in the jaw and kept punching until he pushed me into the dresser.

"The fuck wrong with you? Bitch, you done lost yo fucking mind!" He snapped as he wiped the blood from his mouth. Looking at his hand and then back to me, he spit on my floor.

I'm not gon' lie, the murderous look he gave kind of scared the fuck outda me, but he wasn't gon' keep talking to me like I was one of those scared ass hoes or niggas he dealt with.

"Oh, daddy, I got yo bitch!" With that, I jumped on him again, swinging quick and hard. I caught him with a right fist that smacked hard into his left cheek, then his right eye.

After that hit Blaze grabbed me by the throat then pushed me back hard, making me flip over as I fell to floor.

"You wanna play?" Blaze's face contorted into a hard glare. Once again he spat on the floor before he pulled off his shirt then yanked up his jeans.

Now, I was scared.

Chapter 3

Peaches

Blaze once again grabbed me by my neck. Effortlessly, he slung me across the room.

A loud grunt left my mouth as my back hit the wall hard and I fell to the floor.

"The fuck y'all doing in there?" King yelled from the other side of the door. "Peaches, unlock this damn door!"

With a heavy breath, I looked at the jiggling handle. King was trying hard to get in, it was only a matter of time before he started to kick the door.

"We're talking, now get the fuck away from my door!" I yelled at him.

I didn't even get a chance to hear what King said as Blaze pulled me up by hair. A surprise squeak left my mouth as he pinned me to the wall. I tried to kick him in the stomach, but he caught my leg and then grabbed my throat.

Blaze stared down at me hard as his hand tightened.

"Peaches, you can't whoop my ass, so calm the fuck down," he warned, his face fixed into a scowl.

Maybe not, but I damn sho' was gon' try.

Blaze's words only pissed me off more and my nails dug deep into his wrist before I brought my knee up, trying to hit him in his balls. When I missed, his hand went back then came forward. He slapped the fuck out of me. The loud whack rang out, the sting to my cheek caused me to freeze for a second.

Then I lost it!

"You fucking bitch!" I yelled with a punch to his head. "Punk ass coming over here like you run shit. Bitch, you don't know me!" My voice rose as I continued to swing on him.

Blaze pick me up. My back soon went crashing into the vanity. A loud gasp left my mouth and my head hit the wall before there was another sting to my cheek. This time the hit was harder and louder than the first.

21

"I'm tryin' not to hurt yo stupid ass!" My head smacked into Blaze's before I grabbed the handle to my hand mirror and slapped the back of it across his face. His head went to the side just as the back of his hand shot out. The hit connected to my jaw.

I went to hit him back, but he grabbed my arms. "Let me the fuck go!"

"Man, shut the fuck up before I knock the shit out yo ass!" His arms held tight as he lifted me off the vanity.

His ass had already slapped the shit out of me.

"Blaze, let me-eep!" A loud squeak left my mouth as he slammed me on the bed.

"Calm the fuck down, Peaches, before I hurt you fo'real," he snapped at me.

I opened my mouth and bit into his shoulder. "What the fuck!" He slapped me again.

Those damn slaps were fuckin' hurting like hell, but that last one had my struggle to get free slowed down.

"Blaze—" his mouth covered mine.

Even so, I was mumbling some very foul words with a ton of threats, *but his mouth stayed on mine.* That was until I bit into his bottom lip hard, making him pull away.

"Boss, I'ma slap the fuck out of you, bite me again. Now shut yo ass up," he threatened.

I stopped my movement and looked at him like he was crazy. *What the fuck has he been doing?* I wanted to ask him that so bad because he had already been slapping the hell outda me, but I chose not to, just in case he was serious about that slap.

Even so, that didn't stop my smart ass mouth. "Fuck you, Blaze! Get off of me," my wiggle started and I tried to throw him off.

He paid me no mind as he kissed me roughly. His left hand tightened around my wrists as his other took hold of my thigh, bringing it up to his waist.

Dammit!

Somewhere along my mumbling/cussing him out, I began to kiss him back.

What the fuck was I doing?

After what I saw him do to Sly, I didn't even like him. Even so, it still didn't change the fact I love the way he felt against me, his demanding attitude. Everything I didn't like, deep down I wanted.

He let my wrists go. I wrapped my arms around his neck. Blaze sat us up then grabbed the hem of my shirt, he pulled it up and I stopped him, shaking my head no.

"No, I can't do this with you."

"Look, we can go back and forward on this all day, but at the end I'ma win. I want you, that's what matters. So gon' let that attitude you got about me go. I'm not gon' stop until you give me a chance. I can't promise you a prefect nigga, because I'm not one nor am I a romantic mothafucka. I'm anything but that. Don't shoot me down so quickly, I don't do this bullshit. I fuck and keep going, but I don't want that with you. You're different from any chick I done met, I wanna fuck with you on some real shit. I get you don't want shit serious, but fuck with me and don't give me that 'you ain't feelin' me' bullshit, 'cause we both know that's a damn lie," he said.

How we go from fighting to this? I couldn't begin to explain. What he said ran through my mind. I didn't know about giving him a chance.

This nigga ain't wrapped to tight.

Even so, part of me liked him.

"You're right, I don't want a relationship, but I'm willing to try this friend thing again and see where it goes. If we do this, that little control thing you got going on has to stop. And you can't threaten my male friends, I keep those," was my bargain, apparently he didn't like that idea.

Blaze's hand waved in front of my face. "These little niggas you fuckin' with ain't gon' fly. You gotda let them mothafuckas go. The fuck you mean you keep those?" He fumed with a stare, as if he wanted to choke the hell out of me.

23

"Just like I said, you have yo hoes, bitches, baby mommas or whatnot. This isn't a relationship, we do as we please. There's a no jealousy, shooting rule which means you can't be or do the latter." I explained, serious about every word that left my mouth.

Blaze looked at me like I was stupid.

"Did you hear shit I just said? You ain't bout to have nobody touchin' my shit. You keep the niggas that eat yo pussy? Fuck that. Any nigga come around here gon' end up like Sly's ass. I promise that shit," Blaze threatened.

I knew Blaze was going to be more trouble than any nigga I'd come across. For the simple fact his take charge attitude, I liked a little too much.

"My shit, you meant. Last I checked, you are a man, meaning you don't have a pussy, so you can't claim something you ain't got. And if you want me to give you a chance then we doing it my way. You don't have to agree, regardless, in the end I won't lose sleep one way or another."

True I wasn't going to, but that month without seeing or talking to him, for some reason he did stay on my mind. And I was pretty sure he'd be on my mind even more now.

Though, he don't need to know that.

"I don't agree and I already made claim on yo pussy, so that shit you talkin' don't mean a gotdamn thang. We gon' do this yo way, but I'm saying bet no nigga touch or taste my shit, meaning yo pussy, or I'm shooting his ass point blank. Baby, I don't play by rules, nor am I to fond of games. I'm too old for that bullshit."

This man was unbelievable. With a shake of my head a sigh left my mouth as my right hand combed through my hair.

"This is stupid. Do what you want, Blaze, okay? I see shit with you gon' be stressful when it don't even have to be. But whatever, I got to start on dinner." Hell, I wasn't even going to cook, but just to get away from his ass, I would do so anyway.

Fixing my shirt, I got ready to get off the bed but he stopped me.

24

Blaze pushed me back down then climbed on top of me. He settled himself between my legs.

My arms pushed at his chest trying to get him off of me, but he wouldn't move.

"What, Blaze? Damn, you starting to irritate me now," I made known with a hard roll of my eyes and a loud, irritable breath that left my throat.

Not bothered with the obvious signs of my aggravation, he simply grabbed my arms, then brought them around his neck as well as my legs to his waist.

"Yo ass can't get jealous when we do this either, boss, you can't," he insisted. His eyes locked with mine, the neutral look they held, I didn't like. I couldn't explain why, but there was just something in those light brown orbs of his.

My shoulders moved up then down as I shrugged.

"I won't, I promise, but neither can you." For the oddest reason I had this heavy urge to caress his lower lip. *I wanted to kiss that full set of his.*

Blaze didn't say a word as he moved my right leg from his waist to dig in his pocket.

"Here," he said as he held out a box for me.

I covered my face and laughed. My head shook as a smile plastered on my mouth. "You are bipolar I swear, but thank you." I slowly took the dented Galaxy Note 3 box. I opened it and a bubbly laugh slipped through my lips at the purple case inside. "I love purple."

"No shit. Have you seen your car or your room?" Blaze acknowledged as he glanced around my bedroom before he looked back at me. "We gon' have to change the color in this bitch if I'ma be sleeping in here?"

"Nigga, fuck you! And who said you would stay nights over here?" Blaze laughed as he took the phone from my hands and set it on the nightstand.

"I said it, I'ma stay here," his hands motioned around my bed. "Don't try to play like you didn't love sleeping with me last night. Yo ass was all over my body, grinding and shit."

Blaze's hips rolled against my pelvis at the word grind, which caused a bubbly laugh to leave my throat.

"Get off of me with your lying ass!" I pushed at his shoulders once more as I continued to laugh.

"G, I ain't. You be grinding man, like straight up. I started to bust yo ass open last night. So you stay on yo side and I'll stay on mine."

"You don't have a side... Blaze, stop," I whined out while I made a grab for his wrist.

Blaze sat up, then grabbed the hem of my shorts and began to tug them down.

"Fo'real, I'm not playing with you." I grabbed his wrist to stop his movement.

"Baby girl, pretend all you want, but at end of the day you know I'm right. You liked sleeping with me, you like the way I talk to you, the way I handle you," his deep voice and hard but neutral stare caused my lower abdomen tighten.

"Blaze don't," I began to weakly protest while tightening my hold on his wrist.

Easily, he jerked from my grip, then pinned my arms about my head as his other hand fooled with his jeans.

"My touch, the way I feel," he trailed off saying as he pushed inside of me.

A loud gasp left my mouth before I bit into my lower lip hard to keep the scream imbedded in my throat.

"You ain't got to deny it, I feel the same way," he pushed further inside of me.

I yanked my wrist free, grabbed the back of his neck and pulled him down. My lips attached to his so I wouldn't scream out from the invasion as he reached my barrier, then pulled out, only to push right back in which caused me to scream into his mouth as I closed my eyes.

"What the hell y'all doing? Peaches, open this gotdamn door!" King yelled from the other side while pounding like a fucking maniac.

Damn, King! Shit!

"Get yo fuck ass away from the damn door!" Blaze yelled back, then looked down at me and laughed. "But you don't like me, right." He would have to ruin my lust induced state, but I couldn't even be mad.

"Fuck you, ya yellow bastard."

"I was just 'bout to," he replied with a cocky but crooked smirk.

My hands went to my face and I groaned out a laugh. "Ugh, get off of me." I pushed at his chest, signaling for him to move. Once he did, he pulled me up with him. I winced slightly, trying to ignore the slight pain to my core.

"I'm bullshittin'. Don't pretend with me though," Blaze insisted, as he took hold of my waist. He pulled me to his chest as his thumb and index finger stroked my chin before he tilted my head back.

I didn't like the *want* he had my body craving for. *Him*, I didn't want Blaze. "I don't even know you," I mumbled against his lips.

"That's gon' change. Now get yo ass dressed so you can make me something to eat." He moved away from me and started to fix his jeans. He tucked his still hard soldier in his pants, then zipped them up. "Why the fuck you still standing there fah? Put yo damn clothes on."

This nigga done lost his mind. *Make him something to eat? Who the hell he thought I was?*

"Who I look like? Yo momma? Nigga, if you hungry you better get one of yo hoes to cook for you, the fuck. On second thought, give me my money for cooking. That's fifteen dollas, nigga run it," my hand shot out as my thumb rubbed against the index and middle finger.

"Man, I just bought yo ass a phone and a TV. Fo'real though, you can't make a nigga nothing to eat, Peaches?" His lips contorted into a sexy little smile. Blaze traced his finger up my arm, then tried to grab me.

His tongue swiped over his full sets and the sight of his bottom lip going into his mouth caused my eyes to drop to the floor. Those small actions damn near had me. Blaze was just sexy for no reason and the little gestures had my insides tightening with jitters.

"Peaches?" He called, his thick pink tongue swiped over his mouth.

But the corners of his lips twitched, it revealed the cockiness he tried to cover up. *Bastard.*

"No, nigga, you brought those things because you broke mine. They were just replacements, so give me my fifteen dollars." Pulling up my shorts and then fixing my hair, I looked at him.

"I'ight, man, here. Yo ass sleepin' on the fuckin' couch tonight." The seriousness in his voice got me and I burst out laughing.

"Um, honey, this's my shit—" I started saying, but he cut me off.

"So, and this mines." Once the words left his mouth his hand came down hard on my ass.

Quickly, I turned to face him. "Slap my ass like that again, I'ma fuck you up. That hurt, stupid ass," I punched him in his shoulder then rubbed my booty. "Yo hand print probably on my ass now, damn. You play too much."

A hum left his mouth and his front soon pressed into my back with his arms going around my waist.

"I love a red ass, gon' pull those shorts down and let me see," Blaze mumbled against the side of my neck.

My teeth sank into my lower lip and I let out a shaky breath in order to calm my nerves. His attitude I shouldn't like at all, but for some reason it seemed to continue to make me laugh.

Instead of replying back, I removed his arms from my waist and chose to ignore him altogether. After I unlocked my room door, we walked out.

Chapter 4

Peaches

Blaze stopped at the hallway mirror to look at his face. "Man, I should beat yo ass for hitting me in my fuckin' eye. That shit still hurt. Little violent ass got my shit swollen," he hissed out.

I laughed and quickly left him and walked into the living room. King and Sam looked at me, I turned my head then hurriedly went in the kitchen.

"Peaches, what happened to yo face?" King asked as he walked up to me then grabbed my chin. "That nigga hit you. Fuck that!" King snapped. He shoved me into the counter, then turned to leave the kitchen.

"No! King, stop!" I jerked him back as hard as I could, then ran in front of him to block off the exit. "You told me to handle it and I did okay, stop! So don't, it's cool. I took care of it," my voice rose trying to get him to hear me.

King started to the door, his breathing picked up as his chest rose then fell hard. Finally he stared at me like I was stupid.

"The fuck you mean it's cool? This nigga put his hands on you, Peach. You think that shit cool? N'all, fuck that. Blaze!" He bellowed so loud, I jumped.

"King, don't start that shit, please. I hit him first," I whispered as the will to stand up to him started to leave my body.

"I don't give a fuck!" He screamed, then shoved me back to get me out his way.

"What the fuck you yelling fah?" Blaze asked, coming into the kitchen.

"Bitch, you hit—" King's words ran flat as he looked at Blaze then back to me.

I did the same, looked at Blaze. My lips pressed tight together and my hand covered my mouth so I wouldn't laugh.

"The fuck happened to yo face?" King referred to the dark mark under his right eye, busted lip, and the cut on the side of his head.

Damn! I fell into King as I burst into a fit of laughter.

"Oh, my God, Blaze!" I laughed loudly

"Yeah, I'm about to beat yo ass," Blazes' face formed into a glare as he started toward me.

Leaned all the way against King, I continued to laugh. *How come I didn't notice that in the room? Well, he did have me hella distracted. But I fuck'd him up.*

"Man, I was about to beat yo ass, but shid, Peaches done did that!" King said before he stepped to him. Without warning, King punched Blaze in the face. "I don't give a fuck who hit who first, don't put yo fuckin' hands on her."

"King, what the fuck!" I screamed at him. I pushed him back then went to Blaze. "Why the fuck would you hit him after I told you I started the shit, stupid ass!" I stood in front of Blaze, my eyes roamed all over his face trying to find any new mark. "Are you okay?" My actions didn't register until the arch in his brow formed.

"I'm good, didn't know you cared." Blaze cockily spoke.

My mouth opened, then close. My hands slowly left his face as embarrassment set itself into my body. With a rub of the nape of my neck I step away from him.

"Damn, fo'real Peach? You gon' yell at me because of this nigga?" King asked with a look of disappointment.

The look immediately pissed me off. "No, I yelled at you because you're always starting shit, you had no right to hit him," my thumb jerked in Blazes' direction, "after I told you I handled it! I'm not a fuckin' kid no more. I can take care of myself! Okay? So chill the fuck out." My voice lowered a bit at the hard look on his face.

"Fuck you talkin to? I'll beat yo ass," King snapped as he jumped at me.

Instinctively, I flinched back, but swung on him as an automatic reflex.

"King, gon' fo'real because I'm not scared of you," that was half true, a small part of me wasn't. "I know what I'm doing."

"Mhm, yo ass better, Peaches," King warned before he turned his stare on Blaze. "She fuck'd yo shit up. B, 'cause I know you I'ma step back, but don't be stupid with her." His eyes locked with Blazes'. "I put that on graves my nigga," the unspoken threat chilled my bones because I knew King was serious.

But the chill quickly left and I bit hard into my bottom lip as his words registered.

He was gon fall back...

King tore his eyes from Blaze to look at me. His head nodded toward the sink. "I took that chicken out. Hurry up and cook that shit, I'm hungry as hell." He gave me a push toward the sink with his final words.

My brother was bipolar as hell. I didn't put up and argument, though. Just simply smiled and went to the sink to clean the chicken. Hell, he was going to give me room to breathe. He was about to get a whole ass meal.

"Blaze, don't be stupid, and y'all ain't shit," King told him. I don't know why, but I think King knew Blaze wasn't going to leave me alone. And I guessed Blaze wasn't that bad of guy if he actually stepped back.

"She's already established my nigga, I know she better let them fuck boys know that shit. Sam that goes fah you too. I see you looking my nigga. Established, homie, don't be on no slick shit, that's why Sly's ass got shot," Blaze announced before he slapped hands with King six times, doing a complicated handshake as they both laughed.

"King, don't listen to him. We established a friendship is all, Blaze shut up. Damn, what we talk about?" I asked him as I started seasoning the wings.

"Man, we grown. Fuck that bullshit you talkin and fuck King. His ass know what's up. I told him you was mine before I even came to you. He talked his shit, made his threats, but shid, at the end of the day what we decide on is between us." Blaze spoke freely, in a nonchalant tone.

To my surprise King ain't say nothing and I had to bite my lip so I wouldn't smile at Blaze.

He was most definitely not afraid of King and made a point to get what he wanted. Let that have been any other dude, their asses would've run for the hills the moment King spoke. Blaze didn't though and I like that he had the balls to actually come after me with King knowing.

King whispered something to Blaze before he left out the kitchen. Whatever it may have been didn't move him one bit as he walked over to me.

"You need help?"

"Can you cook?" I replied as he walked up behind me.

He placed his hands on my hips and then brought his mouth to my ear. "Nope, just thought I should ask," he muttered, then bit my lobe.

A laugh slipped through my lips and I elbowed him.

"Didn't I tell you not to worry about him? You can say we have an understanding." Blaze kissed his way to the spot behind my ear as his hand went to my ass.

"Blaze, move. And just because you two are crazy, y'all understand each other? That's not something I'd be proud to tell people," I glanced at him over my shoulder, with a pointed look.

Blaze hit me on the ass hard.

"What I say about hitting my ass? That shit hurt. Get out, go in the living room with King and Sam. You can't cook so I don't need your help, but thanks for asking." His hand squeezed my booty. "Stop playing with my ass, damn. Go wash your hands, get out, I got this."

Blaze's hand suddenly tighten around my ponytail and he jerked my head back, causing an audible gasp to escape from my throat. He gazed down on me.

My body reacted to his slight aggressive action, which caused my chest to rise then fell as my breathing picked up

"This the second time we done got interrupted, next time we gon' finish what we start," he whispered against my lips.

My eyes dropped to his mouth as mine parted. I stood on my tip toes and bit his bottom lip, my teeth sank into the skin. Slowly, my head moved back, in the same motions I released his lip before allowing my tongue to flick over it.

My eyes went back to his and I smiled, "Mm, we'll finish when I say we will. Now get out before yo ass don't eat," I whispered. With a simple peck to his lips, I pushed him back, "Gon' now."

Blaze rubbed his bottom lip as he nodded his head. He then muffed me, making my head go to the side before he slapped my ass.

"You bitch, that shit hurt!" I snapped at him as he walked out the kitchen laughing. "Dumbass," I mumbled and continued to make dinner.

***

We all sat around the kitchen table, just finished with our dinner. Chicken, macaroni, spaghetti and cornbread is what I made. I was stuffed to the point that I had my shirt raised over my stomach and was sucking my teeth, leaning back in my chair unable to move.

"Man, that was good as hell. A nigga done got sleepy," Sam said, leaning back as well.

"I got a guestroom if King's not using it, and a couch," I glanced at King who shook his head.

"N'all, I got a few runs to make, then I'm going to Ebony's," King stated while he ran his hand over his head.

33

"She probably sleep by now," I grabbed our plates then sat them in the sink.

"So, I got a key. Thanks for the meal sis, but I got to go." King stood, came to me, kissed my forehead, then straightened up. "And Sam ass ain't sleeping over here either," King gave Sam a look then looked back to mc. "I'm out," he started to leave the kitchen until I stopped him.

"Nuh uh, nigga, give me my money for making yo ass dinner." My fingers rubbed together before I held my palm out.

"You always got yo hand out, yo ass ain't charge Blaze," he shot back childishly.

What the fuck? King's ass is just stupid. He's my blood and I'm charging him, why the hell wouldn't I charge Blaze?

"She got me in the room for twenty dollas," Blaze lied.

With a frustrated growl, King dug in his pocket then slapped twenty dollars in my hands.

"Thanks bubba. Have fun, be safe King!" After I took King's money, I got Sam's, then put it in my jar on top of the fridge.

"We should be going too, I got a job I need to be at in the morning and you gotda do that thing," Sam discreetly reminded Blaze of something as he stood up.

"Damn, I forgot all about that shit, Fuck! Here, go start the truck, I'll be out in a minute," Blaze tossed Sam the keys, but stayed seated.

"I'ight. Later, Peaches. I'll be here in the morning for breakfast," Sam called over his shoulders.

I waved at him as I sat on the counter drinking some water. Once King and Sam left, Blaze walked over to me. He placed his hands on either side of me on the counter.

"I'll be back in about two hours, i'ight?"

"I'll be sleep." If he thought I was going to wait up for him, then he lost his mind.

"I got my key," he nonchalantly stated.

34

My brows furrowed at that and I started to feel my breast, checking for the key he threw me. Blaze must have caught onto what I was doing and started to explain.

"Oh, that was Sly's key I gave you, I got one made when I got your phone," he said as if it wasn't a problem.

"Blaze, you can't do that." How could he think getting a key made to my apartment was okay? My mouth opened to start fussing, but he cut my words short.

"Shut the fuck up, I ain't tryna hear that shit. I'll be back in two hours." With that said, he pressed his lips to mine once, then turned and walked out without another word.

I don't know how this thing between us gon' work...

***

The dip of my bed had me awakening and quickly reaching under my matters.

"Chill, man, it's me," Blaze announced as he took hold of my arm.

"Boy, I could've shot you! What time is?" A yawn left my mouth as I sat up in the bed.

"Almost four," Blaze said while he peeled off his clothes.

I stared at his back in disbelief. "Why you come here at four in the morning? You should've went home," I spoke slowly, not understanding why he thought to come to my house at that time.

Once he took off all his clothes, he glanced at me before he ran a hand over his head, then down his face.

"Peaches, don't start that shit. It's too early and I'm tired as hell." As if to end the conversation, Blaze pulled the covers back then got in the bed.

"If you didn't want to hear it you should've went home." Truth, he should have. I didn't know what would make him think it was cool to waltz in my house like it would be okay.

35

"Peaches, fo'real man, shut the fuck up," Blaze said with an attitude as he grabbed the hem of my shirt and took it off. "Don't say shit, man, go to sleep." He pulled me on top of him.

"Blaze, let me go." That was not cool at all.

A laugh left my mouth as he grabbed the nape of my neck then kissed my lips. He shut me up, indeed he did. But a fruity scent on him had me not getting into the kiss like I would have. My head moved back and I gave him a funky look before I climbed off him.

Without a word, I got back on my side of the bed, not saying anything. Neither did Blaze as he pulled my back into his chest.

I know I didn't have a right to be mad for the simple fact he wasn't my man, but *let me find out he was with a bitch before he brought his ass back over here to get in my fucking bed.*

Shit gon get ugly real fast.

Why the fuck was I jealous?

Chapter 5

Blaze

"Peaches, so you ain't talkin' to me now?" I caught her arms as she went to walk out the room. But just like the past hour, she said nothing, simply pulled from my grasp and walked out the room.

I didn't know what her problem was or what I did, but shid, she had just been acting funky toward me all morning. I wasn't the type of nigga to bitch and moan over shit, but that was fucking with me bad. I mean, I ain't did shit to her. I tried hugging up with her and she just got off of me. I was tempted to slap the shit outda her. If I wasn't tired as fuck, I probably would've.

Once I left her crib, I stayed at my little spot in Marshall Town with two of my young workers, Mac and Pooh, all fucking night counting money while they cut up and bagged my weed and cocaine. After we finished, they called some hoes over and I closed shop. Niggas be getting stupid so I had to check their asses.

They didn't know those hoes from shit to piss and they invited them in my spot, fuck that. After putting all they asses out, I packed up my money to take it to my lot.

Once everybody left, I locked up and that's when that Trina hoe came at me. Bitch might've smelled good, but she ain't make my dick jump from all the rubbing that bitch was doing. I had to slap the fuck out that hoe once she put her fucking lips on me. I probably would've beat her ass if Mac had not grabbed me. My mom's said not to hit a woman, but she ain't say shit about hoes.

A heavy breathe left my mouth as my hand ran over my head then down my face. The sudden slam of the door made me laugh, it was no winning with that babe, shorty was crazy as hell.

I snatched my keys off the nightstand before I left out her room, then headed straight out the front door.

***

Peaches

"That nigga had the nerve to climb his ol' triflin ass in bed, though. Straight smelling like a bitch. Y'all, I was so fuckin' pissed." I vented to my girls through the phone.

"So wait, let me get this straight. You gave that man a key to your apartment?" Ebony chimed in, the shock evident in her tone.

As I drove my head shook, even though they couldn't see me. "Hell no, his crazy ass took Sly's key and got one made."

"Peach, you cut the fuck up didn't you? I already know yo ass did. You put his ass out at four in the morning?" Angel laughed with her question.

I felt kinda embarrassed about telling them the truth, but those were my bitches, I never kept anything from them. "Eh," my words didn't come out as they got caught in my throat.

"No this bitch didn't just say 'eh'. Am I hearing something or this bitch done got stuck?" Missy blurted into the line.

"Mhm," chorused the girls. "Peach, you let him stay!" Kim questioned loudly.

A sigh left my mouth followed by a groan. "Yeah I did—"

"Oh, hell n'all, Peach! What the fuck is wrong with you?" Ebony shouted.

I felt so damn stupid for letting him. "E, I don't know!" I whined out. Once I stopped at a red light, my forehead hit the steering wheel. "I don't know." God, I felt so stupid.

"So what the hell did you do? I know you knocked that nigga upside the head or something?" Angel pushed for more information.

"Ang, damn," I snapped at her. Hated that she was only being herself right now.

I could hear her smacking her lips. "Bitch, don't *Ang* me. And answer the question."

"Don't tell me you fuck'd him!" Missy boomed through the line.

"No! What the hell?" I shouted into the line as I pulled into the parking lot of my job. "Y'all, I'm at work. I'll call y'all once I get off—." I tried to end the call, but my attempt was quickly cut off.

"No the fuck you don't. Bitch, you better answer the question before we be at your fuckin' job," Ebony added.

"Y'all, leave her alone. If she don't wanna talk about it, she don't have to," Kim came to my defense.

"Kim, shut the fuck up. Bitch, you know yo ass wanna know too. So miss me with that." I could just picture Angel's eyes rolling into her head as she said that.

"If she don't wanna tell y'all ol' nosey asses, then she don't fuckin' have to. Worry about who y'all fuckin'," Kim retaliated, hostility coming off thick in her tone.

"Whatever, Kim," Angel muttered.

"Fo'real, y'all asses need to chill. And we didn't fuck, I didn't do or say anything to Blaze yet. I simply rolled off him and went to sleep. Got up this morning, made us breakfast, then left my place and called y'all," I revealed as I leaned back in my seat.

The line grew quiet, neither of my girls said anything. They were probably just as surprised as me that I hadn't reacted to Blaze.

"You just let him sleep in your bed knowing he was with some bitch?" Angel asked slowly.

"Yep, pretty much," my head nodded as I replied.

"What the fuck is wrong with you?" Angel immediately snapped once again. "That's some dumb shit these bitches do, not you, Peaches?"

My eyes grew wide at her insult. Though it was true, she didn't have to say it. Angel was a no lying, no sugar coating mothafucka. She told it how it was regardless of your feelings, which is why we clicked. She said the shit no one else would, she told you what you didn't want to hear. *The truth.*

"Angel, shut the fuck up!" Pissed, Ebony snapped at her.

"No, you shut the fuck up, E. Peaches, that was dumb, you should've at least clocked that nigga with one of yo guns or tased his black ass. I thought you was gon be the smart one, but you just as dumb as these bitches," Ang continued to go off.

"Angel, shut up fo'real. I do plan on saying something to him. But, man, that mothafucka slap hard as shit and I did not feel like getting slapped again," I admitted. If it wasn't for our little fight earlier that night, I probably would've started some shit. But my damn cheek still hurt from those fuckin' smacks.

"Wait, he slapped you?" Again they chorused loudly.

"Yes, I had to fight his big ass. Let me tell y'all…" After I ran everything that happened between me and Blaze down to them, Missy was the first to break out laughing.

"I swear, only you would do that. Who in the hell locks themselves in a room with a nigga to fight them and make up with him? Are y'all dating?" Missy asked.

"No we not—"

"Peach, what's the point for all the back and forth?" She questioned.

"Miss, I don't know. He won't leave me alone. Though I hate to admit it, I kind of like it because he's not afraid of King. It's complicated," I explained. Whatever it was with Blaze was most definitely complicated as hell.

The girls and I stayed on the phone for another ten to fifteen minutes, going back and forth about Blaze and what they thought I should've done. I was simply going to tell him how foul the shit was and what happened from there just would.

Chapter 6

Blaze

For the next hour I drove through the Bronx, just to see how shit was going. All the while I hoped to run into Joe-Boy or at least someone to point me in his direction.

As I rounded the corner, I spotted this little dude from around the way who was posted up in front of a gas station.

"Yo!" I called out, rollin' up on him.

Once he saw who I was, he walked up to the truck. When I got out we shook up.

"What's up, my dude?" John asked.

My hand ran over my head and I lick my lips as I looked around.

"Shit, working." I grabbed a cigarette from my pocket, then lit it.

John was a young nigga, no more than fifteen. A poster boy was what I liked to call niggas like him because they'd post anywhere just to catch fiends and make a few bucks.

"Working? Then what the fuck you doing out here? Don't yo ass got dealership to run or some shit?" He mimicked me and pulled a square from his pocket, leaned against the side of the store, then lit it.

"That's what I got employees and a manager for, to run shit while I ain't there." I took a long pull from the cigarette, inhaled then glanced down at him. I exhaled the smoke and looked around once more.

"Why you looking round for?" Little John asked me.

"You seen that nigga Joe around?"

John let out a breath before he shook his head. "I knew yo ass was on this side for a reason. What he do to you?" The serious look on his face had me laughing out the smoke I just inhaled.

"It ain't like that. I got a pool hall and a garage on this side of town. I'm just coming to check up on my businesses,

41

seeing as a nigga fresh out. And I heard Joe Boy been holding shit up since I been gone, just wanna show my appreciation is all." Was my explanation.

John shook his head, flicked his cigarette, then pushed his hands in his pockets.

"I heard—" he was cut off when my phone rang.

"Hold that thought," I held up my finger as I answered my phone. "Yo?"

When I saw Mac name flash on the screen I knew it had to be some shit because he knew not to call me. Mac was one of my main street workers. He was hot tempered, but loyal, and kept his ear to the ground. "You talked to Jesse?" Mac asked, making my brows raise.

"N'all, I haven't. Why, what's up?"

"She just called me saying that shit you dropped off to her last night, Joe came in after you left and got it?" Mac explained.

Jesse wasn't a person, but a house. My spot where I had a couple niggas that bag, cut, and sometimes cook cocaine. Joe Boy was one of those niggas that bagged for me, but when I got locked up for those two years for killin' Blue, Joe got beside himself. Nigga started taking my shit to sell for himself. He hit a couple of my spots, but you would've thought after that shit with Blue, niggas would know not to cross me. King wanted to take care of it while I was on lock, but I told him let 'em be for now.

I don't know what the fuck is wrong with Joe's ass.

"The fuck you mean he got it?" I asked in a calm voice, but on the inside I was boiling.

"Yeah, Jesse said him and about two other niggas came in, raided her fridge and cabinets. You know she over there having a fuckin' fit right now." Mac played cool and laughed it off.

"Damn, they took her shit?" The calmness in my voice was slipping when he said *all her shit,* meaning the eight pounds of cocaine and ten pounds of weed I'd just dropped off. "Yo, you know where that nigga Joe Boy staying?" I asked John while walking back to my truck.

"He's prolly on Carolina, if he ain't there, he's at that new spot with Rob and Doe," John quickly replied while following behind me.

With a nod of my head, I hopped in the truck then started it up.

I rolled down the passenger window, signaled for John to get in "Come show me where it's at." Once he got in I put the phone to my ear. "Yo, go check on Jesse and make sure she's straight, we'll meet up later."

"I'ight." With that we hang up as I took off down the street. As I drove, I pulled my burner phone out and shot Sam a quick message. I knew I could trust Sam, shid, we been slanging since we were thirteen, out posted on a corner with rocks, serving fiends. So there wasn't a doubt in my mind about him. There were only three people I trusted in the world and that was my moms, Sam, and King.

King was at the same place as Sam. We got up with King a year or so later and his old G showed us the ropes on how to be in this game and be smart.

Hell, if it wasn't for his ass, neither Sam nor I would've finished high school or went to college for that matter. Like he said, just because you came from the hood didn't mean you had to be stupid. You had to have a cover for slanging. Which is why I owned two car garages, three pool halls and car lot. I wasn't a nine to five type of nigga, I'd pop off in a minute. It was best I had my own so I wouldn't have to work for no one.

I went to school for Law, got a Master's degree in Criminal Justice. I had to know the law, couldn't be in that business and not know it.

"Turn right up here on Carolina. It's the blue house on the left," John directed.

I parked at the corner, reached in my pocket and threw him a few bills.

"This's his spot, no kids, right?" My head nodded toward the blue house with two cars parked in front.

"N'all, don't no kids be in there. Just him and these new niggas he roll with," John told me.

My head nodded, then I pointed toward the door. "Thanks, now get out."

"You don't need help or back up?" The seriousness in his voice caused my brows to raise before I laughed, shaking my head.

This nigga is what? Fifteen? The fuck I look like bringing a kid for back up? In fact...

"Don't yo ass supposed to be in school or some shit?" I asked, kind of fuck'd up about this little nigga, I mean, even though I was slanging way before him, I still went to school first then came to these streets. "Look, don't answer that, let me give yo little ass some advice. Whether you take it or not is up to you. You wanna slang?"

"I am slanging," he replied and even puffed up a bit.

I had to laugh at that, *these kids nowadays think cause they making two maybe three hundred dollars a week they slanging.*

"Get the fuck outda here. Yo ass ain't slanging, you holding for some other nigga, making his ass money. Nigga, you wanna be in this fo'real, finish high school, learn the drug game, the rules, territories. Learn the law, my nigga. Yo ass can't be posted up at no gas station wall waiting for a tweaker to come at you when half those mothafuckas be cops any fuckin' way.

"Get yoself a little crew of two niggas, save yo pennies and buy yo own shit by the pound. Then have yo little crew cut it, bag it, then sell it. Learn to cook yo own shit, if yo ass don't know how to cook then this life ain't fah you. If yo ass scared to drop a nigga on sight, no matter who's around, then you ain't about this life at all. Go get yoself a job and make legal money, pretending to be about this will have yo ass in a body bag within a month to a year. This shit is gruesome," I told his little ass truthfully.

Being a drug dealer, wasn't shit pretty. You couldn't be sensitive in that shit, nor could you be dumb slanging. You had to learn yo shit before you jumped into the devils ring to play with fire.

"I ain't got a choice, its fast money and I need it to look after my mom and my sister. I'm all we got."

I looked at him and nodded my head in understanding. I knew I liked little dude for a reason. Even though he didn't want to slang, he had to, he had priorities and was willing to do what need be for family. That's how I got sucked into the life. "Do you wanna slang?"

"I ain't got shit else," he answered with a shrug.

"Nigga, answer the fucking question straight up. Do you wanna slang?" I snapped at his little ass.

John let out sigh. "No, not really. But what else I got."

Reaching in my arm rest, I grabbed a business card.

"Taking this card means you in, you got one time to fuck me over and I'ma kill you my damn self. Ask for Tameka, tell her Blaze sent you. She'll set everything up. I don't like lazy ass workers and I hope you good with your hands. The sooner you call, the quicker yo ass can get to work. After school hours only. I'm giving you a job at my garage, its legal and I pay well. John, if you take this job you got to leave this life alone and finish school." The only reason I was looking out fah little dude was because I'd been where he was at that moment.

I remember right before I got locked up, he approached me when he was younger, tryna buy some weed to sell. Even though I didn't give his ass shit, the fact that he asked fuck'd me up.

"I will, promise. Thanks, man. My momma gon' flip," he said, snatching the card from my hand and dialing the number.

This mothafucka wasn't about to make that call right then. "Nigga, get the fuck out and do that shit, I got business to take care of. Tell Tameka to call me later."

"Thanks, man."

With a head nod, we bumped fists then he got out the truck. I waited until he rounded the corner before I pulled up at the blue house and blocked the driveway. Opening the glove compartment, I pulled on a pair of latex gloves then some black leather ones. I grabbed my SP2022 with the silencer. Taking the safety off, I got out the truck.

Once I got to the front door, I knocked. As soon as the door opened, I shot dude in the head, his ass dropped and I stepped over his dead body then walked into the house, closing the door behind me.

"Doe, who at the door?" Somebody yelled from the back.

I ain't say nothing as I walked through the living room. Those were some dirty mothafuckas and the place stunk. I ain't know if it was supposed to be the niggas trap or just an abandoned house. "Doe? Oh shit!" Dude called when he came from the back room and saw me. Before he could run, I smacked his ass in the mouth with my gun.

"You know who I am, huh?" Of course he did, otherwise the dummy wouldn't have said 'oh shit'.

"Man, I didn't know it was yo shit or yo spot. I didn't—"

"Fuck that, where's my shit and Joe Boy ass at?" Dude was straight shaking and he was lying. I didn't like fuck ass niggas like him.

"In the floorboard in the back room. I swear I didn't know that was your spot—" His ass wasn't meant for the life, look how quick that nigga was to run his mouth.

"Where, Joe Boy?"

"Upstairs with some hoe. Man I swear—"

"Go get my shit, if you try to run I'ma find you and burn yo ass alive. Boss I am, understand." Dude head was bobbing up and down in a fast motion, shit was comical. But those niggas stole from me, that was automatic death.

I let him go and he ran to the back as I walked up the stairs, going to the room I heard moaning coming from.

Like I did to the front door, I knocked.

"Get the fuck away from the door!" Joe yelled from the other side.

Pissed, I kicked in the door. Joe Boy and the bitch he was with jumped. The chick wiped her mouth, stood, then smiled at me.

"You wanna join?" I hated hoes. I was about to shoot the bitch until I realized she was pregnant.

"Hoe, get the fuck out of here before I stomp yo stupid ass." I wasn't gon' touch her, I mean if she wasn't pregnant I would've killed her, but I wasn't killing no pregnant woman, hoe or not. While the hoe was getting her shit, I shot Joe Boy in the shoulder, making the chick scream. "Bitch, don't even think about it," I told 'em as he made a move for his gun on the nightstand. "The fuck is wrong with you screaming like you stupid?"

Bitch screaming like she ain't got no damn sense. "Bitch, shut the fuck up before I shoot yo dumbass. Get the fuck out." With a tight grip on the back of her neck, I threw her out the room. My gun still on Joe, "Why you gon steal from me? You knew I was gon' come fah yo ass?"

His eyes were wild and wide as he looked around the room nervously. *This mothafucka is high as hell.*

"Blaze, man, it ain't even like that. My momma sick," was the lie he choose to tell me.

"Yo moms' dead, nigga. I helped you bury that bitch. I been knowing yo ass for eight years, baby, you gotda come better than that? Why the fuck you wanna steal from me, nigga? When yo ass didn't have shit, I put yo ass on—"

"I— Blaze, man— I—" The nigga stumbled a minute to long before I emptied my clip into his ass. Niggas nowadays ain't know shit about loyalty, everything was about money. *Greedy mothafuckas.* With a shake of my head I walked back down the stairs.

"Yo?" I called out and dude came from the back with my work. "That's all my shit?"

"Yeah, it's all there."

Nodding, I tucked my empty SP2022 in my pants before I grabbed my 9mm and put three bullets in his face. Picking up the bags, I opened the door and walked out. I tossed the bags in the trunk and hopped in my truck. Once I pulled out, I called Sam.

"What's up?" Sam answered.

"Where you at?" I asked him.

"Just leaving County," he responded.

"Aye, I'm on my way to momma's. Her ass been calling all fuckin' morning, so I'm headed there now. But I just left the store, so tell Jesse to calm her ass down," I told 'em, it wasn't a lie. I'd seen my moms once since I got out, so I was just gon' go chill over there with her for a few hours.

"You got everything?" His tone turned serious.

"Yeah, I'ma assume I do. Shid, if not, I ain't going back." I couldn't go back to get shit since I done killed those mothafuckas. "Come by momma's and get that shit before Jesse be calling me."

"Alright, I'll be there. Aye, you get some orange juice?" He asked.

I looked at my phone and laughed. "The fuck I look like nigga? Y'all ass better drink some damn water, get the fuck off my phone." We always spoke in code, never knowing who was listening. I didn't give a fuck if our phones were tapped or not, it never hurt to be safe.

"Fuck you then, I'll get my own shit," Sam joked.

"Please do. But aye, I'm just pulling up, I'll get with you later."

"Alright." We hung as I parked in the driveway. Getting out the truck, I made my way to the door.

Chapter 7

Blaze

"Ma, where you at?" I yelled once inside the house. Closing and locking the door behind me, I kicked off my shoes.

"Boy, stop yelling… Oh, my— What the hell happened to yo face? Who done put their gotdamn hands on my baby?" My moms dramatic ass grabbed my face. She moved it from one side to the other, pissed.

"Ma, chill. Damn," I kissed her cheek then moved around her.

"Don't tell me to chill. I've seen yo ass once since you been out and you didn't look like this. What happened? You haven't come home with marks on you since the fifth grade," she fussed, following behind me.

We walked in the living room and sat down on the couch.

"Booney, I got you into boxing for a reason and you done let some nigga fuck you up?" She continued her bickering.

I groaned at the nickname she'd been calling me since I was younger.

"Now you know ain't no nigga did this. Remember ol' girl I was telling you about?"

"A bitch did this? Oh, take me to her, I'm 'bout to kick this bitch ass, fucking up my Boon's face. Did you at lease slap her ass? I'm against you hitting women, but that bitch deserved to be slapped." She went off pacing the floor.

"Ma, fah real?"

"Yeah, for real. Did you slap the bitch?" She stopped in front of me, biting hard on her bottom lip. *Moms was pissed.*

"Yeah, I slapped her and her crazy ass slapped me back with a mirror."

My momma laughed at that, actually fell back laughing.

"Booney, you let some girl beat you up?" She asked, hitting the pillow. Wasn't shit funny. Peaches ass hit hard as hell, my damn jaw and eye were still hurting.

"Shit ain't funny."

"I'm sorry, baby. You right, it's not funny. But Booney, your right eye is black, your left cheek is swollen and your lip is busted. She must be a big, cocky, manly bitch, huh?" My moms questioned.

And for the first time in my life I was embarrassed as hell to even tell her how Peaches looked, because truth be told Peaches wasn't big as shit. She was about the same size and height as my sixteen year old sister.

"Booney, if she's built like a man I give you permission to go beat her ass, right now."

Getting up, I walked in the kitchen to get a drink of water.

"What you cooking?" I asked instead, trying to avoid talking about Peaches. My eyes soon landed on the lasagna and I started picking in it with the spoon that sat right beside it. I started eating out the pan while thinking about how I'd gotten out the conversation. Then again, knowing my moms, she wasn't gon' let that shit go.

"Get out of my dinner, I got breakfast in the microwave. Booney, tell me what happened." Her tone serious as she grabbed my face again.

I waved my hand trying to shut her up. "Ma, let it go. Where Britt at? She called me last night talking about—" I was in the middle of talking when she wacked my ass with a metal spatula on my back. "What the hell you hit me fah?"

"You let some nigga beat yo ass—"

"Blaze!" My little sister yelled as the front door slammed shut. A few seconds later, Britt walked in the kitchen. She stopped in her tracks. "Damn, what happened to you?"

It wasn't even that bad for they ass to react like that.

"Some dude beat his ass—" My mom stated with an attitude.

"Peaches ain't no man," I defended, but let it be my moms to take shit up a notch.

"Peaches sound like a transsexual. Who in the hell name their child Peaches? That's some ghetto shit." Moms ass was really going.

Britt started laughing as I shook my head.

"I might need my Taser fah that bitch if she whooped yo ass like this." They laughed, I didn't find shit funny.

"Man, she had on brass knuckles and I don't hit women. Well, I slapped her ass twice," I lied.

"That's all you got was two hits, Booney? She's built like a man, had on brass knuckles, and she slapped yo ass with a mirror. Baby, that's call for an ass whooping." She laughed, but Britt stopped as she started snapping her fingers.

"Ooh, ooh, Peaches? Peaches, light brown skin, a little shorter than me, long, pretty, sandy colored hair, and got deep dimples. My size kinda, beside her ass. Drives a shiny lavender two door car?"

My brows raised at my sister as she described Peaches to a T. *What the fuck?*

"Yeah," I said dumbly. "How you know—"

"Mommy, Peaches!" Britt laughed as my momma got a thoughtful look. "Mommy, Peaches from the center. The MA that works with Dr. Sanchez. He right on the other side of Dr. Karen," Britt explained.

"Oh My God..." my mom trailed off before she looked at me and then fell out laughing. "Booney! You let that little ass girl beat yo ass? What did you do to her? She's so sweet," she asked between laughter.

"Sweet my ass, that chick crazy. Man, her ass shot up my damn truck, then gon' lie like the center ain't got cameras. Plus, Sam told me she did. Ma, that babe crazy as hell, but I'ma marry her ass though," I finished saying, laughing as I thought about Peaches' mean ass.

"You talking marriage? How long have you known this girl?" The seriousness in her voice had me wishing I hadn't said shit about marriage.

"We met the day I got out. So about a month ago if you can really call it that." Even though I'd known her for a month, I only saw her a few times since then.

"And you're talking about marriage? Booney, what the hell is wrong with you? Is she thinking the same?" Moms asked as she moved closer to me.

Leaning against the counter, I ran a hand over my face. "Hell n'all, Peaches don't even wanna date me. She talking 'bout we can be friends. I don't know what to do about her ass, Ma. She got up this morning mad, ain't say shit to me. Made breakfast and left just ignored my ass, but I like her. She's different then these gold digging ass hoes man, fo'real. She got her own and smart as hell, you know.

I told you about the first night we met, she held a knife to my shit and shot Sam in the ear. Man, I don't know what to do about her, I mean she beat my ass and beside slapping and tossing her little, itty bitty ass into the dresser, I ain't do shit but kiss her. I don't know, Ma," I let out a heavy sigh and rubbed my neck.

Man, that shit was stressful. I had never been fuck'd up about a female before. I was wishing I would've followed my first mind and just stayed at the crib the night I got out. If I had, I wouldn't have run into Peaches crazy ass and shit wouldn't have been fuck'd up.

"Aw, Booney, you're in love—"

"Fuck you talkin bout? Stop hitting me, that damn thing hot," I said as my momma hit me with that damn spatula.

"Watch yo mouth. I'm your mother, not your homie, so don't be cussing at me like you do them. Now back to you and this girl. Maybe she's seeing someone else. Have you thought about that?" She put her lasagna in the oven then looked at me.

"Peaches not seeing anybody. Don't get me wrong, she likes me, but—"

"She just don't wanna date you. Well, maybe she likes being single. Plus, I agree with her, y'all should start off as friends and see where it goes. Boon, you can't force the girl to date you, just be sweet like...like... Damn, I cannot think of one time you have ever been sweet to a girl, hell, dated a girl. Booney, you do like girls right?" She tried to hold a serious face but ended up laughing

"On what you just tried to play me? How many times have you walked in one me and chick?" I asked her honestly.

"Sexing a girl and actually dating one is different, Booney. A big difference. You have to be...um...less you," she explained slowly

What the fuck is she talkin 'bout?

"Less me? What the hell that's supposed to mean?" Less me. What type of shit was that? I was a cool, laid back mothafucka. Well, I thought so at least.

My momma looked at me, taping her fingers on the counter as she studied me.

"You have a tendency to want to control things. You can't be like that with a woman, don't no woman want a controlling ass man. So chill, let Peaches have her way for the time being."

My head shook at that.

"She likes getting head from different niggas, that's the only thing I told her not to do." If I couldn't be straight up with my moms, shid, then I couldn't be with nobody.

Her hands started waving as I said that. "Wait, wait, wait! Say what now?" She said looking amused as she let out a small chuckle.

"She likes getting head from these niggas," I told her.

"Like men do? Like you do? Wow, I'm liking her already. Wait. Does she sleeps with them?" She asked and I shook my head.

"No, she's a virgin."

"Even better," my mouth opened to snap, but she waved her hand, shutting me up. "No. But seriously, Booney, if you really like her, then respect her wishes as just being friends for now, don't rush it. Okay? You said she was mad at you this morning so she's staying with you?" She asked.

"No, I'm at hers for the time being. I like sleeping with her," I shrugged.

"Y'all not having no type of sex?" She questioned.

I started laughing as I nodded my head up and down.

"But you said she's a virgin." That woman.

"Ma, she is, Damn we ain't fuckin', if that's what you're askin'."

She hummed at my responses.

"But you giving her head?" She picked, moms just couldn't help herself.

"Hell n'all, damn. Gone, man, I don't know what the hell you talking about." Even though we hadn't fucked, I couldn't stop that stupid smile from forming or the laugh from leaving my mouth. Damn, those were some fuck'd up ass feelings I wasn't tryna have for nobody.

"Why are you laughing? I'm just asking a question. I got to meet this girl if she got you acting like this. So why she's mad?"

Clearing my throat, I shook my head as I laughed a few more times. "Because her ass crazy that's why. I ain't did shit to her. I'm gon' pick her up for lunch, though."

"Bring her here!" My mom stated way too excitedly, causing my head to shake.

"Hell n'all, I'm tryna get the girl to like me. If she meet yo ass she gon run for the hills," I told her, serious as hell. My mom's had just said Peaches sounded like a transsexual, then she wanted to meet her. They couldn't meet until after we were married and Peaches was stuck with my ass.

"Come on, Boon, I'll be nice. I'm always nice, aren't I, Marcus?" My mom's husband walked in the kitchen, shaking his head.

"What's up, Marcus?" I said.

Marcus was a cool ass dude, had a straight and legal business going for his self. He was crazy in love with my moms for the past eight years and he spoiled Britt like she was his own. So I didn't have a problem with him, as long as he made her happy, we were cool.

"Shit, tryin' not to go insane with yo worrisome ass momma and yo spoiled ass sister." Marcus hit my fist before he sat on a stool.

Brittany came back in the kitchen, hearing his last statement.

"Daddy, that's your fault. So don't start complaining now. But, Boon, guess what?" She was excited, bouncing up and down, smiling hard as hell. Shid, I was kinda afraid to find out.

"What?"

"I passed my driver's test! Daddy's buying me a car, Ahhh!" She screamed, making me cover my ears. I looked at Marcus, laughing.

"You have fun with that. Y'all stay up, I got to go."

"Meet Peaches?" My mom asked, smiling.

"Who's Peaches?" Marcus asked, of course my momma had to open her damn mouth.

"Boon's in love—"

"I'm gone, I'll be back for some Lasagna. Bye." I walked to the door, slipped on my white forces then opened the door.

"Boon, hold on!" My mom called after me.

"What's up?" Stopping on the other side of the door, I looked up at her as I messed with my keys.

"Joseph's calling."

Joseph was my father. He left after my mom got pregnant with Britt. I wasn't one of those niggas that held a grudge, it was pointless to me. You dealt with the pain then let it go. Fuck I wanna carry that shit around fah? Even though I don't hold a grudge, I don't fuck with my father either. He one of those 'I'm broke, can you help me out' type of niggas. The ones that only come out when they need some shit or they in trouble. I don't fuck with those types of mothafuckas.

Joseph also don't like Marcus because he got what Joseph could've had if he'd never left. Shit, ain't my problem Marcus beat his ass a couple of times, nigga should've learned. Marcus used to box professionally until he met my momma. He opened up a boxing gym out in Crown Point, shit been good for him.

"What he want?" Joseph didn't have my number and I liked to keep it that way.

"Britt," she said as if it explained everything.

"What's that supposed to mean?"

"Just how it sounds. He called talking shit about wanting custody of Brittany." Hearing that was funny, so much so that I laughed.

"Get the fuck outda here. Ahh, damn!" She better quit hitting me.

"Watch your mouth, but I'm serious, Booney," my mom said, hitting me again.

"Ma, don't worry about it. He just talking, boss, he is. That nigga dumb and broke, ain't no judge in their right mind gon' give his ass Britt. Plus, she old enough to decide who she wants to live with. And with Marcus promising her a car who you think she's gon' pick?" Britt loved the hell out of Marcus. Shid, if he and moms had ever spit up, Britt ass would have probably left to move with him.

"You're right."

"No shit. Now I'm late, bye." She punched me in the stomach while I was kissing her cheek. "Ma, keep on, I'ma kick yo ass."

"I'm not worried about you." She laughed before waving at me. "Love you, Boon, be safe." After checking my trunk to make sure Sam got the bags—he did—I hopped in my truck. Once inside, I grabbed my phone, seeing the missed call from Tameka.

Little dude wasn't bullshittin', he was on his shit already. Sitting the phone back in the cup holder, I pulled off and headed to the garage.

Chapter 8

Blaze

Pulling on the sidewalk in front of my shop, I parked by the front door. After I turned off the truck, I got out then walked through the garage door that was opened.

"Aye, when you finish that you can wash my truck," I called out to a worker who was wiping off a candy red Nissan Altima Coupe. He had that bitch looking nice.

"I got you, just leave your keys on the desk," Paul replied as he glanced up for a second then went back to wiping off the car.

The bell chinned once as I entered the shop. The sound caused Tameka to glance up at me then back down before her eyes quickly snapped back again.

"Look who decided to show up here after how long?" She sat her phone down then stood. "I thought I was gon' have track you down just to see your ugly face again," she joked while coming around the desk to hug me.

Tameka was a cute little high yellow hood bitch. She stood 'bout five-six, thick in the waist with a plump ass to match. Her upper body threw me off a bit because she was flat as fuck up top. I was a tittie man, I had to be able to grab, pull, and suck on 'em. She ain't have shit. But at the end of the day I was a man, so what her upper body lacked, her lower anatomy made up for.

"I was starting to think you were avoiding me." Her lips poked out as she pouted.

"N'all, baby girl, you know it ain't nothing like that. I had other shit to take care of before I came through. I know you had this locked down so I wasn't rushin'." I acknowledged, knowing she was on her shit.

Tameka flipped her bright red hair over her shoulder, smiling. "You know I holds it down, but everything's been good. Business been blooming as usual, so much so I'm waiting on a raise. And yo little friend stopped by, B, he is too young to be working up here," she hinted with a pointed look before walking toward the back, switching harder than need be.

Even so, my eyes went to her ass, watching it sway.

"Did I ask you how old he was? Just get his ass in here, that's all you gotda do."

Tameka stopped at my office door, turning to face me.

"B, don't start with me, okay. You not even in the door good and you talkin' shit."

"What you tell little dude about the job?" I stared down at her and she rolled her eyes while folding her arms. A laugh slipped through my lips as I walked her against the door. "When I'm not talkin' shit, huh? That's me, baby, so kill that. You coming in?" Moving around her, I went into my office.

"I don't know…" Tameka trailed off.

Her doing so irritated me. I needed to get this nut off before I went to see Peaches ass. For a virgin, she was a fuckin' tease and I couldn't be around her ass stiff.

"Man, get yo ass in here and shut the damn door."

She laughed, then jerked away from me. "Don't be snatching on me, Blaze." Tameka closed and locked the door then walked over to the chair I sat in. Then she climbed into my lap. "I missed yo mean ass being around here. Sam and King always came up here to make sure everything was right while you were gone." She informed me of what I already knew. "So, did you miss me?" Her arms wrapped around my neck, bringing her head closer to mine.

"If you kiss me, I'm gon' beat the fuck outda you," I warned, which made her smack her lips and roll her eyes. "Sit up," once she did, I retrieved the condom from my pocket. "Turn around and pull yo skirt up." Again she did as asked with no questions or argument. Bitch was too easy, I didn't like hoes like her. Even so, they ass came in handy when I needed to bust a quick one.

Sliding on the condom, I pushed Tameka's head down. I hiked her leg on the desk, brought my dick to her opening, then thrust deep inside her.

"Fuck!" I couldn't help my groan. It had been two years since I'd been deep inside a pussy.

"Ah, you missed this pussy didn't you, baby?" Bitch ain't know she was only a convenient fuck. "Ooh, fuck, Blaze! Harder baby!" She moaned, grabbing my right hip. Thrusting into her harder, caused the desk to move and Tameka to claw into my hip as she moaned louder. "Oh, my God Blaze! Mmm." Her pussy muscles started to tighten around my dick.

"Damn," I grunted out as Tameka started throwing her ass back while continuing to tighten her inner walls on me.

Shit, it had been two years and that had my manz ready to bust. Pulling out, I turned her around, pushed her down to her knees while pulling the condom off. She didn't hesitate to take me in her mouth. "Fuck, girl, damn!" My hands tightened in her hair as she took me down her throat then released me with a pop. I damn near blew my load.

Taking my balls in her mouth, she started sucking and moaning as her hands stroked my dick faster. My nut grew closer, I brought her mouth back to my dick and started fuckin' her throat while she played with my sack.

My muscles tightened, as did my grip in her bright red hair. "Oh fuck!" I busted down her throat hard. "Shit!" I breathed out as I fell back in my chair.

"Sweet and salty, just like I remember," Tameka moaned, coming between my legs and taking my semi hard dick in her hands, licking the tip. It jumped and she smiled, licking along the rim before taking me in her mouth sucking.

"Ah, fuck!"

"And you gon' tell me you didn't miss me," she moaned on me and my man instantly stood. Tameka peeked up at me through her lashes.

The look was the sexiest thing at that moment. I took another condom from my pocket, tore it open with my teeth, then quickly slipped it on.

"You gon' ride?" I asked her. Again, with a wide smile on her face, she got up and climbed into my lap, handled my soldier and guided it to her contracting sex.

Tameka's head went to my shoulder as she began to slide down.

"Ooh, God, mmm." She mumbled slowly, going down my full length.

My hips bucked as did her head, mouth wide as I thrust up, filling her completely. I slid my forearm under her thighs and started pumping, deep and fast inside her. A nigga was in heaven at that moment, bitch ain't know I was about to slit her ass open.

"Ah, shit, baby! Oh, God! Oh, oh ooh..." Her moans filled the room as she gripped my shoulders, bouncing, meeting my thrust.

"This how you doing it now?" Baby girl was riding the shit out my dick and working her pussy muscles. Slapping Tameka's ass only made her moan louder and bounce faster, bringing my next nut closer. "Oh shit!" Getting out the chair, I laid her on the desk. My hips slammed into her, stroking her long and deep.

"Ooh, baby, like that," she moaned, locking her legs around my waist.

Tameka's nails bit into my sides as she pulled me deeper inside her wet box. The squishy, slapping of our body's sounded loud in the office as our pants mingled together.

"Baby, I'm cumin'! Harder. Ooh, ooh fuck! Ah shit, baby, I'm cumin!"

Bitch pussy tightened as her body went stiff to the point she started to shake with a loud moan. My thrusts became faster as my sack tightened and I quickly pulled out, slapping my dick on her pelvis as I busted in the condom.

"Damn!" A heavy breath left my mouth as I shook the last of my nut into the condom.

Tameka's laugh had me looking up at her smiling face. "Twice? Baby, you wanna see if we can make it a third? I know I can go another round or two."

The idea of it had my sensitive man twitching. Damn. Baby girl sat up, then wrapped her arms around my waist as she kissed my neck.

Shit was tempting as fuck, but I had to go get Peaches' mean ass.

"N'all, we good. I got shit to do." I removed her arms off of me, then reached in my pocket. Pulling off a few bills, I tossed it on the desk next to her then went in the bathroom. Once inside, I took off the condom, wrapped it in some tissue, then flushed it down the toilet. I grabbed some towel paper, got it soapy and wet, then washed my dick off just as the door came open.

"What the fuck is this? You gon' fuckin' pay me fo'real Blaze?" Tameka snapped and pushed me back before throwing the four hundred dollars I gave her back at me.

"Bitch, you push me again I'ma choke the fuck outda you. Why the fuck you mad though?" After I dried my dick off, I fixed my jeans then walked past her, back into the office. "Tameka, where them books at?" I asked, looking in the desk for the record books.

She pushed my hands away from the top drawer, opened the last one, then pulled out the thick black record book. She dropped it hard in front of me and I looked at her. "Tameka, don't make me beat yo ass."

"Fuck you, Blaze, you dirty as hell. I ain't no fuckin' hoe, so don't treat me like I am. I don't know why I even try with yo ass, fo'real." Baby girl was pissed, but I simply ignored her.

I grabbed the book, then got up to leave. Tameka was a good worker that was one thing I could say about her. She took her job seriously no matter the bullshit we went through. That was the only reason I kept her ass around, she could separate business from personal.

"Aye, call John and let 'em know he starts tomorrow after school." I instructed her.

She pushed past me and started down the hall, her hips rocking hard. "I already told him that. Am I going to see you tonight?" She asked, stopping in front of me with her hands on her hips.

"Probably not, but I'll get up with you, I got yo number."

"Blaze, why you always do me like this, huh? Why you won't give me a chance?" My eyes dropped to her flat chest, then to her face. She was a pretty, bright skinned chick.

"Tameka, you don't want me as a nigga. Baby girl, you can do better than me." True, she had a fuck'd up life coming up, and I wasn't that nigga to make her feel good about herself. She was lookin' for that shit in the wrong place. "I'm out," touchin her chin I walked past her and then out of the door to my truck. Once inside, I looked at the time to see it was twelve twenty-five.

Putting a cigarette to my lips, I lit it as I pulled off, headed straight to the crib to shower and change.

Chapter 9

Blaze

I pulled up at the center, parking next to Peaches' car and waited for her to come out. It didn't take her long. Once I turned off the truck, she was coming out with Dane, laughing. I wasn't too fuck'd up about her hanging with him, shid, the nigga was happily married last I heard from him. So I knew he wouldn't try shit with her.

"Peaches!" I called out to her as I got out the truck. With my arms folded I leaned against it.

She looked over her shoulder, glanced at me, then rolled her eyes before turning back around and started talking again.

Laughing, I took off my black and blue, Orlando Magic snapback, and ran my hand over my head.

Man, this chick. She gon make me choke the fuck outda her.

"What got you looking so funky, smell something?" Peaches asked as she walked up to me.

"Just thinking about some shit, can I take you to lunch?" My lips stretched into a smile with the question.

Peaches looked me up, rolled her eyes, then folded her arms over her chest. She popped her hip to the side, staring at me hard.

"Yo ass ain't even got to do all that shit, it's a simple yes or no."

"No, now bye." With that, she turned toward her car.

What the hell?

"N'all, hold the fuck up. Peaches, what the fuck I do to you?" Grabbing her arm, I turned her so she was facing me.

Just then, she jerked away and her face twisted into a mug, looking like a mean ass kitten. Shit was too cute. *Damn she got a nigga feelings shot.* She ain't say nothing.

"Peaches, fo'real, man, what I do?" Her little ass was fucking me up. I ain't want her mad at me, shid. And if she was,

64

then she could at least tell a nigga what he did. *Stubborn ass trick.*

"Okay, fo'real, no bullshit. Where were you last night?" She shot out saying.

I was confused as fuck at the question, but answered it anyways.

"At Jesse's, my spot, why?" If I was confused at first, I was fuck'd up what she got an attitude.

"Who the fuck is Jesse?"

"My spot, man. I'm confused as hell why you mad?" My brows furrowed as I licked my lips. I didn't give a fuck what nobody said, women were confusing as hell, that's exactly why I didn't deal with they emotional asses.

"Well, at least you're honest. But let's get one thing straight, Blaze," she said my name kinda hard, but sexy as she walked me against my truck. Her little bitty ass had me walking backwards as her finger poked in the middle of my chest. "We friends that will occasionally hook up. You can do as you please, I don't have a problem with that, not at all. But what I won't have, is you fucking these dirty ass hoes then come crawling yo nasty, triflin' ass into my bed. That's where our problem will come in.

I don't mind you doing you because we ain't together and we ain't fuckin'. You a man with needs, I get and respect that. But don't ever fuck a bitch then come to me. The next day, fine, cool whatever. That shit you did last night was foul, you should've took yo ass home and showered or showered at mines before crawling yo ass in my bed. This is the first time, so I'ma let it slid. But there won't be a second or I'ma put my hands on you. Got me?" *The fuck is she talking about. Oh...* "Yeah," she said taking in my facial expression. She thought I was fucking a bitch?

After that little speech, I ain't even have the heart to tell her smart-dumbass Jesse was a house and not a person.

"Sorry, won't happen again, promise. Now, can I take you to lunch?" I asked, placing my hands on her hips, pulling her closer to me. She looked away while biting into her lip. *Why she do that?* "Man, you ain't even mad no more, so kill that."

"Boy, whatever. Let me go, I don't know what hoes you been with today," she dissed while giving me a shove back.

Laughing, I picked her short ass up, turning us around, pressing her into the truck then buried my face in the side of her neck.

"Blaze, stop!" She whined out a cute little sound, making my mans jump. "Blaze, fo'real, gone. People are watching us, stop." Peaches whispered as she grasped the nape of my neck.

Ignoring what she said, my hands squeezed her ass as I sucked the skin in my mouth before I made my way to her mouth, only stopping when I got to the corner of her lips, feeling them tug before she jerk her head away.

Peaches moved her head back, smacking it into the window. "Ouch, that's not funny."

"That's what yo mean ass get," I told her before I covered her mouth with mine. That's what fuck'd me up, bitch from last night was rubbing all on a niggas dick and not once did my shit twitch. One kiss with Peaches ass and my nigga standing, ready for war. *What type of shit is that?* My dick done got hard in a matter of seconds. It would probably kill any bitch willing. Putting Peaches down, I moved back. "Get yo ass in the truck so we can go eat."

"Who are you talking to? I didn't say yes," she countered her arms once again, going over her chest. *Stubborn ass wench.*

"You ain't have to, now get in." Opening the driver door, I tried to push her in, but she just stood there with her back toward me and her arms cross. "Come on, man, damn."

"No," she said simply. I pressed against her back and my hand slip into her pants. "Fine. Damn, you play too much. Yo black ass buying too, fucka," Peaches snapped as she started to get in.

I laughed as I slapped her on the ass. Once she got in, she turned around and slapped the shit outda me. I almost forgot who the fuck she was.

"Bitch, what the fuck wrong with you?" I snapped at her.

"I told you that shit hurts. With this thong on, these thin ass pants, and yo heavy handed ass, that shit stings something nasty, so stop. Now, what we eating?" She finished saying with a smile.

Man, I'ma choke the shit out of her one day. Probably when her ass sleep and can't fight back, though.

"So, how was your day?" I glanced at her only to find her brow raised, before a smile came to her lips and then quickly disappeared. "What's that about?"

"It would've been better if Teyo ass hadn't taken over for Sly. He's a fuckin' dick," she snapped off before chewing on her bottom lip.

Peaches ass is just mean and didn't like nobody.

"I want some chicken, what about you?" I asked as I pulled out the parking lot.

"It don't matter, I'll get whatever you get?" She pulled down the mirror, fixed her hair, then put on some lip gloss.

"Why the hell you got to do all that fah?" *The fuck she tryna get cute for? Wasn't nobody gon' be looking at her ass.*

Glancing at me, Peaches rolled her eyes. "Make me slap you."

"Make me beat yo ass." Coming to a stop light, I reached over and muffed her, then messed up her hair. "Stop, damn!"

"Who you tryna look cute fah?"

Looking down at herself, she laughed. "In my Snoopy scrubs, I don't know. You need to stop, jealousy is not a good look on you." Peaches looked back at me with a smile.

Same shit I'm saying, but I can't help it.

"I'm not jealous, I was just fuckin' with you. What time you got to be back at work?"

"At two, why?" Peaches fixed her hair as she answered.

Looking at the clock, it was already one twenty-five.

"I was gon' stop by my place after we ate, but we ain't gon' have time, so I'll do it after I drop you off." I shrugged as I pulled up at BBQ's.

"We don't have to seat, we can just order then go back to yours," Peaches said, pulling out her phone.

"N'all, it's cool. By time the food gets ready, it'll be time for you to get back," I told her as I opened my door. Reaching under my seat, I grabbed my 9mm, making sure the safety was off, then tucked it in the back of my jeans.

"Do you really need that? Blaze, who gon start some shit in here?" She questioned me.

"You never know what might happen, now come on. Why you still sitting there? Get out."

Peaches smacked her lips as she leaned back further in her seat.

"Nigga, come open my door. It's called being a gentleman." She gave me a duh look, then glance at her door and back to me.

Is she serious?

"Man, you better get yo ass out the truck or sit yo ass in here." *Chick crazy, fuck she mean open her damn door? She done lost her fuckin' mind.*

Peaches once again looked from me to the door, her facial expression serious. I closed mine, then walked away from the truck. Just as I made it to the middle of parking lot, I heard the door slam and looked back to see a pissed off Peaches.

"Don't be slamming my damn door."

"Fuck you and that raggedy piece of shit, black ass." She snapped bumping past me.

Damn, she was mad fo'real. "You pissed because I ain't open your fuckin' door? Seriously Peaches?" Man, I swear, I couldn't win with that girl. "Peaches, get in the truck so I can open yo door." She turned around so fast I couldn't help but laugh at the crazy look she gave me. "Man, gone," I said, moving away from her as she tried to hit me. "Get yo ol' violent ass outda here, man, damn. You gon' make me slap the fuck out you. Always tryna swing those little T-rex size arms." I laughed, still moving away from her.

"See, that was just mean. Get away from me, ain't nobody got time to play with you, just make sure you go home tonight." She said, turning away from me, going toward the chicken joint.

I went behind her, wrapped my arms around her waist then put my head on her shoulder.

"Move, Blaze."

"Man, shut up. I was gon' open yo door, I was just fucking with you," I lied in her ear as we reached the door and Peaches stopped to look up at me.

"You lying, you wasn't gon' open the door," she called me out on my shit.

With a shrug of my shoulders, I laughed. "So what? Just go with the lie I'm telling you so we can be good."

She started laughing while shaking her head. "You're helpless, how you gon' get a girl if you can't open her door?" She asked as I pulled the door opened.

"The fuck opening doors got to do with me being with you?" I asked her seriously.

"Everything. Wait, I didn't say me. I said *a girl*, I wouldn't date yo ass because you're rude and a thug. I don't date thugs, dealers, hoods, none of that," she counted off on her fingers, then finished with a roll of her neck.

Fuck?

"The fuck you mean I'm a thug, get that fuck shit outda here."

"And you cuss too damn much," she said and I stopped walking.

"I'm a grown ass man, I say what the fuck I want, whether it's cussin' or not. Fuck you mean, and I ain't no mothafuckin' thug, get that bullshit outda here." Man, I was offended like a mothafucka with her calling me a thug. I was past that bullshit.

"Thug, gangsta, killa or whatever the fuck you wanna call it, that's what you are."

"Peaches, boss, get the fuck outda here with that shit."

Peaches' hands went to her hips, eyes slightly slanted, lips twisted.

"Ever killed someone?" The question left her mouth.

The fuck was wrong with her asking me that shit in public?

My eyes bounced around the chicken spot, looking at the folks that stood around. "What the fuck kinda question is that?" *This babe done lost her fuckin' mind.* I glanced out the door, then back at her.

Again, Peaches arms folded under her chest, her hip cocked to the side as she stared me down. "Have you ever killed someone, Blaze?" She asked, staring me in the eyes.

Why the fuck would she ask me some shit like that out in the open?

"No," I told her and she smacked her lips.

"Nigga you lying—"

"Why the fuck you suddenly asking this shit fah?" I ain't even wanna sit here with her ass no mo, a nigga wasn't even hungry. "Man, lets go."

"What? Why? We haven't even ate—" Grabbing her arm, I jerked Peaches up.

"I don't give a fuck, lets go. Or walk yo ass back to work." Not giving her a choice, I started dragging her out the restaurant.

"Blaze, let me go. What you getting mad for?"

"Peaches, shut the fuck up!" I snapped at her and she stopped walking, yanked her arm away from me.

"Who do you think you're talking too? I was only playing with you, Blaze. Let me go!" She snapped, hitting me.

Grabbing her by the throat, I roughly pushed her against the truck.

"Hit me again, I'ma break yo fucking neck. Now get yo ass in the truck." Letting her go, I opened the passenger side door, pushed her in, then slammed the door before going to my side doing the same thing. Starting up the truck, I quickly pulled off, heading back to the Center.

***

The ride back was quiet, hell, not even the radio was playing. Once we got there, I pulled up to the door, waiting on her to get out. Truth be told, I ain't wanna fuck with her no mo'. I wasn't with that shit, she was on. To publically ask me if I killed somebody? That's what did it for me.

Never trust a nigga male or female that'll ask some shit like that in public. Out of all the places she could've asked me that, she chose the inside of a restaurant. I had no time for no snake ass mothafucka.

"Blaze, I didn't mean to offend you. I was only playing—"

"You didn't, so don't worry about it. Gon' head before you be late." I told her, nodding toward the door.

"I got twenty minutes left." I could feel her looking at me, but I ain't even give a fuck at that moment.

"Well, I got something to do."

"Blaze, look I—"

"Man, I don't even wanna hear that shit you spitting. Yo ass don't know the first thing about me and yo ass judging a mothafucka. You right, Peaches, I'm a thug, I kill people, I own hella traps. But so what? Who I am ain't got shit to do with what I do. I ain't no fuck ass corner boy slanging, mama, I got my shit. But, shid, you ain't even got to worry about a nigga fucking with you no mo'." Putting the truck in park, I turned it off then took my keys out.

"Blaze, I wasn't serious okay, I didn't think you would get mad. Damn, I'm sorry I ain't even mean... What's this?" She asked looking confused before her eyes fell back on me.

"Yo key, I ain't mad, not at all, baby girl. But shid, you were right from jump, this ain't gon' work. You ain't want this anyways so I ain't fuck'd up about it. You ain't got to worry about a nigga no mo', real talk. Gon' head," I told her, started up the truck again as I nodded toward the door. She still didn't move and it was pissing me off that she was still seating here. "Peaches, get the fuck out, man, damn."

"Don't talk to me like that. If you want me out, then you going to have to open my door," she stubbornly stated.

Letting out a heavy sigh, I reached over and pushed her door open.

"Are you serious right now? I was only playing with you," the shocked look on her face didn't faze me one bit.

"I'ight, man, I'll see you." She sat there for a minute before letting out a sigh.

"I'ma hold you to that," Peaches got out and left her apartment key on the seat before closing the door.

I wasn't playing, I was serious. I wasn't fucking with her, on some real shit. Letting the passenger window down, I picked up her key and tossed it out by her before pulling off.

Chapter 10

Blaze

"Nigga, get the fuck outda here. Baby, this ball, you can't be mad, get." I laughed at Wayne. "Baby, that was a three all day, bitch!" I laughed, taking the ball. "Nigga got nut in his mouth so he mad, just hold yo breath and swallow. My babies probably give yo ass some type of game," I told him as I shook up with Sam, laughing.

"Fuck y'all bitches, man. Bellow, these some cheating ass mothafuckas," Wayne said, mad as hell.

Nigga was always pissed when they lost.

"Cheating or not, we won. Now give me my money before I beat yo ass," I told him as I dribbled the ball before shooting.

"Man, hell n'all, fuck that. Double—"

"Nigga, fuck that, ain't nobody about to be doubling all gotdamn night. Anastasia making a nigga dinner," I said, rubbing my stomach, making them laugh, but only Sam knew what I meant. Anastasia was another trap house, but was for pills— Xanax, Ecstasy, Speed, Tylenol one through four with codeine, Crystal Meth, and Acid. If Sly and his people wasn't a big connect on some of the shit I sell, I probably would've killed him.

"Am I invited?" Bellow asked and I looked at Sam, laughing. Bellow and Wayne we knew since our teen days. Bellow was cool, Wayne I ain't really give a fuck about. Even though they never gave me a reason not to trust them, I chose to keep my trust circle small when it came to friends.

"N'all, you cool. Now let me get those two bills up off you."

"You gon' quit betting that nigga," Sam told Wayne as he pulled money from his sock.

I nodded toward Sam so he could give it to him as I shook up with Bellow. "I'll give you a chance to win yo money

73

back, I'm having a Barbeque at the Rex's Friday," I told Bell before dapping him.

"I'm there, you already know," he responded.

"I'ight, my nigga, stay up. I got a date." I picked up the ball, threw it at Sam, then grabbing my shirt, I flung it over my shoulder. "Did you get rid of those chirping birds?" I asked him, referring to the two guns I used on Joe.

"Yeah, they're dead, floating in the lake," he assured me.

I nodded my head, then pulled out my phone. "What you about to get into?" I asked as we walked to the parking lot.

"Shit, about to meet King at Peaches'. I'm hoping she cooked, I'm hungry as hell," Sam was a stupid mothafucka, but he was my nigga.

"What yo ass plan on eating, her or the food?" I asked him straight up. I wasn't no fool ass nigga. Peaches done had this nigga at least once.

His ass laughed at that. "What you mean—"

"Nigga, don't play stupid, you her hoe. You know what the fuck I mean." His ass stopped laughing as I said that. Leaning against the truck, I put my hands in my pockets.

"I'm not her hoe. Don't act like you haven't tasted her ass either." His lips twisted ugly with his accusation.

I snorted. "The fuck I look like? I ain't eating no bitch pussy. If she ain't gon' suck my dick once, I'm done with her ass. Baby, fair is fair, if I'ma make you squirt, its only right you make me nut. Simple as that. But you silly fuck ass niggas desperate just like these hoes. You don't need sex, as long as you're appreciated for something, you feel important for that moment. Key is not to give a fuck and to have patience. I bet she'll be willing to let you fuck, bitch'll be thirsty," I told him.

"What happened to you, yo ass was just threating to kill any nigga that fuck'd her. Now you telling me how to get her to let me fuck."

My brows went up at that. "The fuck gave you the impression I was telling you to use that shit on her?" I asked, looking at him like he was dumb.

"We were just talking about her then you said that," he explained.

My head shook as he was talkin'. "Nigga you dumb ass fuck, if you fuck her I'll kill you. That, I promise you. But shid, she ain't my girl, she could do as she please, not my problem. But yo ass bet not fuck her." Even though those words left my mouth, I knew if I saw her with a nigga I'd flip the fuck out.

"She must have really pissed you off," Sam assumed, staring at me for a long second, his brows furrowed. "This serious, I ain't seen you this stressed since... Shid, never," Sam stated as he posted up against his dark grey, 2014 Navigator truck.

A heavy breath left my mouth and I ran a hand over my face. "Man, I don't know, whatever it was I ain't fucking with it no mo. You know how I am about judgmental mothafuckas and she just that. Bitch gon' label me. But she fuck'd me up when she started asking if I killed somebody in public. I mean really fuck'd me up—"

"Did you check her for a wire?" Sam asked seriously. He knew just like I did how dirty folks could be.

"Shid, I should've. It fuck'd me up, though, when she asked that. I mean, as many times as we've been alone at the crib she could've asked me, but n'all, she wait until we out. I'm done with her ass, though. Aye and just because I'm stepping back don't mean that's a go ahead for you mothafucka, I'd hate to have to kill my brother over a bitch. But it is what it is." My shoulders shrugged nonchalantly. Sam knew I wouldn't kill 'em, but I'd beat the fuck outda him, then her.

"Get your soft ass outda here. I don't want her, barely like her, but that don't change the fact she got a messy ass pussy I like that shit."

Once that left his mouth, I rocked his ass in the jaw.

"You bitch," he laughed it off as he bucked up.

We were thirty, still acting like we were twenty. Shit was crazy, but I squared up with his ass.

We were just boxing when his ass almost fell.

"I got fifty bucks on dreads," a feminine voice called out from behind me.

I turned around at the sound and I see this short, pudgy, thick ass light skin chick. Small, medium, or large, beauty was just that. I could admire a beautiful woman when I saw one and she was a nice, thick, yellow bone bitch. She had a little stomach, titties big as fuck, but her hips... *Damn*. They were wide and her ass poked out, I had to rub my head so I wouldn't grab my twitching dick. Licking my lips after giving her a once over, I smiled at her.

"Well, you might as well give me that fifty because dreads bout to lose, baby girl." I told her.

"I figured that much, his stance was all wrong from the beginning, but seeing as I don't have fifty on me now, how 'bout you let me take you out for a drink? I have a card." She checked me out just as I had done her.

Laughing, I looked at Sam as he tapped my shoulder.

"I have to go, I'll get up with you later. Little lady, you was wrong. If you hadn't come over swinging all that ass, distracting me, I wouldn't have almost fell," Sam lied as he glanced her up before looking at me. "You have fun with that."

She laughed, rolling her eyes before looking back at me.

"I'ight, my nigga. Get word out about Friday." After shaking up with him, Sam hopped in his truck and pulled off. Dusting off my jeans, I turned to look to ol' girl. "I ain't caught yo name."

"Because I ain't throw it," she replied back smartly.

"Damn, ain't even get a niggas name and you getting smart already. I'm about to slap yo ass before I even get to know you. And I'm Blaze." Damn, my mouth was getting dry as fuck.

"Blaze, it suits you. I'm Krystal and believe I ain't worried about you." A cocky little smile came to her thin, pink lips.

I nodded as I looked around me while I talked. "So, Krystal, what you tryna get into?" Looking back at her, I laughed as she bit into her lips, letting her eyes roam. "Tryna get into trouble I see. Get in." She gave me a funky look while folding her arms over her chest. "Don't give that look, we ain't about to fuck. If you ain't got shit to do, get yo ass in the truck," I told her while opening the driver door.

"Do you always talk to folks like this?"

"Just those I like, now get in," I told her, nodding toward the door.

"How I know you ain't gon try nothing, huh?" I laughed at that.

"Man, get that shit outda here. We in an empty parking lot, if I was gon do something I would've knocked yo ass out already. But shid, I ain't gon' beg yo ass either. You riding or you gon' stand there? Please believe, shorty, I don't give a fuck which you choose." With that, I hopped in the truck then started it up.

I had just put the truck in reverse, about to pull off, when she started walking to the passenger side and got in. Once she did, I sped out the parking lot.

***

"She beat yo ass with brass knuckles? No shit?" Krystal asked, laughing hard as hell.

"Man, it ain't that funny. I don't hit women."

"I don't give a fuck, I would've made an exception for that ass." Krystal said, still laughing. When we left the courts we drove around for a bit, then I took her to get something to eat at a rib joint on Cleveland and we had just been kickin' it there.

Krystal was a cool ass chick, crazy as hell, but cool. Straight shit talker and I liked that about her. She wasn't one of those self-conscious ass females, she knew what she had and flaunted that shit sexily. I liked that.

"Yo ass wouldn't have done shit but sat there looking crazy." I doubted shorty was a fighter. She just ain't look like the type to get down, but more of a prissy chick.

I watched as she sat her drink down and pulled her hair into a ponytail on top her head.

"Bring yo ass outside and find out," she said, pressing her tongue against her jaw and smiling with a razor blade in between her teeth. Then she put it back. "Come on, baby, fuck with me," she said, smiling this cute closed mouth smile.

"Yo ass crazy. Who the fuck walks around with a blade in their mouth? I mean, I heard folks doing that but never actually seen that shit. How the fuck you don't cut yo mouth up," I asked, serious as hell, making her laugh. "Ain't shit funny, yo ass talking like you ain't got shit in there when bitches with tongue rings talk tied-tongue as fuck, adding a 'S' at the end of everything, making shit obvious it's something in there."

"A dramatic ass explanation. Fah real, Blaze, you doing too much," she exclaimed with a laugh.

"Fuck you."

Rolling her eyes, she pulled the blade from her mouth. "It has a cover over the sharp part, I stick it between my cheek and teeth I've been doing it since I was fourteen, so it's nothing now," she replied with a shrug.

"You ready?"

"Yep, those were some good ass ribs. I'ma have to come back here," she said while packing up our trash.

"Just let me know when." I would have definitely taken her out again.

She laughed as we got up, threw our shit away then walking out.

"It ain't too many men that'll be willing—"

"Don't go comparing me to these niggas you know or fuck'd with." I cut her off, I thought that was Peaches' problem. Her ass was used to a certain type and probably thought I was like they ass.

"Touchy, aren't we?"

"Fuck you, get in the truck before I leave yo ass out here." Watching her ass sway, I licked my lips. I was so focused on her ass that I hadn't realized she stopped until after I ran into her. I'ma fuck that ass. Boss, shit, just stupid big for no damn reason.

"You ain't heard shit I just said did you?" She asked the obvious while looking at me.

"Hell n'all, walk yo ass on the side or behind me if you want me to listen to you. That ass distracting as fuck." Pushing her out the way, I walked to the driver side, getting in just as she did. "You rushing to get to the crib?"

"It don't matter, I don't have to work tomorrow," she informed me, getting comfortable in the seat.

Not saying anything else, I drove to The Shack, one of my pool halls.

Peaches

Blindly, I flicked through the channels as my mind replayed earlier events. I was still confused as to why he flipped like he had. He couldn't have been offended for real.

"Peaches, leave it here," Kim's hand waved in front of my face.

My head went back and I blinked a few times before I focused on her. "Hm?" I hummed, hadn't heard what she said.

"What's up with you, boo? You've been spacing since I got here. What's up?" Kim pushed my feet off the couch and sat where they once lay.

I cut my eyes at her for that action. All that damn space and she sat her black ass there. "Bitch really?" With a roll of my eyes, I moved over and sat up straight.

"Hoe, don't get funky with me. I didn't do shit to you," Kimmy snapped back before she nudged my shoulder. "Peach, what's up fo'real?"

A loud groan left my mouth and I turned sideways to face her. "I don't know how to explain it. I mean, I don't know, well I do but... I don't know, I'm confused my damn self."

"Okay, now I'm confused because I have no idea what you're going on about." She exclaimed. "So what's got you in a twist?"

Might as well tell her.

"Okay, I don't know man what's up with Blaze. He got pissed at me because I called him a thug and asked if he ever killed anyone. I basically told him I wouldn't date him and all that jazz, but for some reason he just snapped, like seriously got pissed the fuck off. He was slamming doors and he gave me my key. I apologized to him, I mean, I wasn't trying to offend at all.

"Kim, we always talk shit whenever we're together, so it was just kind of unexpected, you know. Anyways, after apologizing and him putting me out his truck, he said we were cool and that he'd see me later or whatever. I left the key on the seat and closed the door, next thing I know, the window is being rolled down and dude throws the fuckin' key out then speeds the fuck off. Man, I don't know, I tried calling him but nothing. This bullshit is really bothering me." A heavy sigh left my mouth and my head fell back. Until I heard her gasp and focused back on her.

"Oh, my God! Peach, you really like him," Kimmy said, completely shocked with wide eyes.

"That's the thing, I don't. Well, I do, but I don't. I don't know, it's fucking confusing as hell. It's like when he's around me I want to literally fuckin' kill him, *hurt him*–shit something. Then when he's not, the fucka seems to pop up and I find myself wondering what he's doing. But now that he's mad at me, all I want to do is fix it." My eyes dropped to my fingers as they twisted together.

"Babe, you have it bad. But, Peaches, you can't ask a nigga no shit like that in public. Shid, the type of dude Blaze is, I can bet any money he looking at yo ass suspicious as hell right now," she began to explain, which had my brow coming together.

"Wait, what you mean?" Confusion set in my body as I took in what she said.

"Did he search you?" The seriousness in her voice threw me for a loop.

Slowly I began to understand why he suddenly got pissed. "No, he didn't. Wait, so you think he got mad because he thought I was asking that shit as a trap?" Knowing what I said was true, she didn't even need to reply. Once my mind wrapped around his reasons, I got mad. "Why the hell would I try to trap him on some bullshit when King hangs with him?"

"Peach, that don't mean shit. What would make you ask that man some bullshit like that in public? Hell, if I ain't know yo ass, I'd be looking at you the same damn way, no lie," she went on to say.

Again, my eyes rolled up in head. "I was playing, though!" The irritation in my voice was evident. I wasn't mad at Kim because I knew she was speaking truth. I was mad at myself for even doing it. Even so, he should've known I was just playing.

"Babe, I know, but you can't play with everybody like that. Especially not Blaze. That nigga just got out and I'm sho he's looking at everybody with the same eyes. You know the reason he was locked up because a bitch snitched on him. So take that in and think about you, *a female*, asking him some bullshit like that in a *public* place, Peaches."

I didn't know a chick snitched on him, but for him to think I would do some dumb shit like that was still crazy, especially given the shit King was into. I would never, but I guess he wasn't King and wouldn't really know. "I fuck'd up, huh?"

Kim's head nodded, "Yep, you did. But you'll fix it because you like him." A smile stretched across her lips as her brows wiggled.

The face made me laugh. "I can't stand yo black ass. You right though, I'ma try to fix it." My eyes rolled up in my head as she continued to give that same stupid look. "Kim, stop. Stupid self."

"Okay, just admit it though, you like him? And don't give me that I do but I don't bullshit, be real with me," she picked.

With a shake of my head, I shrugged my shoulders. "I do but—no Kim let me finish. I like him, I really do. His whole attitude and the fact he's not afraid of King is just a plus. But, Kimmy, you know how these niggas is. He's friends with King, ain't none of them niggas straight, they're all hoes. And I can't deal with that. I mean, I watched my mom go through that shit with my dad, then Ebony put up with the same bullshit with Ha'Keem triflin' ass. Both women I love to death, but I don't want to be like them, stuck in the same place and dumb in love." My head shook as I explained why I didn't want to like Blaze.

"Peaches, you can't judge them all alike. Who's to say he's the same as them?" She questioned.

My lips pursed together and my head tilted slightly to the left. "Kim, name one nigga that hangs with King that's straight? Never cheated, ever. Please, name one." I folded my arms over my chest and leaned back against the couch as I waited for her answer.

"Dane," she started until I cut her off.

"Nope, Dane cheated twice. He may be faithful now, after she left his ass, but he was no different. You see, he barely hangs with King now. And if he do come out, Jennifer right there with that ass. I don't have time to babysit no grown as man and damn sho' can't teach they ass how to be a fuckin' faithful man."

True, wasn't no way I was going to be stuck waiting on a man to grow up. My mom did and at the end of it, nothing, because my father never changed and she never went nowhere. She was too dependent on him. *In love and dumb.*

"You can't just judge that man like that. Maybe he is like them, but maybe he's not. We don't know. And you won't until you get to really know him. I'm not saying jump in bed with him, just give him a chance. Who knows, he could end up surprising you." Kim advised before she let out a laugh.

"Peach, think about it, though, he must really like you. I mean, was you not in the room when he fought King for you? Girl, when King slapped you that man didn't flinch once, he jumped up so gotdamn fast and knocked the shit outda your brother. Now name one nigga you know that would do that for a chick he barely knows?"

The memory had my teeth sinking into my bottom lip in order to contain my smile. But the action failed and I ended up laughing.

Seeing that, Kim hit my thigh. "Point exactly."

I really did like Blaze, but I didn't want to get hurt or played in the end. Even so, what would it hurt to really get to know him? My mind replayed the petty arguments, our flirting with one another. "I have to fix this, huh?"

Kim's head nodded. "Yep, you do, babe."

Chapter 11

Blaze

"Blaze, why you ain't tell me we were going to a club?" She asked, doing the same shit Peaches did, pulling the mirror down. Before she could even start doing whatever it was, I closed the mirror.

"Man, get yo ass out. Who you tryna impress?" I asked as I turned off the truck.

"I don't know who's in there." Krystal answered back honestly.

Shaking my head, I got out and heard Krystal laugh. I glanced back at her only to see she had pulled her hair from its ponytail.

"Don't hate, Mr. Blaze. Haters gets nowhere in life. So a pool hall, you gon' teach me how to play?" She came to my side and I couldn't resist grabbing her ass, *Damn, it was soft.*

"I got you. What's good, Ben," I hit my fist to the bouncer at the door as he pulled it opened.

"Everything good," he replied.

Nodding, I led Krystal to the bar. "Aye, wait up at the bar, I'll be right back." Standing at the bar, I called Vincent over. "Get little mama whatever she want, don't let nobody fuck with her. I'll be right back."

"Alright, Boss," he responded and I made my way to the back.

***

"AYE!" I yelled loudly, making everybody look up as I walked into the room.

"Blaze, my nig, thought yo ass would've been here by now. What took you so gotdamn long?" Monte asked as we shook up.

"Aye, y'all give us a minute," I told the three niggas that was seated in there. Once they left, I turned back to Monte. "Shit, got caught up on this one little thing, but what's been going on? I'm hearing niggas been actin' stupid in this bitch." I pulled out a chair, turned it backwards and sat down.

Monte was the manager of The Shack, meaning he ran shit until niggas start acting stupid in my shit and I had to let they ass know who spot they were in.

"These young mothafuckas thinking they can do what the fuck they want. You know how that shit is. I came in the other day and seen some little nigga snorting on pool table-."

"Wait, snorting on my table?" I asked him.

"Yeah."

"Yo ass know how these mothafucka's is. That's why after you serve 'em, you make 'em leave. If they want a quick hit, you make 'em snort it in the room in front of you. Once you do, you put they asses out. If he don't plan on doing it right then and there, you don't serve his ass. The fuck is wrong with you?" That was that stupid shit.

"I didn't serve him, Benny did," he explained with his hands held up.

"Benny? Benny, that's at the front door?"

"Yeah," Monte responded bleakly.

I hit him hard in the face. His chair went back and he fell out of it. "You let his ass do that and he still working here? The fuck is wrong with you, Monte? Yo ass know better. Let this be the last time this shit happen. Dumbass mothafucka's, man." Pushing out the chair, I left the back room, going back to the front. "Yo! Ben, bring yo ass here!" That nigga looked up at me and held up his finger. I was about to walk over there, but he started coming my way.

"What's up man?"

"Come on." I lead us to my office. Once inside I went to my desk and sat down on it. "Fuck this I hear about you serving some nigga and letting him snort on my tables."

"Oh," A dumb look covered his face and he rubbed the back of his neck.

This nigga just, 'Oh'?

"Before yo ass started working here, I explained the rules to you. Ain't no 'Oh's' or second chances in this bitch, all it take is one time for a fuck up to mess all my shit up. What you did was dumb as fuck. Yo, you done. Go find yo ass a nine to five that pays as good as I did. I don't need any dumbass mothafuckas working for me. Now get the fuck outda here. Just in case you thinking about coming at a nigga sideways, remember who you fucking with." Pulling my 9mm from the back of my jeans, I shot him twice in the shoulder.

"Ahh shit!" He hollered out as he clung to his shoulder.

"Now get the fuck out before you get blood on my fuckin' floors." Just as he got up, my office door was kicked in and I started shooting, not knowing who it was. I ain't give a fuck.

Don't nobody just open my damn door without knocking.

Once the clip was empty, I slid behind the desk as I quickly ejected the magazine I pulled the other from the pouch strapped to my ankle. I slammed it in, then cocked it back.

"Blaze, what the fuck nigga!" King yelled.

When I recognized the voice, I looked up to see him, then Sam peeking over his shoulder.

"What the hell y'all niggas doing just opening up my mothafuckin' door? Get yo dumbasses killed doing that shit, nigga knock. How many times do I gotda tell y'all stupid asses that?" I snapped on 'em, what if I would've shot one of their dumbasses?

"Fuck you shooting fah any damn way?" King asked, looking his self over, then turning to Sam. "Next time yo ass open the fuckin' door, but good looking though." He turned back toward me with a wave of his gun. "Why you shooting?"

"I just fired Ben. I was warning his ass not to try shit, but you niggas came busting in the door. Aye, Sam go out front make sure shit i'ight," I instructed him, then looked around my office. With a quick glance my eyes landed on Ben, who was laid out on the floor with a bullet to the head. "Fuck man! Get his ass up off my floor. You know how hard it is to get blood out a carpet," I asked King, getting pissed off because that nigga was bleeding on my fuckin' floor!

"Nigga show some type of sympathy, you just killed this man. Fuck wrong with you, B?" King asked, looking at me like I was crazy.

"This nigga bleeding on my fuckin' carpet, if it was yo shit I wouldn't let his ass bleed out on yours, damn." That nigga had his fuckin' nerve.

King gave me a funky look that had me sighing.

"Fuck it, you right. Call the twins and tell 'em to come roll this nigga up and take him to the shop with the carpet. Shit was ugly anyways, I need a drink."

Twins were two brothers who disposed of bodies for the right price. I'd known and had done business with them for well over ten years. Whenever I called for them, they never disappointed and I never had a body surface once I called them to clean up. I didn't know exactly where they disposed the bodies, and what I didn't know wouldn't hurt them.

With one last glance at Benny, I stepped over him then left the room.

Sam met us in the hall. "Everything straight out front? Why you fire him?" He questioned as they followed behind me.

"His ass served some nigga and let his ass snort on my pool table. Then when I said something about it, this nigga gon say 'Oh'. Like oops, the fuck. Monte ass 'bout to go too. Shid, I ain't got time for no fuck ups," I told 'em as we walked out the hall to the main room.

"You still with ol' girl?" Sam asked, nodding toward the bar and I laughed, looking at Krystal.

"Hell yeah, she cool man. Crazy bitch carry a razor blade in her mouth."

"Damn, look at her ass," King blurted out, making me laugh.

"I know, just stupid ain't it. My dick crying to bust her ass wide open. I'ma beat the fuck out that shit," I told him as we stood against the wall watching her.

"Wait, what the fuck you mean? I thought you ass so high up on Peaches?" King asked.

"Man, I'm done fucking with her crazy ass, on G. I goes to pick her mean ass up for lunch and she start spitting some bullshit about me being a thug and she don't wanna date me. Then her ass waited right good until we in there and gon' ask if I killed somebody. King, you know me. I ain't with that shit. So shid, I gave her ass her key and that's that." I shrugged then made my way to the bar where Krystal stood.

"Give me a bottle of Hennessy," I reached behind the bar and grabbed three glasses as he handed me the bottle.

"You fucking with that brown, let me get away from you then," she laughed while pushing me away.

"Man, get the fuck outda here. I ain't gon' do shit to yo ass yet." Truthfully, I was most definitely gon' fuck, just not that night.

"Yet? You say that as if you already know you gon' hit. Which you're not by the way." She laughed with a smile stretched across her face.

"Oh, I'm gon bust yo ass open, ain't no denying that. I'm just not gon' do it today because we just met. Now tomorrow, shid, you fair game."

Laughing, Krystal pushed me while rolling her eyes. "Nigga get the fuck outda here."

Moving closer to her, I brought my mouth to her ear. "Okay, when I have that ass folded, don't say shit," I whispered while grabbing a handful of her ass.

Her mouth opened then closed before she settled with just shaking her head.

"B, you ain't gon' introduce us to yo friend?" King asked, putting his arm on my shoulder leaning against me. *This nigga is helpless.*

"Krystal, these my niggas, King and Sam. Y'all this Krystal."

"Hey." She waved her hand and King took it and kissed it.

"Hey to you, beautiful," she raised a brow, glancing at me but smiled nonetheless. She tried to play it cool, but the color to her yellow cheeks told the truth.

"What's up?" Sam nodded at her.

"Dreads, I remember you. So, are we playing pool or what?" She asked.

King pushed me out the way, took Krystal by the waist and led her to the pool tables. "So where yo man at?" King asked her.

I couldn't do shit but laugh at his ass, nigga was dirty.

"You know that nigga gon' try to hit right?" Sam asked, pointing toward King.

"Of course, he ain't tho. But if she let him, I don't give a fuck. She ain't my bitch. Come on." Grabbing the glasses and the bottles of Hen and Don, we went over to the table.

"Come on, Blaze. You said you'd show me how to play." Krystal held out a pool stick as we made it over there to her.

I poured myself a drink then quickly downed it. After I cleared my throat I took the stick and stood behind her.

"You got to bend over the table." My hand pressed against her back, bending her over. She popped me as I did that. "I'm serious, bend over the gotdamn table like this," Once again, I pushed her forward, then leaned over her, showing her how to hold the stick. "Put yo index on top of yo middle, making a little hole, and put the stick between it then push it in. Oof!" She elbowed me as her arm drew back. 'Man, I'm serious, damn. Now break." She broke.

Chapter 12

Blaze

I had put everybody out an hour earlier when the twins came to pick up Benny. So it was just me, Sam, King, Krystal, and Vincent. He was steady bringing us drinks.

"Blaze, you can dance?" Krystal asked.

"I can fuck. What you mean!" I said, making King and Sam laugh. "If you got rhythm then you can fuck and if you can fuck then you can dance. Wanna see?" I said, her licking my lips. She looked at King and Sam. "Man fuck them, y'all call ya girls, hoes, or something, damn. Come on."

"No, Blaze, I'm not having sex with you," she protested, laughing while pushing me away from her.

"You ain't got to, we just dancing. Come on, man." Pulling her up, I walked to a pool table further down. I pulled up my jeans up and stepped to her. Krystal covered her face let out a muffled scream as she laughed.

My hips moved into hers, my dick rubbed against her. I pressed her down on her stomach, then grinded against her ass, thrusting my pelvis into her. It wasn't until she started moving that shit got serious.

My hand tangled in her hair, yanking her head back. I kissed down her neck as I started a slow grind, making sure she felt my dick.

Her movement was in sync with mine until she started shaking that shit, rolling slow then fast.

Bitch is teasing a nigga.

I was hard as fuck.

Turning her around, I picked Krystal up, then sat her on top of the pool table. Grabbing the hem of her shirt, I pulled it off, then unhooked her bra.

Krystal fell back on the table and raised her hips, letting me pull her pants along with her panties off. Once I dropped them to the floor, I pushed her legs open wide.

I sucked on my index and middle finger, getting them wet before I ran them through her slit. Her pussy lips parted and I began playing with her clit. At the same time I pulled one nipple in my mouth while pinching the other.

My fingers pushed inside her pussy. I watched as her back arched and she began to moan. I wasn't up for no foreplay, I just wanted to get her ass wet so I could fuck. Pulling away from her, I undid my jeans, pulled them down my hips, then grabbed a magnum from my back pocket. After I rolled it down, I ran the tip over her clit.

Her legs stretched wider as my dick came to her opening. I pushed my tip inside of her.

Bitch was tight as fuck, abnormally tight, and she had a nerve to clamp her inner muscles down around my shit.

"Ah shit!" Her hand quickly came to my pelvis and she pushed me back.

Shid, I ain't with fucking no bitch that ain't willing. No matter how close we are to fuckin', when she say wait, that means stop, point blank. "Fuck is wrong with you?" She looked away from me, seeming embarrassed. "Man, gon with that bullshit, what's up?" I asked her again and her skin turned red. *Hell n'all, man, on what?* "You a virgin?"

Fucks wrong with me finding these damn virgins suddenly? This shit should be fuckin' illegal.

"Yes, I am, is that a problem?" She shot with a hint of an attitude.

Fuck kinda question is that? "Any other day, hell n'all. Right now, fuck yeah. A nigga hard as hell, I should slap yo dumbass for teasing a mothafucka." I muffed her head back, she sat up and pushed me in the chest.

"Yo ass won't slap another, bet that. Plus, you started it. I'm not a loosely ass bitch you gon' fuck and dump. If that's what you looking for, your eyes done landed on the wrong one. This, what just happened, was caused by to many drinks, I ain't no hoe."

"Man, shut the fuck up. Didn't nobody call yo ass a hoe, so cool it with that shit. I don't fuck with hoes, so if I thought yo ass was one these pass few hours wouldn't have happened, so chill. Ain't nothing wrong with you being a virgin," I told on some real shit. Yeah, I wish she would've said something from jump, but it was what it was. I was still gon' roll with her ass.

Once those words left my mouth, my mind went to Peaches and her bullshit. "Look, check this, if yo ass longing fah a nigga to romance yo ass, then I ain't it. If you a judgmental mothafucka that's gon' label a nigga, then we need to end this here and now. If you stay, then we gon' rock, simple as that. Not on no relationship type shit, we kickin' it, that's it. Now get yo ass dressed and think about what I just said."

Once I fixed my jeans I walked back over to King and Sam.

"Blaze! So y'all just danced?" King asked once I sat down.

"King, yo ass stupid. Shut the fuck up." My head shook as I laughed.

"How the fuck you gon' be this big ass, mean nigga and be dancing?" Sam asked, he glanced away from his phone to me, laughing.

"Believe it or not, some women find men who can dance sexy. You know what they say about dancer's, right?" Krystal added, coming over.

"They can fuck?" I asked, laughing as I slapped hands with King.

"I can roll and pop wanna see?" King's ass was just stupid.

"N'all, sweetie, I'm cool," she told him as she came and sat on my lap. "I'm gon' rock with you. Whatever you may be into doesn't make who you are. So I'ma roll with you."

Nodding my head, I licked my lips. "That's what it is then." Right after the words left my mouth, my phone started ringing as well as someone banging on the door. I ignored my phone, then lifted Krystal off me as I grabbed my gun. "Y'all niggas call somebody over here?" I asked as the impatient mothafuckas started banging harder on the damn door.

"Yeah, I did. Vincent get the door man!" King yelled at him and I sat back down, pulling Krystal into my lap.

"Yo ass ready to go?" I asked as my phone went off again.

"You got to take me back to the courts so I can get my car," she said as I answered the phone.

"Hold up," I told her. "Who dis?" I didn't recognize the number right off bat.

"Where you at?" The female voice kinda fuck'd me up.

"Who the fuck is this?" I asked again.

"Peaches." I looked at my phone again.

"Who?" I heard who she said, I just wanted to make sure I wasn't hearing shit.

"Peaches, Blaze. Stop playing, damn. I know you ain't still mad about earlier." She stated. When I didn't say anything, Peaches sighed heavily into the phone. "Are you still pissed? Blaze, I don't want you mad at me, especially when I was only playing. Honestly, I didn't think you would take it serious, I promise I didn't," she insisted. The line was quiet for a second.

I was trying to wrap my mind around the fact she called me at three in the morning to tell me that.

"Blaze," Peaches whined out.

"N'all man, we good. I already told yo ass that, so don't sweat it." I responded. Before I started talking to her, my mind was on the fact I wasn't gon' fuck with her on that level no mo.

"Okay, as long as we cool," Peaches mumbled into the phone.

"Yeah, we good. But aye, I gotda go so I'll hella at you later." I was ready to hang up, but she started talking again.

'I'ight, were you coming over? I mean you did give me yo key. I'll be up a little longer if you're coming," Peaches willingly invited.

Her invitation caught me off guard. Even so, I was tempted like a mothafucka to push Krystal off me and bolt out the door. But because of that feeling, I didn't, and that's the only reason.

"N'all, I ain't coming over. I'll get up with you later, bye Peaches." I ain't give her a chance to say nothing else as I hung up. I already knew if I kept talking to her, there was no doubt my ass would be at her crib.

"You good?" Krystal asked, her face scrunched up with a worried look.

"Why, you worried with yo nosy ass?" I didn't know why her question irritated me.

She smacked her lips while getting in my face. "You just looked like something was wrong, so don't pop slick with me."

Grabbing her wrist, I jerked her down to me. "Who the fuck you talking to? Make me beat yo ass, Krystal. I'll strangle the fuck outda you." I emphasized my words as my hands went around her neck and I squeezed.

"You won't choke nobody else, I promise. You mean as hell, I swear," muttered Krystal.

"It's just me. If you don't like it, so what. Yo ass ain't complained since we been together, so don't start now." As the last word left my mouth, my name was called. "Yo?" I replied back lazily.

"Hey, Blaze," ol' girl said with an attitude. She looked familiar, but I didn't know where from.

"What's up?" My two fingers waved her way. And ol' girl face scrunched up at me. "The fuck yo problem is?" She was just looking at a nigga funky as hell, like I stank or some shit. I looked at King and pointed to the babe who sat on his lap. "Who the fuck is her?"

"Her is sitting right here and her can speak, so ask her who the fuck she is?" She blurted, attitude thick with the smart remark.

Man what was up with these bitches and they fuck'd up ass attitudes toward me?

"Ebony, man, chill with that shit or get the fuck out," King told her.

She swirled around on him and muffed the fuck outda him. "Who are you talkin' to King? Yo ass called me here, not the other way around. How the fuck you gon' let this nigga play Peaches like that? You a dumb, grimy ass bitch," she snapped at him. Her hand, once again going to the side of his head, she pushed it harder with each ending word.

"Ebony, boss, touch me again, I'ma slap the fuck outda yo dumbass. I ain't letting them do shit, they ain't even together so what the fuck you mean play her," King defended, pushing her ass off him.

"You a dirty ass bitch. How the fuck you gon' be in my girls shit one minute, then hugged up with some bitch the next. What, she ain't wanna fuck yo hoe ass, so you moved on to this ratchet ass bitch?" King's girl snapped at me, lookin' like she was about to run up. If she did, I was gon' beat the fuck outda her ass. But before I could say shit, Krystal was already talkin.

"Who the fuck you calling a bitch? I ain't got shit to do with none of this, so check who the fuck you talking to before that mouth of yours get yo ass beat," Krystal snapped at her.

"I'm calling yo hoe ass a bitch! Why you sitting on my girl niggas lap? Fuck you gon' do, *bitch*?" This Ebony chick bucked up, Krystal got off my lap bout to walk up.

"Sit yo ass down, man," I said, pulling Krystal back down on my lap. "King get yo girl the fuck up outda here. Ain't nobody got time fah that shit she spitting." That chick was crazy, I'm glad I wasn't cheating because a nigga would've been caught like mothafucka.

"N'all, you get yo ass up and put me out, you fuck ass bitch. Come put me out, Blaze, sitting in my bitch shit, all in her ass, sleeping in her shit. Now you tryna play her. The Fuck!" Man why she couldn't be a nigga or a hoe fah that matter, so I could beat her ass.

"Ebony, get the fuck out, damn. Stupid ass don't never know how to act," King pushed her toward the door, but his stupid ass had to make it worse for himself. "Bye Krystal, I'ma see you at the 'Rex' Friday, right?" Ebony turned around and knocked the fuck out his ass in the face, swinging hard as hell. Man, those new age bitches tougher than some of those niggas. I needed to get a few of them on my team, real shit. "Bitch, what the fuck wrong with you hitting me like you stupid?" King snapped at her and push her ass down, but she got right back up swinging.

"Yo ol' disrespectful ass, talking to that bitch like I ain't right here." She was swinging on his ass hard as fuck.

"Sam, go help that nigga." Sam looked away from his phone at me.

"Hell no, you do it."

"Shid, she might whoop my ass if I go over there," I told him, laughing. "Who you textin'?" I asked as I watched King throw Ebony over his shoulder, carrying her out. Those mothafuckas was crazy.

"Brandy. She just pulling up now, so I'll get up with you later," Sam said and we shook up. Brandy was Sam's girl, had been since we were teenagers. "Bye, Krystal."

With a smile, Krystal waved. "Bye, dreads," she called out to him before turning into my lap and pulling something out of her pockets. "Here, I owe you this." The fifty dollar bill made me laugh.

"I thought you ain't have it?" I asked her while grabbing her ass and squeezing it.

Her face took on a serious look as she stared down at me. "I lied, so we rocking?"

I flipped her over on the couch. "Yeah, I'ma fuck with you fah now." My head nodded toward the door Sam just walked out of. "You not gon' ask why ol' girl came at you the way she did?"

She rolled her eyes at that. "I could care less what her beef is as long as she don't step to me wrong again. And you're not seeing her friend, so we cool. But if you are, then this not gon' work for the simple fact I ain't gon' be no niggas side chick. Simple yes or no, I'ma take yo word on this. Is you seeing ol' girl she talkin' 'bout?" She asked straight up.

"N'all, I tried fucking with her girl. But whether I am or not, we ain't together either. You do as you like, just as I'm able too. This ain't no relationship and the first time yo ass start treating this like it is, I'm dropping you." I don't have time to go through the same shit I did with Peaches. I'm good on that note, it ain't worth it.

"I got it, same thing goes for you." Though Krystal said that, she didn't like that. I could see on her face, but I ain't say shit.

"That bullshit don't apply to me."

She rolled her eyes before pushing me. "I should go, it's late." Pushing myself up, I helped her up.

"You live by yoself?"

"Yeah, I just move to Marshall Town." I glance at my watch to see it was almost five in the morning.

"How about I drop you off at yo crib? Then later when you up and about, hit me up and I'll take you to get your car," I offered.

"Why you can't do it now?" She asked as I walked us outside.

After I locked the club up, we went to the truck. But I stopped once I noticed the black on black Dodge Charger I barely drove. I kept it at the hall just in case. I glanced at the car then at Krystal. It was already five in the morning.

"You got license?" I asked and she gave me a look that said 'no shit'. "Don't look like that, a lot niggas rolling without L's nowadays, so I'm just asking. Give me yo license," I instructed while I opened my glove compartment, grabbing the little sliver box and envelope out. I sat it on the seat.

"I'm not lying, see," Krystal held it out in from of her.

Taking the card, I took a picture of her license, zooming in to make sure you could see the info clear.

"What are you doing, Blaze?"

I ignored her as I took the ink pad from the box. "Give me yo hand." Pushing each finger on the on the pad then the paper getting her prints I handed her license back. "It's just in case you try to fuck me over," I said, taking in her shocked expression.

"You just finger printed me?"

"Yeah, I did. Is that a problem?" If I was gon' fuck with her I needed to know everything about her, if she had a record or anything.

Krystal blinked a few times then shook her head. "Okay, so why can't you drop me off to my car?" She asked.

"I have something's to do right now on this side of town, so I'ma let you take my car and I'll get up with you later. Hold up," I quickly ran back inside the club to get the remote to the Charger. Once I returned, I handed it to her.

"How you know I won't just disappear with your car," she asked, smiling hard.

I laughed at that as I opened the envelope. "I don't, which was why I just did all this. Just in case I have to find yo ass. Say ah," she looked at me like I was crazy making me laugh. "Man, say ah, damn."

"Ah," I quickly stuck a Q-tip in her mouth to get saliva. "The fucks wrong with you?" She snapped at me as I put the swab in a tub then in a bag with her prints closing it up. Putting it back into the glove compartment I turned toward her.

"Baby, don't be offended. I have trust issues. I don't wanna get fuck'd over by nobody, so I take precautions as you can see. So don't fuck me over because I'd hate to have to kill you. Don't be mad, I'm just being real. Now, seeing this, do you still wanna fuck with me?"

Man, I didn't know that chick. Even if I thought she was cool and I wanted to fuck her didn't mean she couldn't be a snake ass bitch. Better safe thinking with my head and not my dick, that's how those young mothafuckas got caught up.

"I ain't gon' fuck you over, I'm not even mad about this. Just next time warn a bitch before sticking shit in her mouth," she said, walking closer to me. "You can come through around twelve, I'll make you lunch."

"I don't know, I got hella shit to do today." I had to stop by my other pool halls, my garage, car lot, Anastasia's and Jesse's, but it was what it was.

"It's just lunch for an hour, then you can be on your way, plus you got to get your car," she pressed.

I wasn't fuck'd up about her keeping my car, wasn't shit in there so I wasn't rushing to get it back. "I'll stop thru, but it won't be for an hour. So have my shit already made and hot before I get there. As for the car, keep it for now," I told her, looking down at my phone again. "Get up outda here, I'll see you later." Grabbing the front of her shirt I pulled her to me. "Let me find out you had a nigga in my shit, I'ma kill his ass then beat yours."

"Nigga, please. I'm not worried about you." With that, she stood on her tips, kissed me, then walked off.

"Keep on, I'ma have yo ass bent over the hood of that car."

She threw up her middle finger as she walked to the car. "You just talk, Blaze!"

Bitch gon' say that shit now. "Oh, baby, I can show you I ain't," I told her while walking backwards toward my truck.

"You're too much, bye," she called, laughing.

"I'ight," I hopped in the truck, started it then pulled off.
Why shit couldn't be this easy with Peaches ass?

Chapter 13

Peaches

It had been a few days and I hadn't heard from Blaze nor had I seen him. That shit was starting to piss me off. He was straight avoiding me like I was so type of hoe, when just the other day we were seconds away from having sex. Now we weren't even talking. I even tried being slick with getting to see him by using Sam to come over when they're together, but Blaze never came with him.

This is fucking irritating!

"What we doing today? It seemed like I ain't been out this apartment in years?" I asked Ebony and Kimmy as I lay on my bed, watching Ebony go through my closet.

"That's yo fault you been in a funk these past few days and don't wanna tell nobody why," Ebony said, looking at a white halter dress. "I'm going to try this on. So are you ready to talk about why you've been locked up in here?" Ebony asked as she started to get undressed.

I looked from Ebony to Kimmy then shrugged. "Blaze ol' stupid acting ass. He been straight avoiding the hell outda me. And it's crazy because I wanted him to leave me alone from jump. Now that he has, I miss him. Like I said, it's crazy."

"Not really, it's usually like that with us women. We always what we can't have. When he was chasing you, Peach, you basically blew him off. Now that he's gon' you want him. That's not crazy at all, you've never encountered a man like Blaze, he's not going to put up with your shit like these other softer men will," Kim explained as she played in my hair. "If it's meant to be it will be."

My eyes rolled at that.

"I guess, I mean I can accept the fact if he don't wanna fuck with me no more. Like okay, I can take that. But don't avoid me. The only reason it's really bothering me is because I feel like I really offended him, you know. And I don't want him to be pissed, holding that against me." That whole thing was stressing me out. I was not one to get attached, so I couldn't begin to understand why I was trippin' over Blaze.

Ebony suddenly jumped as her fingers snapped. Her eyes wide with excitement. "Blaze! Bitch I'm sorry I forgot to tell yo ass about that nigga and yo punk ass brotha. Girl I had to beat King's ass," she was so pissed and was talking way too fast.

My hands waved to stop her from talking. "Wait, E, calm down. Now you and King got into a fight?" My brows furrowed in confusions not understanding why she got hyped so suddenly.

"Yeah, the other day he calls at three in the morning, drunk, asking me to pick his ass up at his dude's bar. Not knowing who his dude is, of course I go get him. When I get there I see yo nigga hugged up with some bright skin bitch. I mean ol' girl was all on him like they were the only two there. Girl, I went the fuck off on 'em. Then that bitch gon' have the nerve to get buck, she lucky King grabbed my ass. But King was sittin' his ol' triflin' ass with them like shit was good, I beat his mothafuckin' ass," Ebony popped off, rowdy.

My head tilted to the side as the wheels in my head started to turn. "Wait, the other day when?"

"A few days ago," she responded.

I'd called his ass the other day around that time. That was the last time I'd talked to him. *So he was with some bitch, that's why he couldn't come over that night.* "I don't even care, he ain't my nigga. Blaze free to do as he please, I don't give a fuck. I just thought he was still mad at me for what I said the other day. No, I am pissed. He gon' play me for some bitch when his ass done ran my main nigga away? The fuck?" I said grabbing my phone so I could call and cuss his ass out, but Ebony stopped me.

"Nuh-uh, bitch. He having this thing at the Rex tonight, so don't even sweat it, babe. Though, from the looks of things, shit moving pretty fast with them. Because ol girl be driving his shit," Ebony went on to inform me.

What right did I have to be pissed? None at all, but I couldn't convince the logical part of my brain of that. My body was heated to the point that my nerves kicked up, making both my hands shake violently as my leg bounced up and down vigorously.

"Bitch, how the fuck you know?" Kimmy chimed in.

Ebony rolled her eyes at Kim, but answered nonetheless. "Because yesterday King and I was on our way to his place when he saw this all black Charger and rolled up on ol' girl thinking it was Blaze. I had to slap the fuck outda him for looking at that bitch ass. Nigga sitting there straight tryna spit game to that bitch like I wasn't even there. Both those bitches lucky I ain't have my gun."

He got this bitch driving his car?

"Is the bitch at least pretty?" I asked, making Kimmy laugh. "What? Man, I'm so serious. I want to know." My voice shook, the anger I was feeling seeped through as I tried to laugh along with her, but failed.

"She is, I ain't gon' lie or hate. Bitch thick as fuck, I mean she's got a little stomach, but that bitch got ass for days. Then she has the nerve to have hips on top of that, yellow bitch. I'm gon' deflate that hoe if she try some shit with King and I'ma cut his ass if he fuck with her," Ebony said, making Kimmy laugh, which I didn't find funny now that I knew she was pretty.

"What I'm not understanding is why King didn't tell me about this party," I thought out loud, but seeing as Ebony was pissed off she answered.

"Because he's a snake ass bitch." Once again, Ebony started to snap off and I quickly became irritated.

I didn't feel like dealing with her and King's shit when I was tryna figure out my own. "Shut up, damn. E, you acting as if you don't be talkin' to other niggas. So look at yo damn self before you start calling King out on his shit. Shid, it ain't like you don't know what the fuck he out here doing. So what you mad for? Yo ass ain't trying to change yo situation, so shut the fuck up!" I snapped at her.

I honestly didn't mean for all that to come out, but I couldn't deal with her at that moment, I couldn't deal with none of it right then. Shit was to fuckin' confusing, I didn't even understand why I was fuck'd up about Blaze and the bitch he was supposed to be seeing.

Ugh, I don't fuckin' know.

"Damn, Peach, that was fuck'd up," Kim said, looking at me while shaking her head.

"N'all, it's cool, Kim. Boss, fuck you Peaches. Don't try to play like yo ass A-one, because you not. Kim, I'll talk to you later." Without a second look at me, she walked out my room.

I flopped down on my bed as the front door slammed. "Don't be slamming my fuckin' door!" I yelled out to her, not knowing if she could hear me or not.

"Bitch, you was wrong. Now yo ass know she love that damn man and she don't be trickin'. She just don't want him to think he could do what he want and she just gon' let it slid," Kim snapped at me.

"I know, Kim, damn. I'm sorry—"

"Fuck you apologizing to me for? You ain't just stab me in the heart. If you had, I woulda cut yo ass back harder. Don't take yo shit out on her because you can't understand why you like that fucking man and don't know how to handle what's happening. You too busy trying to pretend it's nothing. But now that he's found something new yo ass wanna get conflicted? Get that bullshit outda here, Peaches.

"King done shielded yo ass so much you blind to realizing when you truly like a nigga. Figure yo shit out, then call Ebony and apologize. That shit was foul you spit at her. You know when it comes to King it hurts her. Yo ass was wrong." Kimmy stared down at me, disappointed. "I'm gone too." With a shake of her head she turned away from me. "And I'm taking these," she grabbed my white Gucci bag from the closet, then her keys and purse. "These too," Kim snatched up the European, sequined, peep toe wedges by the straps then walked out my room and once again the front door was slamming.

"I'm just pissing everyone off this week, damn, man." I knew what I said to Ebony was wrong, Even though what I said was true, didn't mean I had the right to say it.

Ebony loved King, I knew that. And after the shit happened at Mike's party she'd been trying to leave him alone until King changed his ways. His lifestyle she could deal with, but sharing him she wasn't going to keep doing. *So she says. It's been the same story for years.*

They'd been back and forth doing that since they meet. King had literally put Ebony through some shit when it came to him and those hoes. Even so, Ebony continued to deal with him, which I didn't understand, neither did I understand King's ass. *Men are freaking complicated.*

That's just like with Blaze ass. I'd known that nigga for a month, if you can really call it that. He just practically pushed his way into my life, *who does that shit?* No dude I have ever met had done anything like that to me. Blaze was different, he was persistent, possessive, psychotic, rude as fuck. And him being all those things was reason enough for me to stay away from him. But it was also what attracted me more to him.

If he thought for a second I was gon' let that shit fly with him and his new bitch, he had another thing coming. You don't invade my life and get that close to me like he had that past week, then bounce because of a spat. N'all, I don't roll like that. Nigga been sleeping with me, practically fuckin' me and he left because I joked about something he didn't like. *Yeah, okay. If Blaze thought it was going to be that easy to get rid of me, he don't know Peaches.*

"Cherry, what are you doing?" I asked my kitten as I heard her clawing at the bottom of the covers. Picking her up, I got off my bed then grabbed my phone from the nightstand and dialed Ebony.

"You've reached Ebony,' After getting that message five times, I've decided to call King to see if she called him.

"What's up?" He answered on the first ring.

A Dangerous Love 2
Can't Let Go

I rolled my eyes hearing King's voice. I wanted to ask him about this bitch and Blaze, but knowing his ass, he was probably happy Blaze wasn't coming around no more. "King, is Ebony with you?"

'Hell n'all, her ass been trippin'. I ain't talked to her in couple days and her ass ain't been at the crib. She gon' get fuck'd up if she keep playin'," he vented, pissed off.

Again I found myself rolling my eyes at his dumbass. "How you gon get mad at her for not being at home when yo ol' triflin' ass only come around when you wanna fuck any mothafuckin' way? King, you dumb. She gon' get tired of yo stupid ass and find another nigga that's way better then you, who's going to treat her right," I snapped at him.

"Fuck is wrong with you?" He asked while turning down the music in his background.

'Nothing, I gotda go.'

'N'all, fuck that. Yo ass ain't snapping for no gotdamn reason. What happened?" King pushed for more information.

I didn't wanna talk to him no more. "Nothing, King. Bye." After hanging up on him, I tried calling Blaze.

"You've reached two-one-nine..." Hanging up the phone, I sat it down on the kitchen counter along with Cherry so I could feed her.

I wasn't even gon go to that little party thing Blaze was having at the Rex, but since his ass wanted to play, I was gon' do the same. I wouldn't be wrong to act as girlfriend when he didn't seem to have a problem with it when he beat Sly's ass twice and shot him.

Once Cherry was fed, I went to my bathroom and took a long, streaming, hot shower to relax myself, but that shit wasn't working. Throughout all my years I could not remember one time my body had ever been that fuckin' tense. Ever! Especially not over a fuckin' man.

This that bullshit!

Why the fuck did his ass have to fuck everything up? Shit was going great before his ass came along. To get head with

no feelings attached was my routine, but all that changing because of *him*.
    Blaze!

Chapter 14

Peaches

The barbeque started at four and I was starting to back out of going. That had never happened to me, those feelings, the jealously wasn't something I was use too. It was infuriating to have those emotions for someone like Blaze. I'd always said I wouldn't fall for some hood because of the shit my momma went through with my dad. Hell, even the shit Ebony was still going through with King's triflin' ass.

I am going, I'm not about to sit around this fuckin' apartment mopping and let some bitch come around fuckin' with my shit. Blaze and that bitch got life fuck'd up if he think this gon fly.

God, this man has me feeling all types of bipolar.

I stood in my full length mirror and stared at my reflection, I was so nervous. I gave myself a once over, took in the leopard print halter top that tied around my neck with the matching skirt. My shoulders shook as I tried to shake my nerves away.

I went to my dresser, sprayed myself with VS Love Spell. Picked up my rhinestone, leopard print, stiletto sandals from the side of the dresser and slipped them on. I slipped my big, black, oval shaped ring on my index finger, then went to my vanity, grabbed my black chain with my gold brass knuckles and I pulled it over my head.

Standing in the middle of my room, I looked around, not knowing what I was looking for exactly. Maybe it was just that I was trying to stall longer, subconsciously hoping time would fly and the night would end.

My eyes soon landed on my round toe Iron Fist satin skull and floral platforms. Ebony immediately popped in mind.

Quickly, I snatched my VS leopard print tote bag. I laid the shoes in there then went to my closet to get the one shoulder side sliced dress I bought to go with the shoes. With a groan, I folded the dress and sat it on top of the shoes before throwing my phone, wallet and my gun inside.

After I combed through my hair once more, I put on a bit of eyeliner and a little gold eye shadow before swiping my lips with some cherry flavored gloss. Again I gave myself a once over.

I was ready to go.

***

I pulled into the Rex only to pull right back out because it was packed. Niggas were parked any kind of ways and to close to each other. I parked on the street, folks didn't know how to drive and would hit your shit without a problem. I didn't feel like going to jail because I fucked somebody up for scratching my baby. Parking a few blocks down, I grabbed my tote bag and got out just as a black car came speeding past me.

"Fuckin' bitch!" I screamed at the car. "Stupid ass." Closing my door, I hit the alarm button then walked down to the Rex, pissed off. *I swear this is the fuckin' hood for yo ass, niggas just don't give a fuck.*

I made it back to the parking lot and pulled out my phone to call Missy to see where they were, only to end up running into Mya's rude ass.

"Damn, Peaches, watch where you going," Kimmy's sister said with an attitude which had me looking up at her.

"Bitch, you ran into me, what yo ass should be saying is excuse me. I don't know what done crawled up yo ass, Mya, but don't take that shit out on me," I snapped right back at her. I was about to walk away, but what she said next had me stopping again.

"You are my fuckin' problem. Whatever this thing you experimenting with Missy, you gon' have to let it go and find somebody else to fuck with," she informed me, her face contorted into a mean glare.

The confusion on my face was evident as my brows furrowed and my head tilted sideways. "What?" I was confused by what she was saying for the simple fact that I wasn't experimenting shit. Then it hit me. "What Missy and I got going on is between us, Mya. You ain't got shit to do with it. I mean, why do you care? What y'all had wasn't anything serious anyway. If you still wanna fuck around with Missy then do that, we aren't together. So don't come at me with that shit, acting as if we owe you an explanation. Gon' head with that bullshit." Why did it seem like déjà vu with somebody coming at me about fuckin' with what they considered theirs?

Folks got life fuck'd up.

Mya said nothing else, simply mugged and walked past me with a bump to my shoulder. I shook my head and started walking again.

"Damn, baby, can I hit that?" A voice sounded behind me before their hand came down on my ass.

"Stop, you bitch, that shit hurts!" I snapped, hitting Angel in the arm.

"What took yo ass so damn long? And what's this I hear about you going off on Ebony?" She asked and I groaned. "Nuh uh, bitch, none of that. You fuck'd up now. Make it right, Peach. And you know how hard Ebony ass play at forgiving, especially when it comes to King's sexy ass," Angel replied.

I groaned loudly. "I know. I was just a little irritated, then her talking shit about King, I just didn't want to hear it. I shouldn't have said the extra stuff and I'm going to apologize when I find her." Linking our arms, Angel led the way. "You know where she's at?"

Angel nodded while pointing ahead. "Yep, up there fighting with King like always. Hey, don't you and ol' boy suppose too be talking or something? I mean, he was staying at yours right?" She suddenly asked as we got closer to the grill. I already knew what she was talking about.

"Something like that. He's like how Sly and I were, but different. He gets on my nerves." Irritation quickly set into my body and I bit into my bottom lip, looked away from her with a roll of my eyes.

"Oh, my God, Peach, you like him!" Angel squeaked out as she yanked me to a stop.

I couldn't help but laugh, she was so dramatic at times. "No, I don't. Okay, I do a little. I just don't wanna date him, not now anyways. He's practically another King and I don't need two crazy, possessive men in my life right now. I can't deal." There wasn't any point in lying to my best friends about liking Blaze because they'd see right through that bullshit.

"Well, yo new man was with some big booty rat. I had to snap on his ass, girl. Shit was about to get ugly if that Sam dude ain't grab me." I burst out laughing, Angels' little ass was always, and I do mean that literally, always up to fight. She was the smallest of us all, bitch wasn't no bigger than a tooth pick and was buck as fuck.

"Bitch, you did not try to fight ol' girl—" I started, but she cut me off with a wave of a hand.

"N'all, I went at him. I stepped to her, though, but she ain't know about you. Saying Blaze told her that y'all weren't together, it didn't work out or some shit. And you know how bitches is nowadays with believing these lying ass niggas. It might take all of us because Blaze a big mothafucka, but we can beat his ass all through this thang," Ang explained.

Even though I laughed at what she'd just said, I was still pissed by what Blaze said to ol' girl. I couldn't wait to see his ass *and* that bitch. She may not have known, but her ass was about to know. This gon' be her warning. And if she continue to fuck with what's mine, then shit was gon' get nasty real quick.

"What's up, Peaches?" My head turned to the side at the two dudes that spoke. Sam who yelled from afar and the other one was pretty close.

"Who is that?" Angel asked, and I laughed at her as she looked him up.

"Chase, dude I met at Voodoo a while back," I whispered to her before waving at him. "Hey," I spoke as I hugged him.

"Hey, you. You're looking sexy as always," he said, pulling back and giving me an obvious once over, making me laugh. Then he looked at Angel and waved, which she returned.

"Thanks. So what's been good with you?" I asked him while leaning against Angel.

"Shit, really. It's fuck'd how you stopped calling," he stated, staring into my eyes.

If it wasn't for King and that thing with Blaze, I probably would have still been talking to him. Then again, if I had of known he used to fuck with Trina, then that shit would have never had started. I moved his arms from me as I smacked my lips.

"That's because yo hoe ass baby's momma came at me sideways while I was at work." As that day came back to mind, I found myself getting an attitude all over again.

"The fuck you talking about? How would my baby's moms even know who you are?" He looked sincerely confused.

"I'm guessing that night at Voodoo she saw us. But that bitch got an ass whoopin' coming, so you let her ass know that." I was about to walk away, but dude grabbed my arm. He pulled me back, almost making me fall. "Dude, what the fuck yo problem?"

"My bad, I ain't mean to do that. I was just tryna stop you from walking away is all. I don't know who came at you, but it wasn't my daughter's mother. She wasn't even at Voodoo that night. I'm kinda fuck'd up about what you saying, plus my daughter's moms is engaged to be married in a few weeks, you know. So I don't see why she'd come at you or how she know who you are," he explained to me. The serious expression on his face didn't leave once.

I looked at Angel to see her looking at Chase as if he had lost his damn mind.

"Angel, chill. Chase, don't be grabbing on me like that. And yo ass lying because I saw Trina in yo face at the club that night. If I would've known ahead of time that she was yo daughter's mom I wouldn't have even fuck'd with you."

"Who da fuck is Trina?" He asked.

I just started laughing. "Wow, really Chase? Whatever, I'm gone. It was nice running into you, though." I told him, about to walk around him, but he stepped in front of me.

"Damn, nigga get yo thirsty ass the fuck gone. She just said she ain't wanna fuck with you. Now go find yo triflin' ass baby moms," Angel snapped at him.

"Yo, don't be disrespecting my daughter's moms. That ain't even 'bout to go down like that with you talking about her. Peaches, my baby's moms name's Michelle, not no damn Trina." He stopped talking as if a thought finally came to him, and a look of recognition crossed his face.

Without warning, he took hold of my wrist and started walking. So I snatched up Angel's little ass, dragging her with us.

"Damn, Chase, slow yo ass down and let me go." He ignored me as he looked around. He dragged us around looking for that bitch for at least fifteen minutes before we found her with some dude. Chase seemed pissed when he saw her. He let me go, then walked right up to Trina, snatching her by her long weave ponytail and pulling her over to where we stood.

"Is this her?" He asked me, jerking her head up so we could get a look at her face.

"Yep, she came at me while I was at work, saying she was yo baby moms and whatever we had was gon' stop." Relaying her words back, I shrugged, already done with the whole thing.

"You lying bitch, I ain't never fuck'd you. You my daughter's mother, Trina?" He asked before pushing her hard, making her fall down.

That wasn't really necessary. Even though I ain't like the hoe, he ain't have to manhandle her like that.

"No, that bitch lying. I never said you were my baby's father, I ain't even got no kids. I promise all I told her was that you had a baby by my cousin and that you didn't need no gold digging hoes tryna use you, I promise," she lied with a straight face.

This lying... "Bitch, on what, you sitting here lying, though?" As soon as the words left my mouth, Chase slapped the shit out of her. *Oh my...* "Chase what the fuck you doing? No," I said, tryna push his ass away from Trina.

"N'all, that bitch always lying. This ain't the first time she done did this shit. Stupid ass bitch," he snapped, slapping her again.

Why the fuck I always got to meet crazy mothafuckas? *He is definitely showing his ass now.*

"Angel, let's go. This that bullshit." I wasn't about to witness him beating that girls ass.

"Peaches, man wait. Her ass just pissed me off. She the reason me and my baby's mother ain't together now, because her ass be lying," he explained.

My eyes slid from him to Trina, who had pushed herself up off the ground before running up on Chase–*or so I thought.* Until the bitch swung at me. Angel pulled me back just in time, causing her to miss.

Oh, I had been wanting whoop that ass.

"You lying ass bitch!" She was yelling as she missed before she came back.

I moved to the right, dodging her blow. She swung again, missed and I caught her with a left, knocking the hell out of her. Trina went stumbling backwards. Before she could react, I hit her with an uppercut and just kept swinging on her until she fell. Once she did, it was a wrap. My size six stiletto sandal went into her face as I began stomping her. I never talk shit in a fight. Why? Because it's tiresome and shit could easily be flipped around.

"Stupid ass bitch! Dumbass hoe." My main focus was to whoop ass, not talk shit, which was exactly what I was doing to

Trina. I was stomping and kicking the shit out that bitch as she yelled for me to stop and get off her. "Ol' lying ass bitch." I stomped on Trina harder, then kicked her ass in the mouth, tryna knock her teeth out.

I could admit that most of my anger wasn't toward her, but she went picking, so I was letting all my shit out on that bitch.

"Peaches, calm yo ass down," King yelled, yanking me back.

Instinctively, I turned around and punched him hard in the jaw. "Don't fuckin' touch me!" I snapped at him before turning back and kicking Trina in the face one last time. "Stupid ass bitch!" With that, I snatched up my tote bag and started walking away.

I'm done with this bullshit. I don't even know why I fuckin' came here in the first place.

Chapter 15

Peaches

"Peaches, hold the fuck up!" King called from behind me before he finally caught up, grabbing my arm.

"Leave me alone, King. I ain't got shit to say to you." Jerking my arm from his hold, I continued to walk.

"Man, slow yo ass the fuck down." King grabbed me from behind and locked my arms at my sides. "You ass bet not hit me," he snapped, holding me tight. He stopped and held me. "You cool?"

"No, I'm not. That bitch swung on me and got blood on my fucking shoes." It wasn't a lie. I just wanted to go home, that bitch had fuck'd up my whole mood.

King placed me on my feet, then turned me around to face him. "What do you want, King? Don't you have some hoes to be chasing around or something?"

"Man, what the hell is up with you? I ain't did shit to yo ass fah you to be snapping and all that at me." He stared down at me with his arms folded.

Mimicking him, I folded my arms under my chest, rolled my eyes and kept quiet.

"Peaches, make me slap yo ass. You hear me talking to you, now tell me what's up," he snapped.

When I still didn't say anything, he grabbed my arm and began to drag me off to the side of the pavilion where nobody could see. I knew my brother all too well. He pulled me over there just to slap me.

"Nothing, King, dang! I just don't like her is all." It wasn't an entire lie, I didn't like Trina. King glared at me before roughly pressing me into the side of the Rex hall. "King, nothing is wrong with me, I promise, dang. Now let me go." I was not tryna get slapped by him, that shit hurt. King didn't look like he believed me, though.

"Peaches—"

"King, let me go. Ain't nothing wrong with me, okay," sighing, I calmed myself down forcefully, trying to lose the hostility in my voice. "I'm sorry I hit you," I said softly as I hugged him. My brother was such a sucker, it made no fucking sense whatsoever. He was just too soft when it came to me sometimes, especially at times like that.

"I know what yo ass doing and it ain't gon' work, but if yo ass ever snap at me like you did earlier, or hit me like that again, I'ma fuck you up."

My eyes rolled and I pushed him away from me. "Whatever, you love me too much. Plus, I meant what I said earlier, Ebony is going to leave yo dumbass one of these days." I raised a questioning brow at him. "Were you really gon' hit me?"

"Hell yeah! Yo ass hit like a fucking nigga, I almost forgot who the fuck you was. My damn jaw hurt. You hit me again, I'ma punch you back," he threatened.

Rolling my eyes, I linked my arm with his. "Where Ebony at?" I asked him. "I got some ass kissing to do," I wasn't gon' tell him what I said to her because there wasn't a doubt in my mind that he would beat my ass.

"What yo ass do?" He asked.

"Nothing. Now where is she? You know I don't like my friends mad at me for too long, especially Ebony's ass. That bitch will keep this shit going for months and I don't need that." Ebony could hold a grudge for a long ass time. If nothing serious was happening she would ignore you. I loved my bitch just like all my friends and I hated for them to be mad at me.

"Here..." King called while pointing to a fountain. He turned on the water and started rinsing the blood off my foot. He couldn't help not treating me like a kid, I guess because he'd been playing father since I was younger. It was just a natural instinct for him.

"Thanks. So what's this I hear about you and some big booty girl?" I asked, tryna play it cool about Blaze's new friend.

King laughed as he shook his head. "Man, ain't shit happening with that chick. That's Blaze's friend, she cool as hell though," he said, looking around the park before pulling me to where my friends and his were.

"Hey, Peaches," Dane's wife Jennifer called out. We embraced in a hug.

"Hey, girl, don't ever send a message by that wack ass husband of yours," I told her as we pulled away laughing.

"What message?" She asked and I shook my head.

"About me coming over for dinner," I told her.

"Girl, that was like a month ago," she said, looking over at Dane before hitting him.

"Yeah, he just told me last week," I told her as I walked up to Dane, hugging him. "Hey my sexy chocolate bear," I gave him a flirty smile and kissed his cheek.

"See what I go through. And you wanna say how nobody want a nigga," Dane told Jennifer, making her slap him again.

"Boy, don't nobody want yo black ass except for me. Peaches, stop pumping up that big ass ego of his," Jennifer laughed.

"Big Black knows he's on my speed dial. Yeah, I'm waiting for the day he come calling," I teased, winking at Dane, making him smile stupidly.

"Bitch, you wrong. And what yo black ass smiling fah? Dane, make me cut yo dick off, nigga make me. I work with surgeons, I watch they asses, so I know what to do. Keep on," we burst out laughing as he automatically covered himself.

"Y'all some fools, bye," I told them before walking away. As soon as I looked to my left, my eyes locked with Ebony's, but she simply rolled hers and looked away from me. I went up to her and she turned to walk away, but I stopped her. "E, don't do that please," I said while grabbing her arm, but she pulled away.

"Peaches, fo'real, man, I don't even wanna hear it. That shit was foul. Here I am trying to be yo friend, and so what if I was talking about King's triflin' ass, who I checked because he was sitting there kickin' it with that bitch and Blaze, only to have you snap at me. Man n'all, so whatever fuck ass apology you have, keep it," she snapped. I swear she was so stubborn. Rolling her eyes she turned away from me, about to walk away.

"I got you something," I said and she stopped and turned toward me. Ebony cocked her hip to the side as she stared at me. "Are you going to listen to my apology?" I asked her and again she rolled her eyes.

"I'm standing here aren't I?" She snapped at me.

Bitch just wanted to see what I got her. "I'm sorry, E. I was frustrated and shouldn't have took it out on you. I'm a bitch I admit. No matter how frustrated I was, what I said shouldn't have come out. Even though I do think you're completely stupid for putting up with that bullshit, I shouldn't have threw it in your face and I'm really, really sorry. Can you forgive me?"

It may not have seemed like a big deal what I said to her earlier, but it was a painful thing to have to deal with the lies, cheating, and all that after nine years. I mean, something had to give, but King never slowed down, which was why it was hard for me to accept what I was feeling for Blaze. The chemistry was there, wasn't no denying it, but I just didn't want to end up like them.

"It depends on what you got me," she countered.

Hearing a laugh behind me, I turned to see my other three best friends watching us. I nodded toward the picnic table. We walked over to it and I sat my tote bag down. I took out my gun, slid it into the waist band of my skirt before taking out the dress and then the shoes.

"You're giving these to me?" She asked, gesturing toward the dress and shoes I was holding.

"Yes. Now am I forgiven?" I asked her.

She gave me a funky look before snatching the shoes and dress from my hands. "Bitch, don't think you can just buy me off." She barked with an attitude.

I reached from my stuff back. "Then give me my shit back."

Ebony snatch the items out of my reach, holding them against her chest. "I didn't say I didn't want it, I'm just saying you can't always buy me. You're really giving me these? Like I won't see you in a few weeks asking for them back?" She asked for clarification.

I laughed at her while I nodded my head. "Yes, they're yours. Now am I forgiven?"

Ebony was smiling until I said that last bit. "No." She stated simply.

"E, come on—"

Ebony cut me off, shushing and waving her hand as she looked at my bag. "Let me get that bag too, then you are."

Was she serious? "No, I paid fifty dollars for this damn tote," I said, holding my Victoria's Secret bag to my chest.

"So. Plus I need something to put these in," she added, gesturing to the dress and shoes.

I shrugged. "You better walk that shit to your car because you not getting my bag. I just got it, now if you're not going to forgive me, hand me my shit back."

Ebony laughed at that before hugging me, which I gladly returned. "You're forgiven, next time I'ma cut yo ass for talking to me like that." She looked down at me with a serious expression.

"I really am sorry," I told her.

She waved her hand. "Don't worry about it, I understand completely," Ebony muttered as she held the dress against her clothed body.

"Yo ass understand now after I gave you my stuff. You're something else I swear." *This chick.*

"Bitch, you have no idea how long I've been planning on stealing these and blaming it on Kimmy," Ebony said while looking over my shoulder.

"Bitch, why me?" Kimmy asked, walking closer to us with Missy and Angel behind her.

"Because yo ass always taking her stuff without returning it," Ebony pointed, out making us laugh.

"That's true, and bitch, those shoes you took earlier, I want them back," I told her.

"Bitches, whatever. She got some cute shit and I only take her shoes, the ones I can fit. Missy the one that be taking her clothes," she said with a shrug.

My eyes fell on Missy and I hit her in the arm, forgetting all about Kim's last comment.

"Ouch, bitch! Why you hit me?" Missy asked, looking at me like I was crazy while rubbing her arm.

"Why you didn't tell me we were fuckin' around? Or should I say, experimenting?"

All eyes turned toward her then, causing her face to go red.

"I've been meaning to tell you, I just kept forgetting. Wait, Mya came to you?" Missy's eyes grew wide.

"Yep, my reaction exactly," I nodded my head. "She stepped to me in the parking lot saying this little thing we got going on is gon' have to stop."

"What did you say?" Missy asked with a hand to her mouth, shocked.

"I told her that what we got going on is between us and that if she want to keep fuckin' you then she can because we're not together. Missy, I don't mind playing along, but dang give me some type of heads up. I thought Mya was gon' beat my ass in that parking lot," I joked.

"She wasn't happy about that kiss, that crazy bitch slapped the fuck outda me. Girl, we were in the bathroom fighting... Nuh uh, wait. Once we finished in the bathroom, this bitch gon' try and leave with some hoe. I beat her ass again," she said, and we broke out laughing.

"Nuh-uh, bitch, y'all were not fighting." Ebony said, leaning against the bench, laughing.

"Yeah, we were. And then the bitch had a nerve to show up at my house later that night," Missy said with an attitude.

"You beat her ass again, then put her out?" I asked, laughing, causing Missy to look at me like I was crazy.

"Hell n'all, that bitch ate my pussy before fucking the shit outda me with that strap. Had a bitch forgetting everything. I was like I ain't gon' fuck with Peaches no mo, yeah this yours! A bitch was crying, y'all." Missy finished saying with a clap of her hands.

Missy was a damn fool for no reason at all. Why would she tell us all that? Even though I thought that, I was laughing so hard.

"But that was before Mike's party, I ain't fuckin' with that hoe no more."

"I'm done with yo stupid ass, I promise," I stated, still laughing.

"That's some nasty ass shit. I don't wanna hear about my best friend fucking my sister," Kimmy said with a shudder as the rest of continued to laugh.

"Ebony, come here!" King called, but Ebony stuck up her middle finger.

"Fuck you!" She yelled at him.

"What this?" I asked, pointing between the two as she rolled her eyes.

"I'm tired of him. I'm so done, I swear. Been done since he was flirting with that bitch the other day. I told his ass I'm tired of his bullshit, now he won't leave me the fuck alone. Shit got so bad I'm staying at Missy's. I don't have time for King no more. I need something serious, which is the opposite of what he wants. So, it is what it is." Ebony looked so sincere.

She always did.

I loved my brother dearly, but he was never going to find another chick like Ebony. Honestly, I was happy she was finally tired of his shit— if she was serious this time—because she deserved better than what she was getting, so I told her that. I'd been telling her that.

"It's about damn time! I told him this morning that you were gon' leave his triflin' ass. You deserve to be happy, so find yo man. You know this mean you can't be fucking him no mo, right?" I told her and she let out a groan.

"I know, and as long as we're not by one another then I'ma be good. But damn I'ma miss that anaconda. Shit is wicked, he got that 'feel it in my throat dick." A longing look came over her face and she looked at the ground in thought. Ebony's eyes soon snapped to mine. "I ain't got to stop fucking him completely, not just yet anyways. I mean, not until I meet someone new, right?" Her eyes where wide as she asked that.

"Ugh, I don't want to know what my brother is packing. Shit is nasty." Like Kimmy, I shuddered at the thought of King's dick before gagging. I could just picture it with all type of sores. "Ugh!"

"That's ol' girl right there," Angel said, pointing toward the parking lot.

My fake gagging stop immediately as I spotted the black car that rode past, probably tryna find a parking spot.

Oh, hell no!

"That bitch almost hit me when I got out my car," I snapped, remembering the black car.

"That's reason enough to beat her ass. You know I got yo back. That bitch popped slick at me when I told her she was sitting on my girl's nigga," Ebony was mugging hard.

"N'all, we good. I'll be right back though," I told them as I walked over to where Blaze, Sam, and King stood a few sections down at a picnic table. "Hey, Pretty Boy," I said, giving Sam a hug since he was the closest to me.

"What's up, Tyson? I saw you over there," he laughed as we broke apart.

"Boy, shut yo ass up, you stupid." I walked over to Blaze.

My stomach tightened as the nerves once again set in.

Chapter 16

Peaches

"The fuck you got on?" Blaze asked the moment I stepped to him. He pulled at my skirt. "Shit too damn small."

Slapping his hands away, I looked down at my outfit. "No, it's not." I looked to Sam and King. "Can y'all give us a minute?" I asked them. King looked kind of funky about leaving, whereas Sam shook up with Blaze and walked off. "King, come on man, damn. Like five minutes."

"I'ight, don't be on no slick shit either, Peaches." King dapped Blaze then jogged over to where Ebony sat with the girls.

I swear he was never going to let me grow up.

With my focus back on Blaze, I leaned against the bench next to him. "So what, we have one little spat and you just don't fuck with me no more?" I asked him while looking down at my shoes.

"Shid, it is what it is. I ain't got time to play games with yo ass, man. That shit you was spittin' kinda fuck'd me up. I already don't trust mothafuckas and you asking that shit out in public. I ain't with that," he answered.

"What, you thought I was asking that as a setup?" I turned to face him, I now stood directly in front of him.

"I ain't saying shit. My thing is, as many times as we've been alone you could've asked whatever. But yo ass waited right until we in public. The fuck kinda shit is that?" He fussed.

"So, you've been ignoring me because you think I was on some slick shit." The disbelieving was heavy in my voice as I stared at him with the same non-believing look.

"I didn't say that," Blaze stated, making me roll my eyes.

"You just implied it. Why would I do that when King does the same damn thing? Snitching or setting you up would put mothafuckas onto King since y'all be together. I ain't saying you got to trust me, but trust and believe anything that King's

involved in I'ma protect with my life. Even if that means yo
dumbass no matter how fuck'd up the situation is. Blaze, if you
felt like I was on that bullshit you should've been a man about
yours and came to me, not hide like some bitch." I was pissed
that he would think some shit like that.

Call me what you want, a bitch, hoe, a slut, anything but
a fuckin' snitch. In no shape or form was snitching in my blood,
especially with King in that shit. "You know what? Fuck you,
Blaze, if you ass gon' take everything I say to heart—"

"Man, shut the fuck up, I'll slap yo ass in the mouth. I
ain't no bitch, so watch that shit. But you right, I should've came
to you. I didn't, that's my fault. Shid, first sign of shaky shit and
I'm gone, simple as that. I ain't got time for stupid shit, man,
boss, I don't," he explained nonchalantly.

"Whatever," I tried to make my voice sound as non-
caring as his did, but from the curious look on his face I knew he
didn't buy it.

"What you mad because a niggas got lost? Ain't that
what you wanted? I mean, from jump that's all yo ass been
saying. '*I ain't gon' be fuck'd about you.*' That's the shit you
always spitting, right?" He questioned with a cocky little smirk.
"So what you mad fah? I'm doing what you wanted."

I didn't like him. Looking away, I bit into my bottom lip
as my eyes rolled up.

"Yo ass can't talk now?" Blaze grabbed my arm as he
questioned me.

"So what," I started, but didn't know how to finish so I
trailed off.

"Fuck you smiling fah?"

Peaches, stop being a bitch and talk to him. Sighing, I
walked closer to him, closing the space between us.

"Look, I ain't fucking with you on some real shit, man.
Gon' Peaches," he insisted, his hand came out and he gave me a
slight push back.

My lips pursed together as I once again closed the space
between us. I wrapped my arms around his neck. "That's what

124

yo mouth saying, but you know that's a lie, on some real shit. So why pretend?" I used his words on him. My mouth rubbed against his before I bit into his bottom lip.

"I ain't playing man, gon'." Blaze pulled his head back to look down at me, but didn't make any attempt to push me away.

"Stop playing like you ain't miss me, when we know you did." I said, kissing at his bottom lip.

Placing his hands on my hips, Blaze pulled me in between his legs. "What makes you so sho' I missed yo mean, itty bitty ass?" Blaze muttered.

I could not stand him. Even so, I couldn't help but laugh as I pulled back slightly to reach into the pocket of my tote, getting what I needed.

"If you didn't, you wouldn't be taking this." My two fingers raised with his key tucked between them.

"I don't want that shit," he took the key then flung his arm out, pretending to throw it.

"You play too much. See, this why I don't like you," I told him, muffing his head back.

"Man, shut up. If you didn't, you wouldn't be giving me this, now would you." He had a point. Humming, I bit at his bottom lip again.

"So does this mean we made up?" I asked as I watched him put the key on the ring then slide the set back into his pocket.

Blaze pulled me back to him with a head nodded.

"We good as long as you ain't on that bullshit and yo ass stop charging a nigga fah breakfast and dinner," he bargained.

My arms once again found their way around his neck. "I doubt that's gon' happen, but you're more than welcome to eat elsewhere. So, will you be coming over tonight?" I wanted him to spend the night for the simple fact...I kinda like sleeping with him and I felt the need to tell him that.

"Aw, you missed a nigga bad, huh?"

"Fuck you. No," I looked away, making it obvious I was lying. Ugh, I hated those feelings. "Yeah, I missed you."

Blaze's eyes roamed over my face before locking with mine. "Peaches, you missed me in yo bed?" Blaze asked as his head came closer to mine. *God, I didn't want that, but I did.* "I'll be there." From his tone it sounded like a promise. One I hoped he'd keep.

I stood on my tip toes and met him half way, bringing our lips together. My arms tightened around his neck as I bit into his bottom lip, pulling it into my mouth, sucking on it before doing the same to the top.

Blaze's tongue slid through my parted lips. His hands tightened on my hips as our tongues initiated their own sexual dance.

But the clearing of a throat soon ended our moment.

A very loud groan left my mouth to make it known I wasn't happy about being interrupted. *That damn kiss was getting good.* I pulled back slightly and Blaze buried his head into my neck, sucking on the skin. He wasn't at all bothered by the interruption. My eyes rolled and a smile came to my lips. I looked to my left to see a short, bright skin chick just standing there, not saying anything.

"Can I help you?" I asked her as Blaze's hands became friendly and started roaming. "Blaze, stop!" I laughed as I tried to move his hand from my ass, but the fucka wouldn't let go. "Blaze, fo'real, stop before King brings his black ass over because of yo mannish ass." I was being serious whereas he laughed.

"Man, I told you before not to worry about King," he said, bringing his lips back to mine. I leaned into him, pecked his lips through my smile. "Why the hell you smiling? You must've missed a nigga bad," says the fool who was all over me.

I didn't even say anything about that, instead I answered truthfully.

"I told you I did," I whispered low as I let the tip of my tongue flick his bottom lip. Sticking my tongue out, Blaze grabbed it between his teeth then pulled it into his mouth. Laughing through the kiss, I pulled back. "You better stop before I have you kissing my second lips."

Blaze started laughing. "As long as—" The clearing of a throat once again interrupted us, cutting Blaze off. It was that yellow chick.

"What can I do for you, mama?" I asked and she looked at Blaze. "Bae, who is this?" Of course I knew who she was, her ass stood out like candy in a candy store, that damn noticeable.

"Bae?" She asked like there was something funny about it while looking at Blaze once again.

"What's up, Krystal. Took yo ass long enough to get back. Fuck you do, go joy riding?" Blaze asked her, turning around so I was now facing the girl, I leaned into Blaze's front and his arms went to my waist.

"Bae, who's your friend?" I asked again.

"Bae?" She laughed this time.

"What's funny?" I asked her.

"Peaches, this my friend Krystal. Krystal—" Blaze started the introductions, but she cut him off.

"Peaches? Ol' girl that you said you weren't messing with?" She says, looking at me with a stank look.

"Mama, don't be looking at me like that—" I started.

"Peaches, shut yo ass up. Krystal, it ain't even like that. What this is right here ain't got nothing to do with you, so that attitude you bringing, lose that bitch fo'real," he told her and she glared at him. "Man, fix you fuckin' face. Fuck you mad fah?"

"I ain't mad, not at all. You ain't my dude, but a few days ago she wasn't yo bitch either." *Bitch?*

"I got yo bitch, mama. Boss, this ain't even where you want it, sweetie? Don't be mad because he knows where it's at, whether he's with me every fuckin' day or not. This right here," I pointed to Blaze, "every part of that is mine. Yo ass remember that so you won't go catching feelings now," I told her, walking up, but Blaze pulled me back to him.

"Peaches, shut yo ass up and calm down. Krystal, don't come over here starting shit. Yo ass knew from jump this wasn't shit. We cool, meaning friends, so don't come over here being disrespectful and calling her out her name," he told her and she looked shocked by what he said.

"Are you serious right now, Blaze? When I asked you were you fucking with this 'Bitch," *strike two,* "you told me you weren't. But now that she's right here, it's different? What the fuck?" She snapped, yelling at him.

"*She's* standing right here," I informed her. "But I'm confused, you just said he wasn't yo dude which I already knew. But he just said it himself that you're just friends. So I'm not understanding where the hostility is coming from? Like why you mad, sweetie, if you're not dating?" Which I truly didn't understand. "If you're just friends, why are you pissy that he's with me?" I asked curiously. On the other hand I was glad to hear Blaze say they were just friends, now I wasn't fuck'd up about her and him.

"I'm 'pissy' because yo ass wasn't on his mind none these past few days when we were fuckin'."

Chapter 17

Peaches

As soon as the word fuckin' left her mouth, I whirled around on Blaze so fast. "You fuck'd this bitch?" I snapped at him, I was pissed. I knew most women tended to go after the other woman in those types of situations, *but* truth was she owed me no type of explanation, a woman could only believe what she was being told by a man.

When Blaze didn't say anything, I muffed his ass.

"We have one little spat and you take yo triflin' ass out and fuck the first bitch you see? Huh, Blaze? Did you fuck this bitch?" I muffed him harder with every word that left my mouth.

"Peaches, keep yo fuckin' hands off me," Blaze snapped, pushing me back.

"Answer the question. Did you fuck her, Blaze?" I asked pushing him into the bench.

"Peaches, man gon. We ain't together," he snapped, pissed now.

I rocked Blaze hard in the face and keep hitting him as hard as I could.

He got me fuck'd up.

"You gon' fuck that bitch fo'real, Blaze!" Blaze grabbed my wrist, shoved me back. Someone caught me just in time before I hit the ground.

"Peaches, I swear I'ma fuck you up if yo ass hit me again," he threatened, glaring at me with the meanest look ever.

I was pissed so he didn't scare me.

"Fuck with me, Blaze, you gon fuck that bitch fo'real." I snapped, trying to get loose. I ain't know who was holding me, nor did I care. "Let me go!"

"So what if I fuck'd her, we ain't together so why you mad? Yo ass actin' like you ain't had no nigga," he accused.

"I haven't, boss ain't nann nigga had a taste since I decided on doing this bullshit with yo triflin ass! Fuck you,

Blaze, let me go!" I snapped, jerking out of whoever's hold, then turning to that Krystal bitch. "And don't think for a second that he's free, because he ain't. Fuck 'em again and that's yo ass you loosely ass bitch! This yo first and only warning." I shoulder bumped her hard as I went past, making her stumble back.

"Peaches!" Blaze was yelling, but was cut off by ol' girl.

"Blaze, fo'real, you gon' chase her?" She snapped, seeming unable to believe his actions.

"Bitch, shut the fuck up. Peaches, hold up!" Blaze called after me, but I kept walking.

I was so pissed that I was actually scared I would shoot his dumbass with the gun on my hip.

"Peaches, man slow yo ass up!" Blaze yelled as he finally caught up to me. He grabbed my arm, jerking me to a stop.

Once I was facing him, I slapped the fuck out of him.

"Don't touch me you triflin' ass nigga. How you gon' tell me to leave my dudes alone, then you turn around and fuck that bitch? Really Blaze? Man, fuck you!" I started to hit his ass again, but he caught my wrist.

"Yo ass ain't gon' keep hitting me," he stated, jerking me closer to him.

"Fuck you, let go." My feelings were beyond hurt. We had one little spat over a misunderstanding and that nigga went jumping the first bitch willing. *The fuck?* Whereas my dumbass basically stop fucking with niggas because of Blaze. I was taking this friend thing serious with his ass because I didn't want my getting head to be the reason whatever it was between us failed.

My good dumbass.

"Man, gon' with that bullshit, fo'real. Peaches, you said it, baby girl, we ain't together. I can do what the fuck I want," he threw back at me.

I slapped him again with my free hand before jerking away from him. "*And?* We weren't together when you beat Sly's ass. Twice! So what you want me to be cool with you fuckin' that bitch after everything, fo'real? You know what? Don't even worry about it, do you, baby," I snapped, about to walk away until I noticed ol' girl staring. "And his ass still ain't free for you to fuck. Now I dare yo ass to fuck with her again, I'ma beat both y'all ass. Fuck with me! Get the fuck off of me, Blaze." My hands pushed at his chest, trying to get free from his hold. But Blaze wasn't letting go.

"N'all, man. Come on, it ain't even like that, Peaches. G, I ain't fuck that damn girl," he insisted.

"Blaze, why you lying? You just said you did," I repeated what I heard.

Shaking his head, he held me tighter. "No, I didn't, man. I said so what *if* I did. I ain't fuck her, I was about to, but we ain't fuck. So calm yo ass down, man, damn."

I just looked at him, I didn't know if he was lying or not for the simple fact that I didn't understand why she would lie on her shit?

"Whatever, can you let me go, please?" I was done, I just wanted to go.

"Fuck you explaining shit to her fah, Blaze? This how we rockin' now?" Ol' girl yelled, walking toward us.

See this bitch is begging me to tap that ass real bad.

"Bitch, I'm where it's at and he knows that. This is me all damn day. Don't let a fuckin' moment you had with his ass make you think you're official, hoe. You wasn't shit but a distraction fuck, with yo dumbass." Realizing what I said, "Bitch, you ain't even fuck 'em, so get yo thirsty ass the fuck gone. Oh, and best believe he will be getting those keys," I told her.

"Bitch, you come get 'em from me," she screamed, hyped.

Oh, okay!

"Blaze let me-."

"Nah, Peaches, chill. Krystal, shut the fuck up man, damn. Get yo ass up outda here, fah real. Don't nobody have time fah that stupid shit." Blaze snapped at her, looking pissed. But he didn't seem to want to let me go.

"N'all, that bitch," *strike three,* "wanna talk shit. Bitch, bring yo ass over here," she yelled, still walking up.

Kneeing Blaze in his balls, I ran up on Krystal, knocking her ass in the face.

She immediately started swinging back, her only mistake was that she let me walk her dumbass back and once that ass was on that picnic table, shit got crazy.

Grabbing that bitch by her throat, I started to pound into the side of her face with every ounce of strength I had. Not gon' lie, I gave her props because she wasn't stopping. Baby girl kept swinging and bucking her hips trying to throw me off her. But I wasn't letting up, she brought this on herself. All she had to do was shut the fuck up, which she didn't.

"Peaches!" Someone yelled before I was being pulled back. There was no way I was letting go, I wrapped her hair around my fist, yanking her up with me. "Peaches, let her go." *Fuck that, this bitch gon' pop slick after I gave her ass a pass. Not with me she ain't! Bitch got life fuck'd up.* For a few seconds she stopped moving and my fingers were soon pried from her as I was yanked back harder. My foot came up and I kicked her in the face.

Once that happened ol' girl came at me again and I kicked her ass in the stomach as she swung, making her hit my shoulder. Feeling the sting, I kicked her in the mouth one last time before someone grabbed her.

Missy jerked Krystal away from me and started pounding into her ass.

"Bitch yo gon' pull a blade?" Missy snapped as she swung, getting loose, I went to Missy.

"N'all, Miss let her go." I pushed Missy from Krystal as I reached on my side. "Bitch you wanna slice? Huh?" I was reaching for my gun, but it wasn't there. She had better been glad because, I was about beat her with it. I was able to kick her twice in the face before I was pulled away again. "I'm done, let me go." Once loose, I snatched Blaze's car keys off the ground. "Dumbass bitch, next time somebody gives yo triflin' ass a slid, take that shit and shut the fuck up." I stomped on her side one last time, then moved away from her.

"Peaches, the fuck wrong with you kicking me in my dick with yo dumbass?" Blaze yanked me to him, then slapped me hard across the face. I went to hit him, but my back hit a parked car as his hand went to my throat. "Calm yo ass down! I dare you to hit me again." The slant to his eyes held a promising threat that silently begged me try him.

Pissed off and all, I calmed just a little.

"Blaze, let me go. And you bet not touch that bitch or take her ass home, she better walk! Get the fuck off of me." Pushing Blaze away, I started walking again until a thought hit me. His ol triflin ass was gon' help her once I was gone.

"Wait, what the fuck happened?" King asked with a flushed Ebony by his side. Those two were so busy fucking that they missed everything.

"Nothing at all. Blaze, bring yo ass on, nigga. You ain't slick." I snapped at him while grabbing his arm. "Y'all have fun, we gone. Bitches, call me later." With a wave, I was walking away, dragging Blaze with me. To be completely honest, I was surprised he didn't put up a fight and was actually letting me drag him away.

"Peaches, man, slow up. Damn. Where the fuck you park at?"

I didn't say nothing, just kept walking.

"Peaches, you don't hear me talking to yo ass?" He snapped.

Still nothing as we made our way out the Rex and down the few blocks to my car. Once there, I let him go, went to my side only to have him follow me.

"So you ain't talking to me now?" He asked, but I didn't reply. I opened my door only to have Blaze slam it right back. "Man, I'm talking to yo ass."

"So what, you bogus as fuck on the real, man, Blaze, don't even talk to me right now, just get in the car." I didn't want to talk to him at the moment. I was still pissed and it was taking everything in me not to walk back over there just to whoop that bitch again for cutting me on the shoulder.

"Peaches, I'm telling you I ain't fuck—"

"But you did something with that damn girl for her to come at me the way she did. I ain't stupid, Blaze, far from it. You can't lie to me."

"I didn't fuck her, it got close but we ain't fuck. So what, though? From my understanding yo ass said it was cool because we ain't together. So why the fuck you mad?" He said, throwing my words at me.

"Blaze, get out my face." I was pissed already but more so with myself that I told his ass that.

"N'all, man. You just flipped the fuck out back there fah no reason," he exclaimed in a serious tone of voice.

No reason?

"No reason? Blaze, seriously you fuck'd that bitch." Pushing him against the car I got in his face.

"I didn't, but so what if I did? Yo ass said—" He started saying nonchalantly.

"I didn't mean that shit literally, you dumbass!" I screamed at him. I swear I just wanted to hit him again.

"Well, yo ass said—"

"So fucking what? That didn't mean go out and do the shit, God! You know what? Just go back to your party, Blaze, and do you. Take that how you want to," I was so done. I didn't like the jealousy, the anger, the like I had for him. It was simply too much and I wasn't used to it. I honestly didn't know how to handle it.

I was getting so mad about all those different emotions that I actually felt like I wanted to cry because I couldn't deal. It was teeth grinding frustrating to the point that I wanted to scream. To make it worse, I hardly knew him.

Shaking my head, I looked away from him, about to open my car door again.

"You just gon' leave? Peaches, I'm not gon kiss yo ass. I told you I ain't fuck that girl. Why she said that shit, I don't know. But I ain't gotda lie on my dick," he insisted.

"Blaze, I believe you. But I don't do this, like fo'real. How I know next time we have words yo ass ain't gon' run out to find some bitch—"

"Peaches, we ain't together. So why should it matter, baby girl?"

"You right, it shouldn't. Do what you wanna do, Blaze, okay? It's late and I have a class tomorrow, so I gotda go."

Throwing my door open, I threw my tote bag into the passenger seat before getting in myself. After checking that no cars were coming, I pulled off fast.

God I hate this!

Chapter 18

Peaches

"You sure you okay? Because I can stay," Kim offered.

"Girl, gone fo'real. I'm cool, plus I got homework I need to finish. So go, I'm fine," I told Kimmy as my other three best friends stood around my living room, watching me as I held Cherry. "You know what? All you bitches get out my shit, like for real, I'm good."

"We just making sure. I mean, from the way yo ass went in on Blaze and ol' girl, something ain't right," Ebony pushed. "So, what's up Peach?"

"Okay, my feels were slightly hurt. I did tell him he could do what he wanted because we weren't together. I just didn't expect him to actually go and do anything," I told them, shrugging. I didn't want to stress over whether it happened or not.

"Well it didn't—" Missy started and I rolled my eyes.

"Bitch, how you know?" I asked her.

"If yo ass would shut up... Thank you. Now, after you left he came back pissed and snapped on her ass fah lying. Then he made her walk home. Bitch, you did a number on her. Ol' girl face is all fuck'd up. Bitch nose and mouth was bleeding, shit was nasty," Missy said, shaking her head and I shrugged.

"I ain't gon' lie, I may have whooped her ass, but that bitch rocked the fuck outda me in my right eye, shit hurts," I laughed as I rubbed my sore eye.

"Yeah, she got yo ass good. You over there looking a little purple under the eye," Ebony said, laughing as I kicked her.

"Bitch, you wrong. This shit hurts, but shid, her ass better stay away from him, otherwise she gon' get that ass beat again. Same goes for him," I was so serious. I didn't mind fighting for what was mine.

"Missy was telling me about that, I was laughing so hard. You done whooped both they asses, damn. I hate that I missed that shit, ugh," Ebony said and I looked from Angel to Missy then Kimmy and we broke out laughing.

"Bitch, if yo ol' nasty ass wasn't so busy tryna get fuck'd, you wouldn't have missed shit. Nasty ass," Kimmy told her, leaning against Angel, laughing.

"Fuck y'all! You know what? I don't have to take this shit," Ebony said, getting up.

"Now yo nasty ass wanna leave? Nuh uh, bitch, sit yo ass down!" I pulled her ass back down on the couch. "Wait, when her and King's ass finally show up, my bitch was hot in the face, hair every which way, with her shirt inside out and backwards." I laughed harder as I slapped my leg.

"Bitch, you seen me for a second, how you know my shirt was backwards?" She asked the obvious, making us laugh harder.

"It's still on wrong, dumbass!" I laughed out, pointing to shirt.

"Fuck y'all bitches, I'm gone. I have to work tomorrow anyways," she said, pushing my legs off her then standing up.

"Hope y'all nasty asses used a condom!" I said.

"Fuck you, and I'm taking this," she quickly grabbed my tote bag, dumped the contents on the table, and took off.

"No, bitch, fo'real!" Hurriedly, I jumped up to go after her, but fell over my book bag, landing on the floor. "Ebony, I'ma beat yo ass! Bitch, give me my shit!" I yelled, pushing myself up and running to the front door. As I swung it open and fell down again, I ran smack dab into Blaze's chest hard.

"Damn, move yo ass out the way, she got my stuff!" I snapped as I got up again, not even bothering to go after her because she was gone. The laughter behind me only pissed me off more. "That shit ain't funny, y'all asses just gon' sit here while she steal my stuff. Ugh, y'all are not friends." Saying that just made then laugh harder. "Get out my house, all y'all. Including yo ass, Cherry," I laughed as my kitten jumped off the couch and walked to the back with her tail up high like, '*bitch ain't talking to me.*'

"Trick, we were leaving anyway," Angel said before looking over my shoulder and laughing. "Hey. sexy caramel. Bet yo ass won't go creeping again, huh? Got that ass whooped."

Missy and Kimmy burst out laughing at Angel's words as I chuckled.

"Man, shut the fuck up and get yo black ass out." Blaze snapped at Angel and she paused with her mouth slightly parted before looking at me.

"Nuh uh, nigga. Who the fuck you think you talking to? Boy, you better act like yo ass knows who I be before I get Peaches on that ass again. The fuck," she said, snatching up her bag. "Let me go before I have to cut me a nigga, disrespectful ass mothafucka. Peaches, beat his ass again, he just pissed me off," Angel fussed.

My lips pursed together as I shook my head at her.

"Yo ass is crazy. Bye, girl," I said, hugging her, Missy, then Kimmy. "I'ma call y'all tomorrow when I get out of class. Y'all bitches better help me get my shit from Ebony's hoe ass," I said, and Kimmy shook her head.

"Bitch, you might as well charge it to the game. We all know once Ebony take something, that hoe ain't giving it back. She still got my Coach bag," Kimmy said as I walked them to the door, she was right though, that bitch never gave shit back with her black ass. "Be good Peach, no fighting. Bye," Kimmy waved, pushing me back and closing the door in my face.

"Trick!" I said before going back to the living room where Blaze sat. I stood there for a minute because I knew sitting next to him, I would be expected to talk which I didn't want to do. Not right then anyways, because I didn't know what to say exactly.

"Yo ass just gon' stand there?" He asked, looking at me.

Running a hand through my hair, I let out a sigh before walking to the couch opposite him.

"Man, quit playing and get yo ass over here before I slap the shit outda you," he said and I rolled my eyes.

"No, because I'm mad," I looked away from him.

"I don't give a fuck, get yo ass over here."

I didn't say anything, nor did I look at him.

"Boss, make me get up. I'ma beat yo ass," Blaze sat up and I quickly got up.

"Boy, gon' somewhere. I was coming, don't nobody got time to play with you," I said, walking over and pushing him down on the couch. "I don't wanna talk to you."

"The fuck yo problem is?" He asked. "N'all, man, fah real. Yo ass confusing as fuck, yo. What is this? If we gon' be cool then this shit you pulled ain't go fly, sweetheart, no lie. It ain't gon' be too many times I let you put yo hands on me—"

"My hands wouldn't have been on you if you hadn't fuck'd that bitch."

"I didn't fuck her, but so what if I did? I ain't with you nor are we fucking. We friends, right? Ain't that the shit you was spitting at me? If we gon' be friends yo ass ain't got no fucking right jumping the way you did," Blaze exclaimed.

I hopped off the couch so fast. "You did not just sit here and tell me what right I had. Blaze, since I've met yo ass you done took it upon yoself to make my fuckin' business yours. So don't sit here telling me what right I don't have. Nigga, if it involves yo black ass. I got every fuckin' right to know. If you don't like it, so fuckin' what. You can kiss my black ass, na. And if I found out yo ass been with that bitch or any other chick, I'ma fuck you up. What the fuck you thought this was? Baby, you started this, now I'm in. Ain't no going back.

"Daddy, the moment yo ass took it upon yoself to replace Sly, you became mine whether you realize it or not. So don't come in here telling me I had no fucking right when I have every. Fuck outda here." He had life fuck'd up the moment he introduced his dick to my pussy. Shit got real then. The fuck wrong with him? I wasn't no loosely ass hoe he was gon' play with. I took my shit serious. *Fuck!* "We still ain't together. *And what?*" I snapped, muffing his ass.

"Peaches, get the fuck out my face," Blaze said, pushing me back, making me fall onto the table.

"Don't be fuckin' pushing me. Nigga, don't be mad because yo ass got caught—"

"We ain't together, so how the fuck I get caught, Peaches?" He snapped and I jump up in his face again.

"So fuckin' what? I told yo ass we weren't together, but even that ain't changing shit. Yo ass still here, Blaze. Look around, you in my shit tryna explain yo fuckin' self. Nigga yo ass claimed and we still ain't together. But bet no bitch touch, smell, taste my shit, nigga my dick." I grabbed his dick just to get my point across.

The shocked look that came across his face told me he didn't expect me to actually grab, jerk, and slightly squeeze his shit. It took everything in me not to burst out laughing. But it really wasn't a laughing moment, I was being serious as hell.

"Peaches, boss, let my shit go."

"My shit, and I'll let it go when I wanna," Blaze suddenly pushed me hard.

"Get the fuck off me with yo dumbass. Yo ass ain't running shit but yo fuckin' mouth. You got me fuck'd up with that bullshit you spittin'. Yo ass better sit the fuck down and realize who the fuck you talking—"

"Nigga, yo ass don't scare me. The fuck wrong with you? Push me again, nigga, I dare yo ass to," I snapped, getting back in his face.

"Peaches, get the fuck out my face." He muffed me and I punched his ass, only to have him grab me by the throat, throwing me on the couch.

"Blaze, get off of me!" My hips bucked wildly as I screamed at him.

Blaze bit into his bottom lip, his hold tightening. "First, calm yo ass down."

"Blaze, get up!" I yelled, but he wasn't moving.

"Shut the fuck up and once yo ass calm down, I'll get up."

Sighing, I rolled my eyes. "I'm calm, okay. Now get up," I told him.

"Peaches, I ain't playing with yo ass, if you touch me I'm fuckin' you up, on everything. Got me?" The hard look he was giving scared me slightly and I knew he would probably beat my ass this time.

"Okay, damn," I gave in. Once he let me up, I stood to my feet then jumped at his ass like I was gon' hit him.

"Keep on, I'ma beat yo ass. Now get yo ass in the room," he hollered with such bass.

I looked at him like he was crazy. "Last I checked this was my place. In fact, get yo ass out! Bye! I don't know who the hell you talking to. Bye, Blaze," I fussed as I shoved him.

That same hard look returned to his. "Get yo ass in the room before I knock you the fuck out." I didn't move, just crossed my arms over my chest. "Make me tell you again." He suddenly looked ten times bigger while making that threat.

"Fuck you, I was going any damn way," I snapped, going into my room and slamming the door.

"Don't be slamming the damn door, black ass," he yelled.

"Fuck you!" *Stupid ass nigga!* I thought as I pulled my hair into a high ponytail before I turned on the TV. I flicked the light off then climbed in my bed. Just as I got comfortable, my room door opened and I looked at Blaze as he slid his phone in his pocket.

"Yo ass calm now?" He asked and I looked away from him.

I wanted to slap the shit outda myself because my dumbass left out the damn living room then came and got my good dumb ass in the bed.

"Don't talk to me," I glanced his way for a second before looking back at the TV.

"Look, I gotda make a run. I'll be back later." Blaze saying that had me rising.

Chapter 19

Peaches

"Where you about to go?" I asked.

"I just told—"

"On a run is not answering my question, just stating the fact you tryna leave. So where are you about to go?" Regardless of what just happened, I didn't want him to leave.

Blaze set his gun on the nightstand then sat on my bed. He kicked off his shoes then climbed over me.

"Blaze gon' somewhere, I'm still mad." My hands pushed at his chest to keep him at a distance. It didn't work and I ended up leaning into the headboard, sliding down until I was flat on the bed.

"You want me to yoself, huh?" He hovered over me, his lips brushed against mine with every word.

"No, you can leave if you wanna," I lied. I didn't want him to, but I didn't want to seem desperate for him to stay either.

Blaze laughed, "It ain't no winning with you, is it?" He asked while pulling the covers back and getting under them.

"There is, you just have to make everything difficult," I mumbled while sliding my hands under the back of his shirt then wrapping my legs around his waist.

"Me? Yo ass the one that flipped the fuck out," Blaze's words faded out.

Once I stretched my neck up and caught his bottom lip between my teeth, I sucked it into my mouth, then pulled on the top.

Blaze pushed more into me as he deepened the kiss, sliding his tongue in my mouth. My nails dug into his lower back, pulling him closer as I sucked on his tongue, making him groan before he started to kiss me harder. Our heads move from one side to the other as we sucked, pecked, and licked at each other's top and bottom lips and tongues.

My hands pulled at the hem of his shirt. Breaking the kiss, I pulled it over his head and tossed it to the side. Blaze quickly followed suit, he threw my shirt to the floor and made quick work discarding my bra. I undid the button on his jeans and pulled down his zipper. My hands gripped his pants along with his boxers and pushed them down his hips as our lips hungrily moved together.

He soon broke the kiss and went to my shorts, snatching them off, leaving me bare underneath him. He spread my legs and moved down. His hands massaged the back of my thighs as he kissed, licked, and sucked at the skin on my right inner thigh before he kissed my pussy lips.

That action caused my muscles to clench and my hips to thrust up. Blaze moved from my sex to my left thigh kissing, sucking, licking, and biting at the skin.

"Blaze, mm..." My words turned into a moan as he returned to my throbbing sex.

The tip of his tongue ran from the bottom of my slit to the top, parting my lips. He kissed from one lip to the other. His slowness was killing me, I was two seconds away from yanking my own damn hair as my inner muscles continued to suck at air.

"Blaze, ahh..." My hips bucked as he pushed two fingers inside of me at the same time he started sucking on my swollen pearl.

My hand rubbed over his head before cuffing the back, holding him to me as my hips grinded against his face. I kept him in place as my hips became in sync with his mouth and his fingers.

His tongue flattened, he and licked from the bottom of my vulva to the top. The tip of his tongue flicked over my swollen nub before giving it one hard suck then another as his fingers moved faster, hitting my sweet spot with every pump.

"Ah, ah, ah, Blaze. Ooh, baby! Ooh, like that." One of my hand's fisted the sheets as I moaned loudly, not caring who heard. "Mmm, daddy, right there. Right there, baby." Blaze's mouth and fingers wreaked havoc on my body. The pleasurable building caused my muscles to tighten and my body to violently twitch. My back arched as my nails bit into the nap of his neck, holding him to me. "Aahhh!" A loud, orgasmic scream left my mouth as I came hard. "Ah, mm, mm," I rode out my orgasm against his mouth.

Blaze pulled back, groaning as my pussy continued to contract. "Damn, you sweet as fuck," he mumbled before his mouth came to my sex once again, giving my clit a nip then a kiss before he made his way up my body, coming to my lips, kissing me.

That was only one orgasm and it still topped every other one I'd had. Blaze had a bitch sleepy as hell and we ain't even fuck. I was still breathless even as I began kissing him back. God, I was tired like I actually did some fucking work and my pussy was still sucking air.

The vibration to the bed had Blaze lifting up and grabbing his phone. I didn't complain. Hell, I was still trying to catch my damn breath.

Blaze looked at his phone before sitting it down then leaning back over me. "I got to go, but I'll be back in two hours, no longer then three. I'ight?" Blaze said.

"Where you going?" Once again I asked, staring up at him.

He stood, fixed his clothes then stared at me. "Don't worry about it, just know I'll be back," was his reply.

"Yo ass bet not be going to see that bitch—"

"Peaches, shut the fuck up. Boss, don't start that stupid shit." He snatched his shirt up off the floor, then pulled it on. Blaze sat back on the bed to pull on his gym shoes.

With an attitude, I leaned against the headboard, my arms crossed under my chest and I just stared at his back for the longest.

Feeling my stare, he glanced back at me. "Man, I ain't going to see that damn girl, so fix yo fuckin' face," he said, making me roll my eyes.

"You bet not, I ain't playing with you, Blaze. I don't wanna have to fuck you and ol' girl up, but I will," I told him as he hopped up, coming to my side.

"You think that shit funny? You gon' make me fuck yo ass up. You was wrong for doing that damn girl like that—let me finish," he said as I attempted to interrupt him. "She deserved it, I ain't gon' lie, but if you would've shut the fuck up I would've took care of it," he said, making me roll my eyes as I smacked my lips.

"Nigga, please. Yo ass wasn't gon' do shit, but you heard what I said. I'll fuck both you up, I'm serious as hell," I was being so serious.

"I'll let you know when I'm worried, but I'm out. I'll see you later." He leaned in, but I moved back. "Fo'real?"

"I don't see where you got to be at twelve that can't wait until the morning." I felt like a kid pouting, but I didn't want him to go.

Blaze ignored my complaint, he simply took hold of my chin and tilted my head back. "Man, stop that shit. I'll be back," he said before kissing me.

Sighing, I kissed him back. I didn't want him to go, I wanted to lay in bed watching some wack ass midnight show and spoon with him until I dosed off, which wasn't going to happen.

"Go to sleep." He pecked my lips once more, then straightened up grabbed his nine from the nightstand, tucked it in the back of his jeans and then walked out of my room.

It wasn't long after I heard the front door close.

There was no denying it, I was officially in total like with Blaze. So much so, I didn't even want him to leave. I wanted him to caress my breast and stomach until I fell asleep like he did once before.

There was no going back for me. Hell, even if it was, how would I begin to forget about him? Forget the strong like and the attraction I had. How did I rid myself of the giddy feeling that was bubbling inside me? How did I kill the fuckin' butterfly that start going crazy whenever he was around?

Why couldn't I like someone normal like a mailman or the UPS guy? Hell the cable man? At least I would have known what to expect a little. Why Blaze? Out of all people, why him?

A Dangerous Love 2
Can't Let Go

Chapter 20

Blaze

I pulled in front of the green house after I backed into the drive way. I turned off the truck, then got out, pissed as I made my way to the door.

"Nigga, why the fuck you pounding on my door like you fuckin' stupid?" Krystal yelled once she snatched open the door.

Grabbing her by the throat, I slammed her into the wall. "If yo ass ever come at her the way you did earlier, I'll fuckin' kill you. Why the fuck you go popping off at the mouth like you fuckin' stupid? Bitch, yo ass knew what it was from jump, so why the fuck you gon' pull some bullshit like that fah?" I snapped at Krystal.

Whether we fuck'd or not wasn't nobody's business but ours. For her to spit some shit like that to Peaches though. Especially after she done came to me on some shit I wanted only to have this stupid bitch go run off at the mouth.

"So yo ass can't talk now? Huh? Yo fuckin' mouth ain't workin'?" Pulling her from the wall, I slammed her back into it harder than before.

Krystal's eyes watered as she clawed at my hands.

My hand squeezed tighter before I let her go. Immediately she let out a loud gasp, filling her lungs with air before choking. Once her breathing returned to normal she looked at me, mugging hard as tears left her eyes.

"You told me you wasn't fuckin' with that bit—" she caught herself, "girl. Then you gon' try to fuckin' play me in front of her. You were smiling, hugging, and kissing her like y'all together when just a few days ago you were telling me you wasn't fuckin' with her like that. So what's real, Blaze?" She yelled at me.

"When I told yo ass that, I wasn't with her. But that ain't mean go tell her we fuckin' when we ain't even fuck'd. I ain't gotda lie about shit, baby girl, I told yo ass what was real. I ain't fuckin' with you either, though. G, we cool, that's it. You ain't my bitch so kill that jealousy bullshit yo ass got going on. What we do ain't got shit to do with Peaches and vice versa. Bitch, that's between us. If yo ass gon' become loose lipped when you see me with her, then you ain't rockin' with me, period. Think on that shit, if yo ass can't handle it then lose my fuckin' number, yo. I'm out." With that, I turned away from her, headed for the door.

"B, wait. We rockin', but I don't wanna have to share you." Krystal, grabbed the back of my shirt then quickly walked in front of me, closing the door. "I don't wanna have to do that nor do I want to become a side piece," she stated.

Licking my lips, I started at her. What the fuck was she expecting me to say? Dropping Peaches wasn't even an option, especially not when I just got her back.

"Good thing I ain't yours then, huh? Krystal, I ain't 'bout to be on this dumb shit with you, man. Yo feelings don't mean shit to me. You bring them mothafuckas in this, that's yo fault. You ain't my bitch, yo, and I ain't tryna make you mine. We cool, that's it." Wasn't no sugarcoating, I was gon' be straight with her. "If you wanna fuck with me knowing this, then that's what you wanna do. I ain't forcing yo ass to do shit you don't want to."

"But you are, Blaze. If I don't agree, then you don't wanna fuck with me no more. How is that fair or right? You wasn't even thinking about her a few days ago when you were here, though. Now it's something different?"

"Why the fuck you still thinkin' bout Peaches? This ain't got shit to do with her and I plan on keeping it that way. Like I said, if you can't handle that then ain't no point of me even standing here talkin' to yo ass, on some real shit," I explained, not really giving a fuck which she choose to do. It wasn't gon' fuck me up either way. "Look, man, think on it then shoot me a text. I gotda go." Krystal rolled her eyes, not moving from the door. "You gon' just stand there or get the fuck out the way so I can go?"

"Where you 'bout to go?" When I didn't answer, she let out a sigh. "Well, am I gon see you later on then?" After the bullshit she just tried to pull with Peaches, I ain't even think I wanted to fuck with her ass no mo.

"N'all, probably not. Serious shit though, I don't even wanna fuck you man, you childish as fuck. That shit you pulled earlier, why the fuck you lying on yo pussy fah? I don't fuck with liars, man." I shook my head at her, laughing. I ain't never had a bitch lie on my dick before, that shit was comical.

"It was stupid I know, but that shit hurt me seeing you hugged up on her. You ain't even acknowledge the fact I was there, Blaze, so yeah I got pissed and lied. I'm sorry, okay?" Krystal let out a sigh as she walked up to me. "You was right, I shouldn't have said nothing, I'm sorry. B, I'm rockin' with you." Her hands moved up my chest as she stood on her tip toes.

When I didn't duck my head down for her, she grabbed the back of my neck, pulling my head down, pressing her lips to mine. "Stay with me for a few hours, then you can go or come back once you finish your business." Krystal's ass was clingy, I noticed that after a few days of us chillin'. I ain't like that shit at all, but Krystal ass gave good head. That was probably the only reason I went against my better judgment to stop fuckin' with her.

My hands went to her ass, getting a good grip, picking her up. Going to the living room, I sat on the couch. Krystal smiled and I shook my head, grabbing ahold of her face and moving it from one side to the other. She was a beautiful chick hands down, even with the busted lip.

Peaches fuck'd the side of her face.

"Damn, she worked yo ass good," my eyes roamed over her face and a laugh left my mouth. Peaches ass played no games. The right side of her face was swollen and had turned a mixture of green, purple, and black. Krystal was a yellow bitch, it wasn't no hiding that shit.

Peaches beat her ass.

"N'all, she really didn't, this ain't shit. If I hadn't tripped and her girl ain't jump in then..." She stopped talking, probably because the look I gave her.

My brows rose at what she was saying. "Then what? You would've whooped her ass? Man, get that bullshit outda here. Yo ass ain't trip and her girl ain't jump in until you pulled that razor out yo mouth. And even then, Peaches pushed her back. Baby girl, if you ain't got hands you can't go around popping slick at the mouth." Letting out a few chuckles. "Real shit, though, yo ass ain't have a chance with Peaches. But you pull another razor on her, I'ma beat yo ass, I promise you. If you see her, don't say shit. This shit that happened today can't happen again. If it do it's a wrap. Get up," I tapped her leg then pulled out my phone, shooting a quick message to Dre, one of house packers, letting him know I was gon' be about an hour or two late.

"Come on, let's go in the room." She pulled at my hand, but I jerked her down. "Blaze stop," Krystal laughed, straddling my hips. Pushing her hair over her shoulder, she leaned down, bringing her lips to mine again. My tongue slid into her mouth as my hands held her grinding hips, my dick twitched at her movement.

Moving her panties to the side, my fingers ran through her slit before going to her clit, pinching the little nub, making her jerk slightly. My two fingers thrust into her pussy at the same time she pressed her hips down to get more pressure on her clit, not realizing I had already moved my fingers. That was until she screamed into my mouth then jumped up holding her pussy, with wide eyes.

"Oh, my God!" Looking at her confused, tryna figure out what the fuck was wrong with her, I followed her eyes to my fingers.

"Ah fuck!" I cussed before getting up and going to the bathroom to wash my hands. "Why the fuck yo dumb ass move?" I snapped at her.

"How the fuck was I supposed to know you were about to stick yo long, thick ass finger into my pussy. Don't get no fuckin' attitude with me, you think I wanted that shit to happen?" Krystal yelled, coming into the bathroom and sitting on the towel. "Fuck! That shit hurt. I'm still bleeding."

Hell n'all, I wasn't even about to deal with that shit. "Aye, I'm out, I'll get with you later." Krystal looked at me, shocked. "What? Why the fuck you looking at me like that fah?"

"You really gon' leave after doing this?" Her expression was serious.

My hand ran over my head and I shrugged. "I told you I had shit to do."

"Blaze, yo fingers just popped my cherry and you seriously gon' leave me? You wasn't just thinking about having shit to do," she fussed.

Shrugging again, I walked out the bathroom. Shid, what the fuck was I supposed to do, stay there and hold her hand? *Fuck n'all.*

"Blaze," Krystal screamed out to me.

I heard the shakiness in her voice followed by the toilet flushing and my ass hurried to the door, not thinking about closing it behind me. I already knew if I was still in that house when she got out the bathroom her ass was gon' try to convince me to stay and I wasn't for that crying shit when I told her ass no.

Once inside the truck, I started it, throwing it into gear. I was about to pull off just as Krystal yanked opened my back door.

"Blaze, you a dirty ass nigga for that shit! Yo ass was really about to leave? You wasn't gon make sure I was okay or nothing?" Krystal whined as she got in the back then climbed into the front seat.

My hand came down my face before looking over at her. "You look i'ight, Krystal. Get out— what the fuck is you doing?" I asked her as she climbed into my seat.

"Why not finish what you started."

My dick jump at her words, but I wasn't fuckin' her. "Hell n'all, get the fuck off me, I ain't fuckin' you, man. Krystal, take yo ass in the house," I pushed my door open then motioned for her to get out.

"No, Blaze. We both want this, so why not?" Leaning down, she caught my bottom lip between her teeth as her hand found the front of my jeans, undoing the button then zipper.

"Krystal, get out. We ain't fuckin'," I pushed her ass out the truck, closed the driver's door, locked it and then pulled out her drive way. I pushed my stiff dick back in my boxers then buttoned and zipped my pants up as I drove.

Coming to a stop light, my phone started ringing.

"Yo?"

"B, where you at?" King asked.

"On my way to Anastasia, why? What's up?" I asked while going on US30.

"Aye, I'm about to come through."

"I'ight." Hanging up the phone, I drove out to Hammond where I moved Anastasia to.

Chapter 21

Blaze

I backed into the driveway of Anastasia.

It wasn't long after King pulled up and parked on the street. I flicked the headlights at King and we both got out of our trucks. He went to the passenger side of his while I walked over to him. We slapped hands six times then shook up.

"What's up?"

"Shit, just came to fuck with you," he spoke with a shrug.

"I'ight, come on," we walked to the house. I pulled on a pair of latex gloves before I unlocked the door.

Once inside, I left King in the front as I went to the back room. I tapped on the door and Dre opened it.

The room was nice and big enough to fit three large rectangle tables to weigh, cut, and bag without getting shit mixed up. I had a person at each table, which made the process a little faster.

Going to the last table, I grabbed a black duffle bag off the floor, sat it on top, and started counting the thirteen bricks in there. Then I did the same to the ten other bags that sat on the floor.

After I finished counting, I zipped up the last bag. I went to the closet and took out the large moving boxes.

"Trey, aye, I need you to put everything in these duffle's into the boxes, i'ight?" I informed him. I helped him take the duffels and boxes to the next room.

"It'll be done." He pulled the box of brand new T-shirts and jeans out the closet and started wrapping the bricks inside the clothes. Once the boxes were half full we filled the rest of the box with empty clothes.

Finishing the second box, I left out of the room and went back to the front where I left King, who stood off to the side on the phone.

"B, you gotda make a drop or some shit?" King looked around at the boxes in the living room, then back to me.

I hummed at his question, counting the boxes before I replied. "Yeah. This little nigga from Ohio called needing some work. He just made it here about an hour ago, so I'm about to drop this shit off." My phone vibrated and Sam's name popped up on the screen. 'What's up? You here?'

"Yeah, pulling up now," Sam said and I hang up the phone.

"Dre, Mike?" I called to my other two workers.

"What's up?" They both asked, walking into the room.

"Aye, load that truck out front." With a head nod, they went to work.

"What he want?" King asked, looking from me to the boxes.

"Thirteen bricks."

King let out a whistle. "Kilos? No shit?" Humming, I nodded my head. Again he whistled. "What's all this other shit?" He asked, pointing to the other four boxes.

"Shit, 'bout to take it the spot." King nodded in understanding knowing the spot I was referring to was the storage building Sam and his girl owned. That's where I kept my shit once it was packed. "Dre, the one with thirteen on it, go in my truck."

"You want the other boxes out the basement in the big truck too?" Mike stood with his hand above the door that lead to the basement.

"Yeah, them too, I don't want shit up in here." The lab was in the basement where they cooked everything. "Hurry up," I rushed Mike after looking at the time to see it was four-thirty in the morning. "Aye, I'm out. I gotda meet dude in ten minutes." Shaking up with Dre, I started for the door. "Yo, don't leave this place looking like shit. Wipe everything down with bleach before y'all leave this mothafucka, i'ight?" Dre and Mike laughed.

"I'ight, boss. You say that every time you leave. We got you, baby, so don't sweat it." Mike and Dre were some cool niggas and took what they did seriously. It was never bullshit, but straight work and they moved fast as hell. Best workers I'd had so far.

King followed me out the house and hopped in my passenger seat as I made my way to Sam, who stood at the back of the truck.

"I gotda meet dude in 'bout ten minutes. Call me once you got this stored away, bet?"

Sam nodded, shaking up with me. "I got you. You know it's like twenty boxes in here right?" I peeked inside the bed of the U-Haul.

"Come on, baby, you gon bitch up on me and start crying 'bout work?" I joked with him before taking the safety deposit box he held out for me, then lead us back into the house.

Sam didn't get his hands dirty as much as me, but when he did his ass always complained. Even so, he did it. With his job, I didn't really want him involved with my shit unless I really needed him and right now was one of those times.

"I'm not bitchin'. Brandy ass is though, you know she don't like this shit," he explained what I already knew.

"Man, I don't even wanna hear that shit. That's yo bitch, check her ass, teach that bitch her place," I told him honestly. I ain't know what Sam saw in that bitch, he should've left that hoe back in high school.

Brandy was a straight leech with nothing going for herself, but I guess Sam liked that shit.

"B, cool it with that bitch word," the hostility in his voice didn't go unnoticed.

He knew I ain't like his bitch.

"You got it," my head bobbed, acknowledging him all the while I pulled forty stacks from the safety box. I handed it to Sam before locking the metal box back.

"I'll give this to them now. We'll meet up later."

"T'ight, I'm out. Call me once you got that shit done though."

"Alright," Sam shook up with me then made his way to the back rooms.

With the safety deposit box tucked under my arm, I left the house, going back to my truck where King still sat.

"Why the fuck yo ass in here straight chillin'?" I asked while taking the blunt he handed me.

"Nigga, I'm on guard patrol. You know I ain't letting you roll by yoself. Niggas might get stupid, you know?" King spoke real as he reclined his seat.

This wasn't nothing odd of King. My nigga was always down to ride regardless of the situation. I wasn't worried about no mothafucka getting stupid. Those niggas out there knew that, so I didn't have no trouble with folks getting outda pocket. Everybody knew I'd let whatever piece I was holding rip at the sign of any shaky shit.

With a shrug, I pointed to his ride.

"What about yo truck?" With a mouth full of smoke I asked, while handing the blunt back.

He waved me off. "I'll have Ebony bring me out here later on to get it."

I hummed my reply, pulling out the driveway and headed straight to the warehouse.

***

Pulling into the loading dock of the warehouse, I drove inside. Right after I pulled in, a red Navigator drove in after me. King and I got out the car at the same time Tommy and his boy Lamar did the same.

I met Tommy through another buyer, he had a taste of that pure and wanted to get on, but since I ain't know him like that I had to do some research on the little nigga.

"What's up, Blaze?" Tommy greeted with a tap to my fist.

I reached in my pocket, pulling out a baggy. "Everything, everything you know." I replied back as Tommy tossed the baggy back to me.

"We good folks, I know you good. Them fiends out in Columbus go crazy for that shit," Tommy commented. "Check it though, this nigga Perry out in Akron, we use to fuck with the same connect. Dude got ahold of one of my vials and wanted to know who I was coppin' from. I ain't tell him shit, I wanted to get at you first see what you think. I mean you ain't take too easy or quick to put me on so I didn't wanna be throwing yo name out, you know," he informed while nodding toward his boy.

I looked down at my phone, checking the time. "Come on, what's yo take on dude?" I asked him while walking to the back of my truck.

"I wouldn't fuck with him if that's what you asking. I mean, his team shystie as fuck and they mouth stay running," advised Tommy.

"Then why the fuck you even bring that nigga up if yo ass wouldn't fuck with 'em?" I spit out, *mothafucka was stupid.*

"I ain't wanna seem like no hating ass cat, you know. Shid, if a nigga talkin' 'bout bringing money yo way I'ma give you word on it. If you take it then you do, if not then it's that. At least I told you," he finished saying with a shrug.

"Not all money is worth going after same with business. Shit, you wouldn't fuck with it, don't bring it to me. Understand?" The trunk opened as I explained to him.

"I got you, Lamar give him the bag. I put a little extra in there, to show my appreciation."

My brows rose at that. "You on it like that you giving a nigga extra? King, you hear this shit?" Looking over at King we laughed.

"Damn, why you tryna play me? I mean, shit, I can take that fifty back home. Shid, a nigga still hungry." Tommy rubbed his stomach, emphasizing being hungry.

Shaking my head, I laughed again. "Fifty thou, though? Damn. Shid, if you doing it like that to give me an extra fifty,

I'ma have to bring yo young ass out here and put you to work."
Shid, I had some hungry young niggas, but they ass wasn't
molded with Tommy's hungriness, not yet anyway. I still had
work to do with my youngins.

"Same shit I'm thinkin. Fuck you find this little dude
at?" King asked, sizing Tommy up.

"Shid, we met before I got locked up. When I got out he
was with yo boy Mark and stepped to me about a week or so
after I got home. After talkin' to him, I went out to Ohio for two
weeks to see how he and his boys get it. Now you see, nigga
done gave me something extra in my bag."

"Man, fuck you, Blaze. We out, though. It's a five hour
drive back home, traffic 'bout gon' be a bitch. Aye, you should
come back down one day and kick it—" Tommy started saying,
until Lamar cut him off.

"No the fuck he shouldn't, them bitches still be asking
'bout his ass. My main topper, every time that bitch came over
she askin' bout the big dude that came through with Tommy. I
had to let her ass go, my dick still miss that bitch's throat and
that was about a month ago," Lamar blurted out.

We broke out laughing.

"Hell yell, this big mothafucka come out there for two
weeks and hoes still askin' bout his ass like he done made this
big ass impression on their lives and shit," Tommy stated,
shaking up with Lamar.

"Ain't it, though?" Lamar agreed.

"Yeah, I'ma have to make a trip back down soon. I'ma
bring my man's with me though." My head nodded in King's
direction.

Tommy nodded his head, looking at King then back to
me. "Shid, he welcome my crib, yours. It ain't shit but love my
way. Good lookin' though, Blaze man." Shaking up, he gave a
one armed hug.

"It's good."

"Yo, why you keep looking at yah phone fah? Got somewhere to be?" Lamar peeped, his gaze moved from my phone back to me.

"Fuck you little nigga, yo young ass wouldn't understand," I bluffed. Shid, I ain't even understand this bullshit with Peaches ass. But what I did know was I needed to be there before her ass woke up. "We out though. And don't be too quick to get rid of that shit either. Don't come callin' me in a week talkin' 'bout you need a re-up." Starting up the truck, I closed the door then let the window down.

"I'ight, we gon' link up soon, though, fly y'all niggas out to Columbus, Ohio." Tommy called out as he walked around to his ride.

Nodding at him, I pulled off.

"Why the fuck my meeting can't go this fuckin' smooth? So you out there hoein', huh? Peaches gon' know about all this shit when I see her," King said before sitting up straight. "Aye, that Krystal bitch just dumb, Peaches smashed that hoe," King boasted, making me shake my head.

"Man, that bitch Krystal though, let me tell you what the fuck that bitch did." After telling King what went down at Krystal's crib, he was leaning against the door holding his stomach laughing.

"Wait, you popped that bitch cherry with yo fingers. Hell n'all. That bitch pushed down on purpose, fuck you thinkin?" King stated, the seriousness in his voice had me laughing. "Shid, I would've finished breakin' her ass in."

"I couldn't fuck her, especially not after that shit she pulled at the Rex. I might not fuck that bitch, but her ass can blow me any day. Boss, Krystal throat be having a niggas toes curling. You should try it, yo."

A hum left his mouth as a thoughtful look came across his face. "Shid, I plan on getting all in her guts. I gotda play good guy, though, gotda be that friend she can talk to, soothe that bitch first."

159

Laughing, I grabbed a cigarette from the cup holder and lit it. "Do what you do, my nigga." The conversation ended and I turned up the stereo, headed back to Anastasia to take King back to his truck.

***

Pulling up on the side of his all black Range Rover, I looked at the time again. Five forty-five a.m.

"Good lookin', my nig," I told him. After slapping hands we shook up.

King got out the truck and waved me off. "It ain't shit, what you 'bout to do now?" He asked, stretching.

"Shid, bout to go creep my ass in Peaches bed before she wake up," I spoke honestly. Shid, wasn't no point in lying. He wasn't gon' whoop my ass.

King shook his head before leaning on the door. "Yo, if you gon' be fuckin' with my sista, these hoes, my nigga, you gotda let them go or stop fuckin' with her all together. She ain't use to this shit. Hell, I don't want her mixed up in this life period, but after seeing her go at ol' girl, it look like her minds made up about yo ass. Don't hurt my sista, otherwise we gon' have problems, my nigga. School and work come first, know that. I don't want her missing or skipping shit, I'ight?" The hostility in his voice didn't go unnoticed, but I got a sista so it was understandable.

"Peaches where it's at for me, on some real shit, though. I mean, like yo ass, I'ma look, might even get blow, but at the end of the day Peaches where I wanna be. You might not like it, but that's how it is. Plus, we ain't official so it's any other bitch game, right?" I joked.

The look he gave me was the dirtiest I'd ever seen King's face contort into and I couldn't help but laugh.

"Nigga, you gon' make me fuck you up," he threatened.

Licking my lips, I inhaled the cigarette smoke, releasing it as I talked. "You can try it, my nigga, but I'm out. Peaches will be up in a minute, like I said I'm tryna get there before she wake up. I hear you, though. Aye, check this tho, when you get straight with yo bitch and leave these hoes alone, then I'll take yo advice. Bet?" Dumping the ashes from the square, I hit it again.

"Nigga, fuck you. Ebony know I ain't shit, though." The serious look on his face had me laughing again.

"Yeah, i'ight, man. I'm gone, yo ass stupid. Close my fuckin' door." Laughing, he slammed my door, him doing so stopped my laughter. "Nigga, slam my fuckin' door again." Sticking up his middle finger, he hopped in his truck, starting it up. Once he did, I drove off, going straight to Peaches' apartment, turning a half hour drive into a fifteen minute one as I sped all the way back to Gary.

***

I made it back to Peaches' crib at ten after six. I unlocked the outside door then took the stairs by two, quickly making my way up to the third floor. I unlocked the door hoping she wasn't awake. I didn't wanna fight with her about where I'd been if she was. Just thinking that had me laughing to myself, Peaches' little ass was most definitely unlike any chick I'd ever met. She had a little naiveté to her, even so, her ass was on point about every other thing.

Her ass fuck'd me up when she went at Krystal the way she did. The way she turned on my ass when she heard I fuck'd her, the crazed look she gave kinda scared my ass.

Peaches was the first chick to ever make me feel like that and now that she came to me, I couldn't let her go.

When I walked fully into the apartment, not hearing anything, I let out a relieved breath while silently making my way to her room. Seeing her with her back to the door, still asleep, I kicked off my shoes, then pulled off my clothes before I climbed in bed with her. After getting comfortable, I wrapped my arm around her waist, bringing her to my chest.

Baby girl was different and had me feeling the hell outda her. I couldn't promise not to fuck shit up, but I damn sho' was gon' try to keep her as long as I could.

Chapter 22

Peaches

"Blaze, stop before you make me fall." I laughed as he kept pushing me toward the edge of the bed. "Blaze—"

"Then get yo ass up man, I'm hungry as hell," he said, and a thought came to me. Rolling on top of him I pecked his lips before kissing my way to his ear, biting on his lobe.

"If you're that hungry, I got something you can eat."

"Get the fuck off me," Blaze laughed, rolling us over. "Yo ass gon' quit fuckin' with me. Never sucked a dick or not, yo ass better go get a cucumber and start to practicing. Baby, this a two way street, a nigga on strike, boss," he clarified and my mouth popped opened. "Open a little wider," he insisted, with two of his fingers in front of my parted lips.

Laughing, I hit him on his chest. "You a bitch, get off me. Take yo ass on strike all you want. I'm sure I can find a willing occupant." My smile grew wider from his hard stare.

"Get fuck'd up. On everything, you gon' make me strangle yo ass, man." Blaze's hand went to my neck to emphasize his threat.

I rolled my eyes as I wrapped my arms around his neck. "You're cute when you get all jealous." I bit at his bottom lip then licked the top.

"Don't ever call me cute again. Now get yo funky ass up and go make breakfast," Blaze said, making me laugh.

"I don't want to. Why can't we just go out for breakfast. Blaze, seriously?" A little whine slipped through my lips as he bit my nipple then pulled it into his mouth.

All too soon he was pulled away by the vibration of his phone. With a groan, Blaze scooted to his side of the bed to grab his phone.

"Yo?" He answered.

I rolled my eyes, he could've ignored that call.

"Yeah…" I sat up, pulling the covers over my bare chest as Blaze suddenly hopped out of bed. "Nah, I packed Anastasia's shit up this morning and took her ass to the spot."

My brows furrowed as I listened to him, so he was with a bitch last night and he had the nerve to talk about the bitch in front of me? *Fo'real?*

"Shid, I'm about to go pick Jesse's ass up now and take her to the lot, bitch car should be fixed…" He continued his conversation as if I wasn't even right here.

Who the fuck Jesse? This mothafucka was so disrespectful.

"The fuck wrong with you hitting me like yo ass stupid?" Blaze snapped at me as I slapped the fuck outda him in the back of his head.

"Yo ass seriously gon' talk about a bitch while I'm sitting here?"

Blaze looked at me like I was crazy, before pushing me back.

"Man, shut the fuck up. I'm the phone." Blaze turned away, dismissing me.

This dude done lost his mind! "I don't care about you being on the damn phone! Who the fuck is Anastasia? She the reason yo ass ain't answer when I called, huh?" I asked, muffing his ass.

"Keep yo fuckin' hands off me, Peaches, before I slap the shit out you!" He pushed me back and stood up, looking pissed.

"Fuck yo black ass!" Throwing the pillow at him, I got out the bed, going to the bathroom. The door slammed hard behind me. I hoped his ass didn't think it was over, if I didn't have to use the bathroom I'd would've been beating his ass.

After I finished taking care of my business, I washed my hands then brushed my teeth. Once done, I slipped off my shorts, deciding to just hop in the shower.

***

I was in the middle of washing my body for the second time when the shower door came sliding open. Glancing at Blaze, I rolled my eyes at him. I turned my back on him and rinsed off.

"Where you going?" He turned me to face him. Blaze brought our body close.

"Gon', like for real, I wanna slap the shit out yo ass right now. Blaze, let me go." I tried to push him away but he wouldn't let me go, he simply walked me back until I was under the shower head. "Blaze—"

"N'all, lose that fuck ass attitude you got and talk to me. Ask what you wanna know," he licked his lips as he stared down at me.

Smacking my lips, I looked away from Blaze only to have him grab my chin and turn my head back so I was facing him once again.

"I don't wanna know anything. Can you let me go now?" My eyes averted from his as I bit the inside of my bottom lip, trying my hardest not to let this stupid ass smile come to my lips.

"Shid, could've fool me with how hard yo ass hit a nigga. Now ask what you wanna know," Blaze talked while gripping the back of my right thigh. He pulled it to his waist as his hardening dick pushed between my legs. My eyes quickly snapped up, locking with his. "So now that I'm off the phone you ain't got shit to say?" He asked as his head dropped down.

How the hell was I suppose too focus on shit he was saying when his ass got this whole sexy thing going on? *Damn, I was weak.*

Even knowing I was being stupid, I couldn't help it.

My tongue swiped over my lips as I leaned more into the wall, which caused the handle to dig into the middle of my back. Ignoring the slight pain, I wrapped my right arm around his neck. My hand went to the back of his head and I met him the rest of the way, bringing our lips together.

My left hand found its way to his lower back, pulling him closer to me. Blaze suddenly picked me up before he pulled and turned the knob to cut the water back on. A surprised squeak escaped my mouth, making him laugh.

"I don't like you," I mumbled against his lips, but a gasp soon followed after as his hand ran through my slit. His fingers flicked over my clit before he pushed one finger inside me, then another. My head fell back against the wall, my lips parted as I moaned in the back of my throat.

Blaze sucked and kissed his way down my neck to my breast. His tongue lapped over my right nipple, then my left before pulling the little nub into his mouth.

I felt Blaze's fingers widen inside of me before he pushed in a third, moving faster. His fingers were wide and thick, causing discomfort as well as pain to my sex.

"Ah, wait, wait, wait." Quickly, I grabbed Blaze's wrist as his fingers began to move faster, deeper, pushing against my hymen. One, maybe even two fingers I could take, but three I couldn't. That shit was hurting too badly. My grip on his wrist tightened as I panted, trying to get myself under control before I made that decision.

"You wanna stop?"

He tilted my head down toward his so he could peck my lips. He moved back and licked his lips. My eyes followed the slither of his tongue before they locked with his. I searched his pretty, light brown orbs. I didn't want to stop, but I didn't want to be stupid either.

"Who's Anastasia and Jesse? If you're fuckin' them be honest." Straight to the point I asked the questions that nagged my mind.

Blaze let out a chuckle as he shook his head. "They're houses, my spots on the West and East Side. Peaches, I ain't fuckin' nobody man, boss I ain't..." He trailed off as he started moving his fingers again.

If possible, my hand tightened even more as he began to rub my sweet spot, causing my breathing to pick up once more.

A Dangerous Love 2
Can't Let Go

Maybe it was due to the lust induced state my body was in, I don't know, but I believed him. And as bad as I wanted to think it was wrong, it felt so right.

"Don't hurt me," I hated that it came out sounding desperate, but in the end no girl wanted to get hurt. And I was taking a huge chance with him.

Blaze didn't say anything as he pulled his fingers out then ran his tip through my fold before going to my opening. His mouth soon covered mine as he pushed inside of me. He pushed against my hymen, then pulled out again. He did that a few times, stretching me. His hands tightened on my hips and he pulled out before entering me fully.

A scream left my mouth as my nails bit into his shoulder blades. "Wait, wait, wait, wait, wait!" It seemed like he grew within the time he was stretching me until he entered me fully. Hell I felt like I was being split into two.

"You straight?" He asked that dumb ass question and I hit him.

"No, you dumbass. My pussy feel like it's being split in half." He laughed, like actually chuckled. "Wait, don't move." He wasn't even moving.

Taking a deep breath, I relaxed my body so I could get used to his monstrous invasion. After a few minutes the pain eased a bit, gripping his shoulders harder I began to move up and down slowly. Even doing so, it still felt like I was being stretched.

"*Fuck!*" Blaze groaned out as he began to move with me. Pulling out, he thrust back in fast, hard, making me cry out. "*Shit!*" Again, he groaned as he thrust deep inside of me. His mouth went to my neck and he bit into the skin as his hips thrust upward.

"Ooh, ooh," my nails bit into the back of his neck as I held onto him tightly. The mixture of both pleasure and pain made my body jittery as my inner sex muscles sucked on him rapidly.

Blaze's hold on my hips like a vice grip as his pelvis smacked hard against mine. Without detaching our bodies, Blaze turned off the water, got out the shower and went straight to the counter. He placed me on top then pushed me back.

Pulling out, he slowly slid back in until our pelvis touched and his balls pushed against my ass. He repeated the action a second time before he started up again. Blaze was relentless as he began to pound into my body roughly. The sound of our skin coming together echoed throughout the bathroom.

He did not know the meaning of gentle, my pussy was sore from him taking my virginity, but I was enjoying every moment of the pleasurable pain.

"Ah, ah, ah, ooh, ooh! Mmm fuck!" I moaned loudly before biting into my lip to silent the loud embarrassing sound. Doing so didn't last long as he hit my sweet spot repeatedly. "Sss, ooh, ooh." My hand went to his pelvis trying to push him back as I damn near lost my mind.

God I was loving the pleasurable sensation of his roughness.

Grabbing my right leg, he put it on his shoulder, his hips rolled before he started a deep stroke. Sitting up, I put my hands behind me on the counter and began moving with him. My head fell back as Blaze's fingers went to my clit.

"Oh, God! Ooh, no, no, no, no, no." All I could do was moan and cry out in pleasure as he pinched, rubbed and spanked my clit, causing my pussy muscles to milk faster around him.

My muscles soon tightened, thighs became stiff, and my body shook I was at the edge of my peak.

"Ah, fuck!" Blaze breathed out as his movements became frantic.

With three more deep strokes I was cumming all over his dick while screaming like a fucking banshee.

Blaze quickly pulled out, his hand jerked his dick fast before he began slapping it against my pelvis. "Mm, shit," he cussed as his cream shot onto my mound. "Mm, fuck," he squeezed his tip, then pushed back inside of me.

168

My mouth parted, hips raised and loud gasps slipped from my throat.

Ebony's cat like cries and banshee screams were now understandable.

"Oh, my God," breathless, I panted. My eyes fell closed for a few seconds before they opened and stared straight at Blaze.

My face went hot as Blaze leaned into me, kissing up my shoulder to my neck before his face just lay against mine. We stayed like that for a minute until our pants slowed and our breathing returned to normal.

Once they did, Blaze sat up, looked down at me, and I suddenly felt embarrassed as he walked away to turn on the shower.

When he returned I looked away from him. Grabbing me by the waist, he pulled me to him.

"You straight?" He gripped my chin then turned my face so I was looking at him.

If having sex was like this with him all the time, a bitch would quickly become addicted.

"Yeah," I trailed off. Then looking at Blaze, I just started laughing. "Oh, my God!" I was so embarrassed. Not only was my moaning on replay in my head, but... Blaze went to pick me up, but I stopped him. "No, wait."

"What's wrong with you?" Blaze asked, looking amused as I shook my head.

"Nothing, I just want to stay here for an hour," I confessed truthfully. I glanced down at myself. I went to move my legs.

"Come on. The fuck you doing?" He caught me.

I wanted to cry, it was beyond embarrassing. "Promise you won't laugh?"

"Man, I ain't gon laugh if you hurt? Are you?" He checked with a look of concern.

I bit into my bottom lip. "No, but... my legs are numb..." I mumbled low, but loud enough so he could hear me.

"What?" If amusement wasn't noticeable before in those light brown eyes of his, it clearly was now.

"Blaze, stop. Don't laugh, I'm serious." Covering my face, I laughed.

"Man, stop it. Ain't nothing to be embarrassed about. Come on." He laughed as he picked me up, carrying me to the shower. "Fuck yo ass was screaming no fah? Shid, had me watching the damn door waiting on it to be kicked in," Blaze joked.

I burst out laughing, hitting him. "That's not funny, yo ass stupid. Ugh, why would you say that?" I whined out.

"Shid, I was good."

"You were okay," I said, and Blaze stopped washing me up. He glance down at me and within a second he had me pinned to the shower wall, with my leg hooked at his waist. "Blaze, no."

"Nah, fuck that. I was okay? I'm always better the second time." He start saying as he wrapped my leg around his waist.

"I was playing and if I wasn't sore I wouldn't mind doing this again and again and some more then some more after that..." I trailed off, licking his lips as my hands found their way down to his ass, pulling him more into me.

"If you sore you better stop now," the warning was very clear. "Get yo hand off my ass."

My hand move to his lower back. I bit into his bottom lip, my nails dug into his back as my other hand came between our bodies, taking ahold of his erection.

"You mean my ass." I bit the side of his mouth.

"Get that shit outda here, this me, baby. But, shid, I'd play along if it ends with me getting some. Just keep yo hands off my ass," he bargained.

Laughing, I pushed him away. "No, you not getting anything. You can't even make me breakfast, but you wanna get in."

"Yo ass knew you weren't getting breakfast outda me before we fuck'd. The fuck you mean?" Blaze argued with a nonchalant shrug.

Ignoring him, I raised off before getting out the shower. *My damn legs ached and my coochie was sore.*

Chapter 23

Peaches

Once I got in my room, I didn't even bother to put on clothes. I took my black ass straight to my bed crawling in and getting under the covers. My body suddenly felt so tired, I honesty just wanted to go to sleep.

"Peaches, what you doing? I thought yo ass wanted something to eat?" Blaze asked, entering the room.

With a groan, I pulled the covers over my head. That did nothing as Blaze came and pulled them back.

"You mad? I was only playing, damn."

"I'm not mad, just a little tired. Here," I scooted over, patting the spot next to me.

Blaze looked from the spot then to me, confused.

"Dude, get yo ass in this bed before I slap you." Laughing, Blaze slid in next to me and I laid on his chest closing my eyes.

"I done worked yo ass, huh?" His arm went to my side, pulling me closer to him.

"You're not funny." To make what he said worse, a yawn slipped through my lips, making him laugh. "It's not funny."

"I'm not tryna be, shid, I'm only being honest. Check this though, I'm hungry. Yo ass can go make us something to eat or get yo lazy ass up, put on some clothes, and come take this ride with me. I got some running I need to do," he said, making me roll my eyes.

"Blaze, you are so romantic," I spoke sarcastically as I climbed on top of him.

"I ain't tryna be romantic, I done already told you that."

"Get yo hands off my ass," Blaze simply squeezed my ass before letting go for a second. "Damn, Blaze, that shit hurts. I

told you about slapping my ass like you fucking crazy. Damn!"
Now with an attitude, I sat up, hitting him in the chest.

"Man, get yo ass up and put on some damn clothes so
we can go."

"Fine, but we have to go by the park, I lost my damn gun
fucking with y'all yesterday." Climbing off him, I went to my
dresser to put on some lotion.

"I got yo gun."

After clamping my bra together, I looked at him. "Why
do you have my gun?" I asked him.

"Shid, with the way yo ass was going I thought you was
gonna pop my ass. I snatched that thang off yo hip the moment
yo crazy ass started swinging. It was cute though, yo whole little
jealousy thing. On the real though, I started to smack yo ass fah
tryna hoe me, boss. Had mothafuckas out there laughing. You
lucky I kinda like yo itty bitty black ass, otherwise I would've
fuck'd you up."

I started laughing. "I did beat y'all ass, though."

"Fuck you, man. I let you do that. Yo ass better stop
hitting me though, my moms already wanna beat yo ass for that
one time," he claimed.

If possible, I laughed harder. "You told your mom on
me? Oh, my God, how old are you, Blaze, seriously?"

"Shut yo ass up. But fah real, you better watch out,
moms slick ass fuck, boss. Her ass will pop up on you." The
sudden seriousness in his tone had my laughter stopping as I
took him in.

"You really told your mother on me?" Hell, I thought he
was joking and if his ass crazy, I'm pretty sure his momma a
little rough around the edges too. Damn, I didn't wanna beat his
momma's ass. "Yo momma gon' try to fight me or something?"
Even though I liked Blaze a lot, that didn't mean I wouldn't
whoop his momma's ass if she came at me tryna fight. Blaze
suddenly started laughing.

"Fuck you talking about? My moms don't fight, her
crazy ass shoot. Why the fuck you think I'm telling you to watch

yo back. She know who you is and what you look like," he said and I nodded before shrugging.

"I'm always strapped so—"

"Peaches, I'm playing. Yo crazy ass probably would shoot at my momma." He laughed, cutting me off.

"Hell yeah I would, but only if I thought she was going to shoot me." I shrugged again before hitting him. "You play too much."

"Get yo crazy ass ready."

Stupid ass.

I went to my closet, took my long sleeve, Elizabeth Jacquard body con dress off the hanger. I stepped into it then grab my black high heeled, peek toed booties. Sitting on the bed, I put them on.

"Damn, we just going to breakfast. Yo ass ridiculous, man. Who you tryna look good fah?" Blaze asked, looking me up, licking his lips.

Laughing, I shrugged while taking out my Sienna quilted tote and black leather jacket from the closet. "That dress to damn tight, gon' take that shit off." The seriousness in his tone had me glancing over my shoulder at him.

"Hating, daddy, gets you nowhere. Where you get a change of clothes from?" I asked, looking at his black, Louis Vuitton jeans that hung low, showing off his red boxer briefs. Blaze then pulled on a red Louis Vuitton shirt before stepping into his fire red, white, and cement grey IV Jordan's.

"I always keep extra clothes with me," he told me. "Man, I ain't playing with yo ass, you not wearing that dress." Blaze said, coming up behind me, pressing his lower body into my back.

I combed my hair down the side of my face and back. "You get on my nerves, there's nothing wrong with what I have on." I moved my head forward as his dropped down to bury in the side of my neck. "Nuh uh, don't kiss or try to smell me." I laughed, turned around to face him then pushed his head back.

"I'ight, nigga, boss. Remember that."

"I'm playing." Standing on my tips I gave him a simple peck. My eyes locked with his light brown ones and for a moment I seemed to get lost staring at him. Clearing my throat, I looked away, tryna hide the smile that had spread across my lips. Even doing so, I couldn't contain the small laugh that slipped through my lips. My thumb pressed against his lips, wiping the gloss from his mouth.

Still smiling, I looked away from him as that giddy feeling started up again. "Here, zip me up," I turned my back to him.

Blaze did as I asked, zipping up my dress before grabbing my ass.

"You ready? I'm starving," I said, pushing him back so I could walk around him.

Things were moving way too fast for me, but I didn't know how to slow it down and I honestly didn't think I wanted to.

Grabbing my jacket, I put it on before transferring everything of out my other purse and into the one I was carrying.

"Blaze, give me my gun." That was one thing I never left without. My baby. She may have been small, but she hurt something nasty. After getting my black chain with the white spike brass knuckles hanging from it, I put it on then turned to Blaze.

"Why yo ass need a gun if you got that on?" He gestured to my necklace, making me roll my eyes.

"Sometimes a bitch or a nigga needs that ass spiked before they get shot. Now give me my baby." I held my hand out as I explained my reasons for needing both.

Blaze grabbed his keys then turned off the TV and Lights before pushing me out my room door.

"Yo ass violent as hell. Man, a nigga gon' start sleeping with one eye open in this bitch. On G, I ain't bullshittin'" Laughing, I muffed his head to the side. "Gon' before I beat yo ass."

"Whatever, I ain't worried about it. Then again, that may be what I want." I licked my lips then bit into my bottom, sucking the corner into my mouth.

"Get yo nasty ass outda here before you be around here talking about you can't feel yo damn legs."

My face went hot as a blush crept up my neck to my cheeks.

"Blaze, that's not funny. In my defense, this was my first time so maybe it's normal. I mean, my body wasn't use to that kind of—"

"Shit was mind boggling, huh?"

Laughing, I rolled my eyes. "Yo ass wasn't that, like I said it was my first time—"

"And I tore yo shit up," Blaze said as we made it to his truck.

"I hate you fo'real." I got in the truck and closed the door, then turned in my seat so I was facing him.

"Fuck you looking at?" His hand pushed my face back.

"Stop." My hand slapped his as I whined

"What?"

"Nothing," I shrugged before looking out the window as he drove down the street.

***

"Peaches?" My shoulder shook as I heard Blaze call my name. "Peaches"

"Hmm?" I mumbled, turning around.

"We here," his words faded as I began to doze back off, I was so tired. "Peaches, man get up." My shoulder shook again.

"Stop," I whined out, it wasn't too long after I heard a door close, then a few seconds later another opened before I felt myself being turned. "Blaze stop, dang."

"Fuck you looking at?" The hostility in his voice had me opening my eyes only to find him staring to the side of him. That's when I noticed I was half way out the truck.

What the fuck was he gon' do, drag me out?

"This ain't got shit to do with you, nosy ass mothafucka," Blaze continued to go off at whoever was staring at us.

Sighing, I rolled my eyes. He did not wake me up for that shit.

"Fuck you rolling yo damn eyes fah?" He turned on me. My brow rose and I smacked my lips about to push him away, but Blaze leaned into me.

"Don't start with me," I cut myself off as I yawned. God, I was tired.

Blaze helped me out the truck, complaining. "Man, I can't fuck with yo ass during the morning, tired ass." He joked.

I didn't find anything funny. He did not wear me out, I was simply tired because I only got a few hours of sleep waiting for his ass to get home. That's why I was tired. He slept just as long, and up like the fuckin' Energizer bunny.

"Dude, I stayed up all night. I slept for an hour and a half this morning, it would've been longer if you hadn't woke me up talking about breakfast." We walked into Broadway's Café.

He blocked the second doors as he turned to me. "What yo ass was doing up all night?" He questioned.

Without thinking, I told him the truth. "Waiting for your dumbass to get home. I even tried to call but you didn't answer." My mouth snapped shut, realizing too late what I was saying. Then again, there was no reason to hide the fact that I was in strong like with him. Hell, if yesterday wasn't a dead giveaway, I didn't know what was.

"You were worried about me?" Why did he have to ask so lowly, smooth, sexy?

My cheeks grew hot fast, causing me to look away.

"No, I just like sleeping with you." *The fuck is wrong with me?* Clearing my throat, I glanced at Blaze, then the double doors. "Um, we should go inside, I'm hungry," I tried with a pout.

177

"Shid, it's cool. Don't be embarrassed about it," Blaze said, licking his lips. "Ain't nothing wrong with worrying. Last night was crazy, that's why I didn't call or text you back. I had to get some shit right. Now that I know you worry about a nigga, I'll text or call you back next time."

"You don't have to." I didn't want it to seem like it was a big deal, so I shrugged.

"Man, get that bullshit outda here. Yo ass ain't got to play that *I don't give a fuck attitude* all the fuckin' time, man. Damn, be real with a nigga, like I be with yo ass." He had a point, but I was not the worrying type if it didn't come to King.

I just didn't want Blaze to see me getting too attached and then turn around and use that against me, which would somehow leave me hurt in the end.

This is already moving too fast and we aren't even dating.

When I didn't say anything, Blaze shook his head. He led me inside the restaurant. I didn't say anything else, just followed in behind him.

Chapter 24

Peaches

The hostess handed Blaze two menus and he took us to a booth in the back where the lighting was dimmed. The restaurant was a nice, big family diner. Simple but nice. And where we sat was quiet, sort of private. Not too many people were in the back, which made it better.

I glanced away from my menu to Blaze, only to find him on his phone. *I took it.*

His head snap up so fast. "What the fuck—?"

"No phones at the table, remember?" A smile crossed my lips at my reminder.

He gave me a slight glare. "This ain't yo apartment and I don't see no damn signs. Now give me my phone," he fussed, holding his hand out. I sat his phone down on the side of me and stared at him. "What?"

"Look I don't—" I started saying, but was interrupted.

"Hey, my name's Megan and I'll be your server today. I can take your drink order and give you a few minutes to look over your menus if you need more time," The waitress says, smiling a little too damn hard for my liking.

Picking up my menu, I looked over it for a second, already knowing what I was getting.

"You know what you're ordering?" I asked Blaze who was looking at his menu before closing it with a nod of his head. "We'll order now. I'll have the Denver Omelet and instead of the sausage links can you make it bacon," I said as she wrote it down.

"How would like your eggs, and what would you like to drink?"

"Scrambled and I'll just have an orange juice."

"And you, sir?" She asked Blaze.

"Give me the steak and eggs with a sprite," he told her and for some reason after she wrote it down she was still standing there. Blaze opened his mouth to say something to me when he noticed her. "Why the fuck you still standing here staring and shit? Get yo ass gone, damn. We don't wanna sit here looking at yo ass all fuckin' morning."

My eyes widen and my mouth parted. Hell, the waitress looked just as surprised. "Blaze—"

"What man? Bitch looking all in my fuckin' face. Ain't nobody looking at yo ass." Bad thing ol' girl was still standing there. "Close your fuckin' mouth and go get our shit," he snapped at her before his stare turned toward me. "Fuck you kick me fah?"

What is wrong with this man? You can't just talk to people like that.

"He just lost his job and he's irritated right now, so don't be offended," I lied, looking at Blaze.

"Fuck you looking at?" He asked me. I looked to ol' girl who had quickly grabbed our menus, walking off fast.

"I would slap the shit outda you, don't talk to me like that. What makes you think it's cool to talk to folks the way you do?" I had to ask. And to think it was his rudeness that attracted me.

I'm dumb.

"Who said it wasn't? I don't see no fuckin' signs hanging around saying I can't," he offered to say.

Grabbing a pack of sugar, I threw it at him, then another.

"What? Shid, I'm just saying it ain't no written law or rule saying I can't talk to people the way I do. Plus, that bitch was all in my face. I could see if her ass was saying something, but the bitch wasn't. She was just staring," he went to explain.

And I like him? Out of everybody in the world, I like him? Blaze.

"Fuck you shaking yo head fah?"

Ignoring that question, I went back to what I was about to say before the waitress came.

"Look, Blaze, I care okay. Don't expect me to just become this sudden open book. I mean, I don't do this, whatever this is, I don't know…" I trailed off, letting out a frustrated groan, making Blaze laugh.

"Yo ass acting like you ain't ever had a boyfriend before." He chuckled, but stopped when I looked away from him. "You're shitting me, on what?" I ain't say nothing, again he laughed.

"It's not funny."

"Seriously, you have never dated nobody?" He asked, making me roll my eyes.

"If yo ass gon' be laughing then ain't no point in me tryna be real with you. So forget it."

Blaze laughing kinda pissed me off. It wasn't a laughing matter, I was tryna be real with him on why I acted the way I did, but his ass wanted to laugh.

Besides Sly, I'd never had a boyfriend. Everything Sly and I did was behind closed doors, never public, so I really couldn't say he was my boyfriend.

"I'm sorry, it's not. I just wouldn't have expected someone like you—"

My hands waved in front of us, signaling him to stop talking. "Someone like me? What's that supposed to mean?" Now I was offended.

"Man, shut the fuck up. I ain't mean it in a bad way. I mean, with as many hoes as you had around, you never caught feelings?" He asked, and I shrugged.

"Have you met my brother? King is way too overprotective, especially after my dad died. His ass went from ten to a thousand, you couldn't pay a nigga that knew King and I were cool to come near me," I told him, and he snorted.

"It didn't stop that nigga Sly," Blaze responded, not seeming happy about that little bit.

Shrugging, a laugh slipped through my lips. "Sly was unexpected, the first to ever give me head. So it's his fault I'm this way, shit was crazy good." I boasted with a smile.

"I don't wanna hear that bullshit!" He snapped at me and again I shrugged. "That's some hoe shit—"

"Did you just call me a hoe?" I was about to jump all on his ass.

"Man, why the fuck would I call you a hoe? I was talking about Sly's ass, that shit he pulled," Blaze explained.

"I guess." How could you be real with someone like that? I mean, it was already hard to express those new feelings. I'd rather keep them to my damn self. Grabbing the sugar box, I started fixing them making sure they were all the same way.

"You mad now, huh?" He asked.

"Nope, not at all." I couldn't be mad because his dumbass probably never had anything serious either besides a fuck buddy.

"Yo ass lying. Why you mad?"

"I'm not mad, there's nothing to be mad about." With a glance at him, I shrugged before putting the sugar packages back just as our food came. The waitress put our food down, about to walk away, but Blaze grabbed her arm, stopping her.

"Yo ass ain't do shit to our food, did you?" His eyes were hard, his face contorted into a mean mug.

"No, I didn't. I swear—" the waitress shakily spoke.

"Blaze, leave that damn girl alone," I snapped at him, the girl seriously looked scared. Hell, I probably would've been too, if some guy suddenly snapped at me. Then again, me personally, I would've snapped right back, ready to fight. "Gone, mama, you good." She quickly pulled her arm from Blaze and took off speed walking. Bet her damn ass would watch who she smiled at next time. "What the hell is wrong with you?"

"Ain't shit wrong with me, I was just tryna make sho' her ass wasn't tryna be slick," he said, pushing his plate away then putting his elbows on the table, staring at me. "Now why you mad?"

Rolling my eyes, I grabbed my fork and knife. "I'm not mad. Blaze, gone somewhere for real," I told him as he got out his seat. Sliding in next to me, he pushed the table over to the side he'd just left. "Blaze I'm not mad. What are you doing?" I asked, grabbing his wrist as he rubbed along my thigh.

"I ain't doing shit, just talking. You ain't the only one new to this. The only different between us is you tryna hide it. Sweetheart, I'm thirty, I'm grown as hell. A nigga ain't never want for shit until I met yo mean ass. Shid, the moment yo ass held that knife to my shit you was got, boss. Even with this shit going too fast, at the end of the day it ain't gon' matter whether it's two weeks, a month, or a year, I'ma still have yo ass. So you getting an attitude because you think I ain't hearing you is bullshit. I'm listening to you, baby girl, but I done already warned yo ass of me. I am who I am, it ain't no changing shit."

Throughout his whole explanation his hands moved between my legs and began rubbing my clit through my panties.

"Blaze," I panted out.

"I'm just talkin', now you can't hear me out?" He was so slick with it. And the fact that my body was reacting to what his fingers were doing wasn't good.

Biting into my bottom lip hard, I tried to keep from moaning out loud. I was surprised I hadn't broke skin with how hard I was biting.

"It ain't no running, not no more. I hear you, boss, I got you." Blaze suddenly moved his finger from my pussy and dug in his back pocket. He pulled out a condom.

No, no he isn't thinking…

My eyes widened as he undid his jeans.

Looking around, there was only a few people a little distance away. But still, we were in a restaurant whether we were in the back or not.

"Blaze, no. I'm not about to do that in here," I whispered lowly, but loud enough for him to hear. My protest did nothing but fall on deaf ears.

"Come here," he was already pulling me into his lap so I was straddling him.

"Blaze we can't—" I started grabbing his wrist as he pulled my thong to the side. The tip of his erection poked at my contracting sex.

"We just talking, we can't do that?" *Is he serious right now?* "Huh? You don't wanna talk to me, Peaches?" His mouth covered mine as he pushed inside of me, causing a small scream to leave my mouth and go into his.

Blaze's hands went to my hips as he slowly sat me down on him, filling me completely.

Oh, my God!

"Blaze, no, we can't." A soft moan slipped through my lips as I wrapped my arms tightly around his neck. My breathing quickened, my pants heavy.

"Shush," Blaze mumbled against my lips as he gripped my hips tightly, moving them back and forth.

I couldn't believe we were having sex for the second time and in a restaurant no less. Even so, I was enjoying every moment of it, loving the feel of him.

My hips began to rotate on him, causing his hold to tighten even more as he started lifting me up and down on his dick. Blaze thrust up hard every time I came down, making it hard for me to keep quiet.

"*Fuck!*" Blaze groaned out as our movements became in sync. He soon placed my thighs on his forearms, my hands gripped his shoulders and I started to bounce faster on him.

Being discrete was no longer an option, shit was feeling too good. I simply couldn't hold in my moans. Blaze must have sense it because his lips came to mine swallowing my sounds.

"Harder," I moaned out against his lips and he complied, kissing me harder as hips thrust forward. It was so wrong, God it wasn't right, but it felt amazing! My inner muscles began to milk him as my body started shaking. I buried my head into the side of his neck. "Ah, ah, Blaze."

He held my hips tightly to him as his thrusting turned into jerking as we both reached our peak.

"Ah shit! Fuck!" Blaze cussed out lowly, making me groan as we came down from our orgasmic high.
"I can't believe you," I groaned out, making Blaze laugh. "It's not funny, my brother warned me about niggas like you."

"Niggas like me? That's should be a good thing then," he said, his hands rubbing across my ass.

"It isn't, not at all." I mumbled against his neck, panting heavily. Blaze suddenly leaned forward, making me groan once more. "No, don't move." This orgasm was just like the first. I came so hard it seems like every nerve in my body just went haywire before going numb. Moving at that moment made my body feel so funny.

Am I going to tell Blaze I'm numb yet again?
Hell no, he'll probably laugh or something.

"Peaches?" He called lowly.

"Hm?" I hummed against his neck, I did not wanna move at all. "Blaze, stop," I whined as he lifted my lower body, causing him to slide out of me.

"Shid, I thought yo ass was sleep," he joked.

Laughing at that, I sat up and looked down at him. "You did not put me to sleep, so shut up." I said, popping the P while leaning down once more to peck his lips. "You done got me twice this morning and still haven't fed me."

"'Cause a nigga that good," he claimed,—*true*—as his hips pushed up.

Sliding off his lap, my butt hit the seat just as a tall, sexy, dark skin man came up to where we were. He didn't look better than Blaze, but he was still sexy no doubt.

Blazes' hand suddenly smacked hard against the back of my head. "What the fuck yo ass looking at?"

Chapter 25

Peaches

Blaze acted as if I was checking the man out. I just so happened to turn around when he was coming. *The fuck I look like?*

"You bet not hit me again, black ass," I whispered as the man stopped at our table. *Oh, my God, I hope he wasn't the owner. If so, he was about put our asses out. Damn, I ain't even ate yet.*

"Blaze, my man." The guy greeted and I was relieved as Blaze stood to pound the man's fist.

When he moved from the booth, I slid out the seat. "What's good Mark? Where you going?" Blaze grabbed my waist, pulling me into his side.

"To wash my hands, I'll be back."

"Mark, I'll be right back. Call yo waiter and ask her to warm this up and wrap mine. Shid, she probably ain't gon' come back. My girl scared her," Blaze lied.

My eyes widened and my mouth opened, not believing what just left his mouth. "You lying—"

Blaze pushed me forward, cutting me off. "We'll be back," he said, still walking. Once we got to the empty hallway by the bathroom, I turned around and hit him.

"Yo lying butt get on my nerves." Blaze pushed me into the women's restroom, laughing. "What are you doing?" I asked him as he walked in behind me. Ignoring my question, Blaze walked to a stall and flushed the toilet. Going to the stall next to him I took the baby wipes out my purse and started cleaning between my legs. Once finished, I flushed the toilet with my foot, then went to the sink.

"I had to flush the condom I wrapped in napkins, damn. Now can I wash my hands? Do you wanna know why I wanna wash my hands? Yo ass got my pants wet," Blaze suddenly said. "Can't be fuckin' yo ass in public, got me looking like I done pissed my damn self."

Why would he say that?

"I hate you. Ugh, I swear," I was blushing so hard.

"You done turned bright red in this bitch. Why you embarrassed?" He asked as we finished washing our hands.

"I'm not, damn. Ugh, fuck you." I walked away from him and out the door. Blaze soon followed, coming behind me.

"Hold up, damn, I'm playing. What's up with you taking everything to heart? What happened to I don't give a fuck Peaches?"

She admitted to liking yo dumbass and started giving a fuck about what you thought.

Ignoring what he asked, my head nodded toward our table. "Blaze, whatever. Who's ol' boy?"

"Somebody I met around the way. He owns this place and stop eye fuckin' him before I beat yo ass."

"I wasn't, I turned around when he came up."

"I don't give a fuck for reasons, you heard what I said," he snapped at me.

Rolling my eyes, I flipped him off. "I'll let you know when I'm worried about you tryna beat my ass," I told him as we came to the table and I slid in with Blaze right behind me. As soon as we sat down, dude looked from Blaze to me nodding, then back. Before I could say something, Blaze started talking.

"This my girl, she good. So what's up?" He said and dude shrugged.

"Shid, living you know. I talked to yo mans and shit was good. Nigga said momma did her thang cooking, dude still talking about it." I was beyond confused. Why the hell were they talking about food?

"What he want?" Blaze asked and again dude looked at me. "Why the fuck you keep looking at her fah? Nigga, I'm over here. Now what the fuck he want?" Blaze snapped. Dude quickly looked away from me, clearing his throat.

Okay.

Pursing my lips together, I contained my laughter. With a shake of my head I began eating my food.

"Both," he said, pulling out a piece of paper and sliding it across the table. Blaze picked it up and looked it over before taking a lighter from his pocket and burning the paper, then dropping it in his sprite.

"I got you," he said, pulling out his phone and doing something to it before looking at me. "You finished?"

Taking a drink from my juice, I wiped my mouth with a napkin. I had just started eating and he was ready to go.

"No, but I can take it to go. You didn't eat," I pointed out, he was the main one talking about being hungry.

"I had mine wrapped to go," Blaze said, taking money from his pocket, but Mark stopped him.

Mark took another glance my way. "I'll take care of it."

Looking away from him, I turned to Blaze. "Can you put my food with yours?" I asked him, about to grab the bag that was sitting on the table when we returned from the bathroom. Blaze pulled the bag from me, sitting it on the floor.

"N'all, I don't want yo syrup and shit on my steak," he said before calling the waiter. "Aye, bring me another box." Nodding, she quickly made her way to the back, returning a few seconds later with a container and a bag.

"Thanks," giving her a polite smile, I put my food in the container then the bag.

"She's new, huh? You—" Whatever Mark was about to say, Blaze quickly shut him up.

"Mark, yo business don't mean shit to me, homey. Watch what's about to come out yo damn mouth. She ain't yo mothafuckin' concern, yah dig? This my last time telling yo ass that. Let's go, bae," Blaze grabbed my hand, pulling me up from my seat, almost making me drop my purse.

"My bad, just wondering who she is, that's all. But I'll get up with you later." His gaze fell on me before his hands went up and he started moving back.

Punk ass nigga.

Shaking my head with a slight laugh, I held Blaze's hand, letting him lead the way out. Once we got outside to the truck, Blaze let me go, walking around to his side and opening his door.

"Why yo ass just standing there? Get in," he stood at his opened door.

My hip cocked to the side as my arms folded over my chest. "Blaze, come open my door." There was no hope for this damn man.

"I got it," some random guy who was park next to us said, opening my door.

Blaze looked murderous, so much so, my black ass moved the fuck away from the truck as he slammed his door and then came around to my side.

"Bitch, yo ass did not just open…" Blaze dropped his ass, "…my…fuckin' door?" He finished saying, stomping dude as soon as he hit the floor.

It wasn't that serious, was it?

Blaze was literally stomping the shit out that man. "Man, stop, come on." I tried to grab him only to be pushed away. I was about to hit him until I heard.

Woop, woop

Fuck!

***

The police sirens sounded before they pulled into the parking lot.

"Come on, man, damn. It's not that serious, Blaze. Stop!" He still wasn't listening. I just wanted to go home, it was like being out with King's dumbass, I swear.

The police officers got out the car, both of them grabbed ahold of Blaze and pulled him off the man. Once they had him back, his dumbass snatched away from them.

"Get the fuck off of me!" He snapped as he snatched away.

"Blaze?" Both the officers said at the same time when he turned around. Blaze looked from one officer to the other, then started smiling.

"Davie, boy, what's good my nigga? Damn, it's been long," Blaze said as he shook up with the tall bright skinned officer. That Davie person acted like he was hella excited to see Blaze, just as the dark skinned officer did. "Pete, yo punk ass finally got that damn badge, huh, bitch?" They laughed, doing the whole man hug thing.

Okay, so did they forget about the bleeding man over there on the ground? Blaze put his ass to sleep.

"Fuck that, when did you get out?" Pete, the dark one asked as Blaze leaned against their car.

This shit is crazy. Aren't they suppose too be arresting his ass or something?

"About two months now. But I need to talk to yo pops about that shit, nigga was sweet as fuck," Pete nodded his head at that.

"How's business going?" David asked.

This was beyond crazy. Like who stood in the middle of a parking lot chatting with the police with an unconscious man lying on the ground?

Where they do this at?

"Which one?" He laughed, making me roll my eyes. "N'all, the lot doing good as well as the pool halls. I'm on my way to the lot now. What you niggas getting into later?" They were still having a conversation like nothing happened.

"My momma having some dinner, but after that I'm free," David said.

"You know me, wherever food at that's where I'll be. So I'm with this nigga," Pete added, laughing.

"T'ight then. I'll get up with y'all later—" Blaze started, but Pete cut him off, looking over at me.

"Who that?" He nodded toward me.

"That's my girl," Blaze told 'em.

Hearing him say that had my insides twisting into knots. God, I hoped it didn't show on my face.

"Fuck y'all looking so damn hard fah?"

"My bad, no disrespect. Little mama look familiar as hell, though," David said starting at me hard.

"Take a picture, it'll last longer." I said. He looked at Blaze then back to me, licking his lips. Him doing so drew my attention to them. Nice, full.

"I don't think my mans would appreciate that, I ain't caught yo name," Davie said.

"Because I ain't throw it," I told 'em.

"I can arrest you for that mouth of yours."

"And I can just put yours to work." Blaze swirled around so fast I jumped back as he yanked me toward him by the front of my dress.

"Man, I'll slap the fuck out yo ass! Get the fuck in the truck." Blaze demanded in a low, hard tone before he pushed me back. The two officers behind him started laughing.

"I was only playing. Now that I think about it, you do look familiar. You know Cornell?" I asked him and he snapped his fingers together.

"I knew I seen you around—" he started, but Blaze cut him off.

"Who the fuck is Cornell?" He asked, making me laugh.

"A friend is all." Cornell was one of my head buddies, but his ass started to get too damn clingy, showing up to my job, at my apartment. Dude was crazy and I didn't do those. He gave good head no doubt, but his clingy had me looking past all that.

"Make me slap yo ass," Blaze warned again and I laughed, walking up to him.

"Don't be jealous, yo head game is better—" I whispered in a cute, flirty voice.

"Get the fuck off me. Didn't I just tell you to get in the truck?" Again, he pushed me toward the truck then turned back to the cops. "I'll get up with y'all later." He shook up with them once more before pulling me into his side.

"I'ight, we'll get at you." Nodding, Blaze turned around, walking to the truck. "Aye, hold up!" Pete called after us and as we looked back he pointed to ol' dude on the ground.

Well it's about damn time they noticed him, even though dude was still out.

"Shid, I don't know, I saw his ass like that when we came out. I was looking at him when y'all pulled up," Blaze lied smoothly, making the other two laughed.

"Yo ass, nigga. Get the fuck outda here," David said, shaking his head. "What he do?" He asked Blaze as he opened the passenger door for me.

"I don't know what you talkin' about. I found his ass like that. I'm out, don't forget to tell yo pops to get at me," he said, closing my door then walking around to his side. Blaze started the truck then pulled out, blowing once at the two officers before pulling off.

"They just gon' let you leave like that? I mean, they know you lying. Hell, they had to pull you off dude." That was some crazy shit.

"I don't know what you're talking about," he said, plain and simple. Coming to a stop light, Blaze grabbed the Broadway Café bag, sitting it in his lap and pulling out a white food container.

"You can't eat and drive, Blaze. You should've ate before we left."

"Shut up." He opened the container just as the light turned green. "Shit, here." Blaze handed the food container to me, so I opened it.

"What the fuck is this?" I asked, looking at the money in the container. He didn't... No... "You used me? Oh my..." Turning around in my seat, I looked at him.

"Man, I don't know what you talking about," he nonchalantly stated as he drove.

I punched his ass.

"What the fuck wrong with you? Don't you see me driving?" He snapped as he swirved the truck.

I punched his ass harder.

"You used me, wanting to go out to breakfast so you can sell this man shit? Are you serious, Blaze? Wow! God, I should've known that's why the fucking conversation didn't make sense and why he kept looking at me. What the fuck is wrong with you? Ugh." As soon as he stopped at another red light I started hitting him. That was so low for him to do that. There I was thinking he was doing that for me, but it was to make some type of deal.

"Get the fuck off me," Blaze snapped, pushing me back into the door, then slapping the shit outda me.

"You *bitch!*" Getting out of my seat, I jumped on him, punching his ass as hard as I could. "Yo dumbass gon' fuckin' use me," I snapped, still punching him. Blaze suddenly got his hand around my neck, pushing me back into the steering wheel, slapping me again, then throwing me into my seat as he threw the truck in park.

"Bitch, you hit me again I'ma beat the fuck outda you!" Kicking his ass in the chin and making his head go back, I sat up before jumping back at him. This time Blaze knocked the shit outda me. I fell into my seat with my back hitting the door. "Yo dumbass—"

"Fuck you! That shit was foul as fuck, you dumb bitch. King ain't never done no shit like that." My feelings were so hurt.

"Bitch, I ain't King—" The back of his hand hit hard across my face. I tried to hit him again only to have him jerk his head out the way before he slapped me again. "Yo ass better stop hitting me. Boss, you gon make me beat yo ass."

"Fuck you! Take me home," I snapped at him, I was so done with his dumbass.

"You'll go home when I finish doing what the fuck I gotda do. Peaches, on G, if you hit me—" He started.

"Shut the fuck up talkin to me. Pull over, I'll walk home." I did not want to be in the car with him anymore. That was what I got for playing every guy whoever became clingy or caught feelings for me. was Karma was fucking me raw and hard.

He wanted to talk about keeping shit real when he couldn't do the same. I didn't care about him living the life because that was his choice, but he sholdn't have dragged me into that shit. Even if he did, he should've told me me about it and not been fuckin' sneaky.

"Blaze, pull over."

"Man, shut the fuck up."

"No, you shut the fuck up and stop the fucking truck." His ass knew he was making this deal when he hopped his triflin' ass in the shower with me.

Once Blaze came to another stop light, I opened my door, about get out, only to have him yank me back.

"Man, close that fuckin' door, damn. Yo ass always gotda act fuckin' stupid," Blaze snapped as he reached over, slamming my door.

I muffed him. "Me? You know what? You're absolutely right, me. Now can you please take me home?" There was no point going back and forth with him.

"Now yo ass wanna go home? Why the fuck you mad? Yo ass wanted to go to breakfast, so I took you," was his reply.

My head nodded as I stared out the window. "You right, so let's drop it. Just get to where you going," I said, leaving it at that. I wasn't about to keep arguing with him.

His ass was foul, plain and simple.

Chapter 26

Peaches

Throughout the rest of the ride I didn't say anything to Blaze. Maybe it was petty, but then again, I wasn't taking any risks, shit was foul. If he would have told me what was about go down, I probably wouldn't have accepted it, but I would of went along with it.

"I think yo ass busted my lip," Blaze gazed in the mirror as he pulled into Carter's Motors.

Why we were there, I didn't know. But I wasn't gon' ask Blaze because I wasn't talking to him. *God, I hope he isn't pretending to like me. I would think this now, after I done fuck'd his dumbass, not once, but twice.*

Blaze drove to the huge white and glass building, drove on the walkway and parked in front of a big window.

Now his ass know he ain't supposed to park on these people sidewalk. Shrugging, I didn't say anything, I hoped they towed his shit.

"I should slap the fuck out yo crazy ass. You busted my damn lip." He fussed in the mirror.

I simply rolled my eyes, still not saying anything as I looked out the window.

"Man, pick my money up off the floor," he continued to go off.

This time I did look at him. "Yo money? You pick that shit up."

Blaze reached over the seat, grabbed and snatched me over to him, and slapped me in the mouth. "Fuck you think you talkin to, huh?"

I went to hit him back, but he grabbed my wrist, pushing me back into my seat, holding me against the door. "Blaze, I swear to God, let go," I snapped, but that only made his grip tighten. "Blaze, let me the fuck go!" I screamed at him. In none of my years had I ever had to fight with a man as much as I had that past week.

Man, this shit ain't even worth it, I promise.

"Blaze—"

"Fuck that, calm yo dumbass down," he said, still holding me.

"Bitch, you just slapped me! Let me the fuck go!" Yanking one of my hands free, I started swinging with one arm.

Blaze pushed me harder into the door, his ass came over in my seat grabbing my swinging hand and pinned it to my chest as his other hand came to my neck. "Yo ass gon' make me fuckin' hurt you, Peaches. Boss, calm the fuck down."

That was some fuckin' bullshit, I swear. "Blaze, get off of me, damn!"

"Calm yo ass down."

"Bitch, I am calm. Now get up," I snapped at him, I just wanted to get the fuck out his truck and away from him. That was just too fuckin' much to go through with a guy.

Blaze, still held onto me, staring. I rolled my eyes and looked away from him.

"Peaches, boss, yo ass bet not hit me," he said, pushing into me before letting me go. As soon as he did, I punched his ass again before quickly throwing the truck door open and hopping out. I snatched my purse off the floor then slammed his door.

Angrily I searched my bag for my phone as I walked down the sidewalk.

"Peaches, get yo ass back here, man, damn." For some strange reason this heavy urge to cry came over me. I seriously just wanted to cry and I was only a crier when it came to King.

Piss couldn't even begin to explain how I felt. My hands were itching to start swinging on him again.

"Man, slow yo ass up," Blaze called out.

I didn't say anything to him, I called Kimmy.

"What's up bitch—" Her words were cut off as my phone was snatched out of my hand and I quickly swirled around on Blaze.

"Blaze, give me my phone, damn. Why the fuck you wanna play?"

My chest rose and fell hard, my nerves were going crazy. I held my shaky hand out, *God,* I wanted to hit him. Blaze turned off my phone, then put it in his pocket. "Can you stop playing and give me– You know what? Keep it." I wasn't about to keep going back and forth with him so I started walking again, but he stopped me.

"Fo'real, Peaches, chill the fuck out man, damn. Why the fuck you so gotdamn mad? Yo ass know what I do—"

"It's not about what you do, Blaze! I can look past all that, but the fact that you brought me in it without telling me is what I'm pissed about. Anything could've happened and I would've been stuck there looking stupid, not knowing shit. You know what? Even that I can get over, but the fact yo ass pretended— Forget it."

"N'all, pretend what? Yo ass wanted to go to breakfast—"

"But you didn't do it for *me!* You did it for you." My hands shot out as I screamed at him.

"So what? I still brought yo ass," he blurted out.

Shaking my head, I laughed. He simply didn't care. *God, I'm stupid.* "That you did. Now can I go?" I asked, pulling my arm from him, only to have him grab it back as he started pulling me to the truck. Stopping, I jerked my arm from him.

"Yo ass gon chill with that attitude," he said, opening the passenger side door and picking up the stacks of money. He put them back in the container, then closed and locked the door.

"Blaze, let me go, I can walk," I snapped, snatching my arm from him, only to have him grab it right back.

"What I tell you about that attitude? Calm yo ass down."

"Why can't I just stay in the truck until you finish here?" I asked as I ran a hand through my hair tryna fix it.

"Bring yo ass on." Again, he started pulling me to the door.

Sighing, I just followed behind him, not even tryna fight his dumbass. Blaze pulled opened the glass door, nodding his head, gesturing for me to go in. That had me raising a brow at him, but I didn't say anything. I simply walked in.

"Hey Mr. Carter," A brown skin woman around my age called, waving at Blaze as we walked in. Her cubical was right in front so she was the first to see everything.

God I hope she ain't see us out there.

"Mr. Carter?" Blaze asked her before laughing. "Tish, has Sam been here yet?" She nodded before reaching in her bottom drawer, pulling out a metal safety deposit box.

"Yeah, he said give you this, then he left," she said, smiling at me.

After taking the box, Blaze jerked on my hand, pulling me along. I went to hit him in the back as something finally hit me, my eyes reading the label on the wooden door.

"Carter? Blaze Carter," I read the label out loud as he opened the door. Letting his hand go, I walked further in before going to the big black chair, sitting down, then looking at Blaze as he closed and locked the door. "I'm not big on coincidences so I'm taking with your last name and the building this is some kinda family thing?" I asked, he didn't say anything at first as he sat the container and safety deposit box on the desk.

"N'all, this me," he said, going to a file cabinet, pulling it from the wall then lifting up the rug and removing a tile piece from the floor.

Of course my nosy ass got up to see what he was doing. I hovered over his shoulder only to see a safe. "Get yo nosy ass back, breathing all down my neck," Blaze said, still putting in the four digit code, causing the board to push up. He opened it, pulling out two different machines. Underneath the machines was money, a lot of money.

"You know I could be like a robber or something and you showing me this," I told as he stood up, leaving the floor board open. "I ain't worried about you stealing shit. So you not mad no mo?" He asked and I rolled my eyes.

"Yes I am," I told him, sitting back down in the big black chair. Coming around to where I was, Blaze let out a sigh before running a hand over his face as he leaned against the desk.

"I'm sorry, i'ight? I didn't think you would've got mad with me meeting Mark."

"If you'd have told me then maybe it would've been different, but the fact you made it seem like you were doing it for me when you wasn't is fuck'd up." Damn, I needed to get out my feelings.

Blaze pulled me out his seat, to him. "Yo ass becoming too damn needy and you ain't even tryna date a nigga."

I stood in between his legs. Slowly, his hands moved down to my ass.

"I'm not—"

"Bullshit, but I'ma let it fly. Check this, though, if you gon' be involved with me, then you gon' be dealing with my lifestyle. Meeting people at breakfast, lunch, or dinner is a must at times, but next time I'll say something. What happened today can't happen again, real talk. If you can't handle it then this ain't gon work," he said, staring me in the eyes.

"Then this ain't gon' work."

Every cell in my body wanted that sentence to be true, I just wanted to grab my purse and get as far away from him as possible, but I couldn't. Even though it hadn't been that long, I was too deep into him to just walk away. I wanted to see how things would play out, if the thing between us could work.

"Yo ass ain't going nowhere," he boldly stated.

Was I that predictable to the fact that I wasn't? "Whatever, can you finish here so we can go?" I asked, about to pull away, but his grip tightened on my ass.

"You better lose that attitude. I just fuckin' apologized, what else yo ol' needy ass want?" He asked.

"I'm not needy and yo ass slapped me, that shit hurt." He had slapped the fuck outda me, my damn cheek was numb.

"I ain't apologizing for that shit, yo ass hit like a fuckin' nigga, boss. I almost forgot who the fuck you was. You might as well suck that shit up, so we cool?"

No.

"No."

"Make me slap yo ass," he threatened as he slickly moved his hands to the hem of my dress.

"We cool for now, Blaze. Gone," I said, tryna push his hands away as he lifted my dress.

"Don't be stingy," his head lowered to mine.

A stupid smile came to my lips and I laughed as I shook my head. "I don't like you and I'm not having sex with you in this office. Seriously?" I asked as his hardness poked against my stomach.

"A nigga been locked up for two years, I can't control that beast." He called it right and that beast was not about to have me embarrassing myself again.

"Not my problem. I think I have lotion in my purse. Stop!" I laughed as he muffed my head back. "Now finish this so we can go," I said, biting at his bottom lips before kissing him.

Groaning, Blaze squeezed my ass then pulled back. "Yo ass playing, that shit ain't cool." Blaze stood up and I took a step back as he walked around the desk, grabbing the two machines sitting it in front of me as well as the container. "Run all this through the counterfeit, then the bill—"

"Wait, a counterfeit detector? Really?" I asked, staring at him.

"Really, niggas be shystie and be tryna get over. Have you ever done this before?" He asked a dumb question.

"No, I didn't even know they made counterfeit detectors," I told him truthfully, making him laugh.

"Don't ever tell nobody that. Just sit the money on the tray. Green light means good red light bad."

"How the hell am I suppose too catch it before—"

"Shut up and listen, damn. It'll go through if it's good, if it ain't it'll come back out toward you. Here," he explained before opening a drawer and handing me brown and mustard colored money strips. "It should be at least six, tens and a five whatever else sit it to the side," he said before walking back to the safe.

This is going be a lot. Am I even ready for this?

Chapter 27

Peaches

Sixty-seven thousand, five hundred, forty dollars. *Damn*! Writing the number on a piece of paper, I took out two thousand, five hundred and forty dollas from the last stack I ran through, sat it to the side, then ran what I had in my hands to make five thousand even. I put a brown strip on it. Looking up at Blaze, he was on the phone so I choose to leave him alone as I got up.

"Where you going?" Blaze asked, looking up at me.

"To the bathroom, wanna come?" I asked, only joking.

"Aye, let me call you back." With him saying that, he hung up the phone and got up.

"I was playing about the bathroom thing, you know that, right?" I asked as he came up to me.

"Shut up. Unlock the door when you come back," he said, pressing a key into my hand.

"Oh,right. I wrote the amount down on here," I said, walking back to the desk, grabbing the paper, then handing it to him. "I sat the rest to the side. I really have to use the bathroom," I rushed out, heading for the door.

"Go back the way we came, it's down the first hall on the right," Blaze said.

"What?" I asked him, confused. My brain was not functioning right, I had use it.

"The bathroom, dumbass."

"Oh," I mumbled while opening the door, letting it slam behind me as I twitched my black ass to the bathroom. Once I relieved myself, I left the stall, going to wash my hands just as two girls walked in. The one from earlier and some bright skinned chick.

They just stood by the wall, neither saying anything. "Is there a problem?" They were just standing there, staring, I hoped they ain't have some type of crush on Blaze and came in there to start some shit. I had no problem with getting down with those chicks if need be.

"I saw y'all out front, just wanna make sure you were okay?" I think Blaze called her Tish something.

"I'm cool, thanks for asking." I knew she saw us.

"I'm Tishana by the way, and this Laquanda. So—" The moment so left Tishana mouth, I waved her off.

"If you're coming in here to tell me he's yo man and all that other jazz—" They suddenly started laughing, hell I ain't find shit funny. Why would two females follow me into a bathroom just to see how I was doing? "What's funny?" I done had two people come up to me about messing with their dude or girl, I didn't have time to play no games.

"My brother would kill the both of us if I tried something with Blaze." Tishana said, laughing.

Still, I found nothing funny.

"We'll, if he ain't have that no fuckin' employees rule then it would've been different," Laquanda said sighing. "Plus, I have a man, don't nobody want yours," Laquanda informed me, not seeming bothered by me taking offence.

That made me relax a bit. "He's not my man—"

"Bullshit, I've been working here for six years and not once has Blaze brought a girl here, especially not in his office. Hell, him and my brother been friends since elementary and he hasn't even been in that office," Tishana said.

"I been here for five and I agree, I ain't never seen no one in that man's office either," Laquanda co-signed her agreement.

I'd have been lying if I said hearing that didn't have me feeling a certain giddiness. "Who's your brother?" I asked Tishana.

"Sam—" The bathroom door suddenly opened, cutting her off. Blaze looked from them to me then back.

"What the fuck is y'all in here doing?" Blaze asked like his ass caught us doing something.

"Just introducing ourselves," I told him.

"I can't wait to tell my momma you got a girl," Tishana started smiling.

"Man, get yo ass to work, both of y'all," Blaze snapped at them before pushing Tishana out the door. Stopping at the door, she turned to look at me.

"Wait, I didn't get yo name," Laquanda hit her before pushing Tishana the rest of the way out.

"She just told him we were introducing ourselves and you gon' ask her name in front of him, fah real Tish?" Like she did any better when we just heard everything she just said.

"Don't listen to shit they said, especially Tishana black ass," Blaze said, making me laugh.

"They didn't say nothing, really. Ol' girl saw us out front. Why she ain't call the police is beyond me," I pushed past him and opened the door only to have him close it. "Blaze, gon', I'm not fuckin' you in this bathroom either. So gon', nigga, I'm on strike. Yo ass is not about to be jumping on me every fuckin' hour," I told him, laughing. As good as having sex was with him was, whatever thing we had was not about to be built around that.

I kind of had morals.

"If I wanted to fuck, we'd be fuckin'. I stopped yo dumb, smartass because you left the damn key on the counter," Blaze said, holding the key in front of my face. I couldn't do anything but laugh.

"Maybe so, but yo ass still would've tried if I hadn't said nothing." Snatching the key from him, I walked out, going back to his office. Sitting at his desk, I turned around to face him. "Am I really the first person you ever brought back here?" I asked.

Glancing at me, he grabbed the money in front of me. "You sure this number right?" He asked instead holding up the paper I wrote the amount on.

Nodding my head, I picked up the two-thousand five hundred and forty dollars then, opened the same drawer he had earlier. I grabbed a violet and red strap and put it around the right amount.

"Blaze, do you trust me?" I asked instead, seeing as he didn't answer my first question.

"No," he said simply, making me roll my eyes.

"Now who's pretending?" I mumbled, but loud enough so he could hear me.

"Don't believe shit Tishana lying ass said. She has a habit of putting her nose where it don't belong, I'ma fire her ass," he said and I laughed.

"She didn't say anything—"

"Yeah, you are," he finally answered, cutting me off.

"So, you trust me?"

"No—"

"Bullshit," I hit the desk, making him glare at me.

"I don't, so stop tryna make it seem like it's more than what it is?" He wiped off the two machines then putting them into the safe.

"What is it then?"

"Peaches, I'ma slap the fuck outda you. Shut up, damn. You making me lose my concentration," he snapped.

Holding my hands up, I sat back in my seat trying not to laugh.

Taking three of the six tens I wrapped, he put it in the safety deposit box. Then he put the rest into the floor safe. You could never tell there was a safe in the floor because the tile fit and matched the floor board perfectly. After fixing the rug, he pushed the file cabinet back.

"Wait you forgot this—"

"You got a bank account, right?" Blaze suddenly asked as he grabbed the container, putting it back in the bag. Then he picked up safety deposit box.

"I would think so," I stated slowly, "seeing as I work."

"Hold this for me," he said and threw me the two thousand, five hundred. I laughed.

"Dude, I will spend yo damn money. Giving me money is like giving a geeka a free hit. So no, because I ain't paying shit back," I told him truthfully. "Ask King, he don't let me hold money no more." King gave me money to hold twice and never again. It always started off with a couple of dollars then after that I don't know how I spent the rest. Blaze looked as if he didn't believe me. "You ain't gon' be no different, especially since we're fuckin' now—"

Blaze burst out laughing. "Yo ass crazy, man. Just hold it. Come on, I have two more stops, then we can really get something to eat." He nodded toward the door.

Throwing him his key, I grabbed his money. Tossed it in my purse then followed him out the room. I went ahead as he locked the door, going straight to Tishana, who stood talking to Laquanda. I walked over and tapped her.

"What's up?" She asked.

"You sure I'm the only person ever been back there?" I asked her and she nodded.

"Yep, six years I've been here and never seen him take anyone to his office. Sam and Blaze been friends for years, he ain't never been back there," she told me.

"Okay, that's all I wanted." I was about to walk away, but she stopped me by grabbing my arm.

"I know he's rough, but don't hurt him, I mean, if he brought you here he must really like you. So be patient with him, he'll... We'll he probably won't get better, but he likes you. I've never seen him fight with a girl only to turn around and chase after her. So yeah, go in there and tell them I sent you," she suddenly said.

What? How she go from talking about Blaze to... shid, I didn't even know.

"Tishana, I'ma fire yo black ass," Blaze'svoice boomed, making me jump.

Oh she was playing it off.

"Yeah right, you love me too much," Tishana told Blaze before turning to me. "It was nice meeting you..."

"Peaches," I finished for her and she looked at Blaze then back to me.

"You Peaches?" She asked, seeming in disbelief.

"Yeah, I just said that," I said slowly, looking at Blaze and he shrugged.

"Oh, my God! Girl my momma and his had a two hour conversation about yo ass. Wait, you are the one that beat him up right?" She asked. How was I suppose too answer that. "Yep, it was you—"

"Tishana, shut yo ass up, damn! We got costumers," Blaze said and I bit into my lip so I wouldn't laugh. There were no costumers in the building at all. Grabbing my hand, Blaze began to drag me out the building. "The fuck you talking to her fah?" He snapped.

"Stop, pulling me. I was asking about her shoes, now stop…" My words trailed off as he opened my door and I just stared at him, unsure if he realized what he just did. It would take beating some dude's ass for them to start opening my damn door.

"What?" He questioned.

Shaking my head, I said nothing, just climbed in the truck. "Thanks."

He walked around to his side then got in, starting the truck. Blaze opened the glove compartment then handed me my gun.

"My baby, she bet not have no bodies on her," I told him and he slapped my thigh hard. "Bitch, stop! That shit hurt," I snapped, punching him. "What the fuck wrong with you?"

"Man, stop hitting me."

"Look at my leg?" Hitting him again, I pointed to his hand print that was forming on my thigh. "I do not like you," I said as Blaze's phone started ringing.

Pulling the phone from his pocket, he looked at the screen then at me before he cussed. Of course I, being me and thinking it was a chick, quickly snatched it.

"Hello?" I answered, looking at Blaze.

"Who is this?" I didn't expect an older woman to be on the line. I looked at the screen and my eyes went wide.

"Here," whispering lowly, I tried to give him back the phone. "Blaze, it's your mom."

He looked at me like I was stupid. "Get on the damn phone with yo nosy ass." I was about to hang up the phone. "Yo ass bet not."

"Shut up," I whispered to him. "Hello?" I repeated.

"Who the hell is this playing on the damn phone?" She snapped and I put her on speaker.

'This Blaze's friend, I'm sorry it must be a bad connection or something—'

"Yah lying, I heard you whispering, 'it's your mom'. Now who is his friend?' I looked at Blaze and he started laughing, making me glare at him.

"Hey, ma. What's up?" I let out a relieved breath once Blaze started talking.

"Hey, Boon. Who was that answering the phone?' She asked him.

Boon?

"Peaches scary ass. But what's up?" He asked her again.

"Peaches, the girl that got yo feelings in a twist?"

"Aye! Yo, you on speaker, damn!" He yelled at her and I had to cover my mouth so I wouldn't laugh.

"Sorry, Booney. You should've said something, and don't be yelling at me. Hey Peaches." Blaze groaned, looking at me.

"Hello," I spoke as Blaze started mouthing for me to hang up on her.

"How you doing, sweetie?" She questioned as I shook my head no at Blaze.

"I'm fine, and you?"

"Good. So you're the one marking up my Booney?"

"No, ma'am," I replied back with wide eyes.

He really told his mother on me.

"Bullshit! He came here all busted up in the face. See my Booney likes yo little ass—'

"Peaches, hang up on her, damn," Blaze mumbled. I was not about to hang up on his momma.

"He don't wanna hurt you, but I ain't gon' have you scratching up my baby's face and shit—" She fussed at me.

Oh, hell no!

"Hello," I pretended I didn't hear her.

"I'm here-.' I cut her off.

"Hello?" I stretched out the O.

"Yeah, Boon—' She spoke much louder this time.

"I think she hung up. Hello." I told Blaze, still pretending like I couldn't hear her.

"No, Peaches—" His momma began saying, but I started talking again.

"She hung up," I hung up the phone and broke out laughing. "Oh, my God. Boon, Booney? Seriously Blaze? I can't believe I just hung up on your mom, though," I said, laughing hard.

"Shit ain't funny," he stated, laughing with me.

"Booney?" I asked, laughing.

"Don't ask why, she just calls me that," he said, pulling into a nice neighborhood.

"She does know you're thirty, right?" He glanced at me, licking his lips as he shook his head.

"I don't know what her crazy ass thinks." He shrugged while pulling in front of a nice two story brick house. It was a really nice looking family home.

"Please tell me this isn't your mom's place if so I'll stay in the car." I just hung up on the woman, I am not about to go into her house.

"Man, get out." Smiling, I turned in my seat to face him. "What?"

"You not gon' open my door?" I asked, pressing my lips together before running my tongue over them. His eyes following the movement had me leaning into him. "Wanna a kiss?" My lips were already brushing against his as I finished my sentence.

Blaze's hand tangled into my hair as he kissed me, his tongue thrusting into my mouth twisting with mine. He took hold of my waist, then placed me in his lap. All too soon we were interrupted.

The ringing of his phone had me pulling back as I panted. I bit hard into my bottom lip as I gazed at him through my lashes.

"Reach in the condom—"

"Condom?" I laughed.

"Shut yo ass up, you know what I meant. Reach in the glove compartment and get the gloves outda there." Laughing, I did what he asked, getting and handing him the latex gloves. "Here, put these on." I slipped on the gloves, Blaze did the same before opening the door. "Come on." Getting out the truck he grabbed my hand, leading me up the walk way.

I was a little worried as to why he had me putting on gloves, but I didn't say anything. I just followed him. We walked up the five little steps leading to the front door and Blaze stopped, pulling out his keys.

"You live here?" I asked.

"Peaches, meet Jesse."

Chapter 28

Peaches

Jesse was really a house? I groaned out loud. Now that I was actually seeing the house I felt even more stupid. I snapped at and smacked him. I was embarrassed.

"You wanna beat her ass and tell her to stop fuckin' me?" He asked, laughing.

"That's not funny, yo black ass get on my nerves."

"Come on, I ain't gon' be here long. Just a few minutes," he said, unlocking the door and letting me in. We walked into the house, straight into the living room. It was nice, definitely didn't look like how I imagined a drug spot to be. I would actually live there. Nice hardwood floors, brown, leather sectional to match. And a huge, flat screen TV mounted on the wall.

"I like this. Ooh, those lamps would go good in my living room. Remind me to take those when we leave," I whispered as if I was talking to one of my girls. Looking at Blaze, I laughed. "I mean, can I have those? They would look so good in my living room."

"Your living room is purple."

"And gold. Well, it will be once I have these lamps." My living room was cream and lavender, but it didn't matter, those lamps were cute as hell. The lamps were of two naked bodies intertwined, they were simply beautiful. "I could spray paint these cream or purple. Ooh, one of each!"

"Yo ass is not taking them lamps, so stop making plans. Now come on," he insisted.

I'm getting those lamps.

Pursing my lips together, Blaze pushed me toward the back, not paying my look any attention.

"Stop pushing me, Booney. Ouch! *Bitch!*" I snapped as he slapped me on my ass.

"Don't ever call me that, only my moms can. Don't make me beat yo ass."

All I could do was smile at him. I didn't say anything as he pushed open a door.

"Don't say shit, just go," he ordered.

He walked in front of me, but I paid him no mind. My eyes were too busy jumping from the three men at the three different tables. One looked like had separated the different pills and was now filling the capsules with a white powder. At the other table a man was putting pills in baggies, while the last man was weighing.

Why the hell would he bring me here? This man done lost his gotdamn mind.

"Come on," I didn't move at first. I know King's in the same line of work and so was my dad, but they didn't bring my mom and me into it. They kept it separate from us. Now to actually see them doing it was a sight, it made what they do real.

Grabbing my hand, Blaze began to pull me out the room and into another. That room was the same as other with the tables, but it was empty and instead of pills it was marijuana packed on the first table, the last two where empty, wiped cleaned it looked like.

"Why would you bring me here?" I whispered.

Blaze didn't say anything as he removed four floor boards, then grabbed a duffle bag from under the table. He put ten bricks inside, then zipped up the bag before looking at me.

"What you wanted me to leave you in the truck?" He said while throwing the bag over his shoulder, turning back toward the door.

"Blaze, wait. I'm serious. I don't do this, you of all people should know that being friends with King. The fighting, shooting, cutting I can get down with, but this…" I pointed to the bag but before I could even finish what I was saying, he cut me off.

He's rude as hell…

"Let's go." Placing my hand in his, he led me out the room and back into the other one. "Yo," he called to the man packing. Picking up another duffle, he handed it to Blaze. With a nod we were headed toward the front door.

"Blaze, wait."

"Man, we'll talk in the truck. Now come on," he said, making me roll my eyes.

That was not why I was stopping, shid, I wanted them lamps.

I watched him open the front door before going over and unplugging the first lamp, thinking I was gon' be slick with it. But the damn thing had the nerve to be heavy.

Shit.

"What the fuck you doing?" Blaze asked, looking back at me.

"Tryna steal these damn lamps, but they heavy. Can you get them for me?" Shaking his head, Blaze walked out the front door. "Bitch," I mumbled as I pushed my purse up my shoulder then picked up the heavy ass lamp.

"On what, yo ass really taking my shit?" Blaze said, taking the lamp from me.

"It ain't like you need them, you can have the ones at my apartment." I bargained and he laughed.

"Man, come on. And don't nobody want them ugly ass lamps." They weren't ugly, just plain oval shaped.

Giving him the finger, I walked out the house to the truck and got in. Blaze put the lamp in the truck then ran back inside to get the other one. He returned a short while later. I watched him lock the front door then jog back to the truck.

"Thanks for the lamps, my apartment will really enjoy them." I turned in my seat to face him while he backed out the driveway. "Look, I get this what you do, but I don't want to see it. Same thing with King, I know what he does, I just don't want to get involved in this life. Like I said, shooting, stabbing, fighting, I'm a go—if it ever comes to that—but this, I can't."

It was true, I didn't want to be a part of it. I liked Blaze and all, hell, I loved King to death, but even that wasn't enough to get me involved, to even want to be around it.

"Don't worry about this, it'll be the first and maybe last time you'll ever come here. I'm just showing you what you're getting yourself into fuckin' with me. Every day this is what I'm doing. I'm either here, Anastasia's, the lot, any one of the pool hall's, or making sells like you saw earlier. Now if you gon' fuck with me, this the shit you gon' have to deal with."

"So you do trust me?" Stopping at a light, Blaze looked at me.

"No."

"So why go through the trouble of showing me this, not knowing for sure whether or not I'm all the way in?" I asked.

"Why the hell you always got to make sense of some shit? Damn. Whether I do or I don't, I'm trusting yo ass with this and giving you a chance to decide on what you really wanna do."

Now he thinks of this!

"Why couldn't you have showed me this before I decided to have sex with you?" I asked seriously.

Blaze laughed, looking at me. "Yo ass, man, damn. So you in, Peaches? On everything, don't fuck me over. I'ight?"

Why him? That was all I could think as I answered. "I won't as long as you don't do the same to me. I'm in."

"I'ight. I got to drop this off then we can get something to eat."

"I want Red Lobster!" I told 'em, all ready tasting the snow crab legs dipped in butter.

***

"I'ight, Tameka, we out. Man, watch yo eyes, damn," Blaze said to the red head I was two seconds away from jumping on.

"Bitch, better. Fuck she mugging for?" I ain't had no problems with no chicks about Blaze ass, but as soon as I walked into his auto body shop this bitch started glaring hard.

"Peaches, shut up. Ain't nobody tryna deal with that shit." Blaze pulled me to him.

"Whatever. Are you almost done here?" I asked, rolling my eyes.

"I guess you were, I can do better. But damn, Blaze, I didn't know you like hoes, ratchet ass hoes at that," she insulted, staring at me distastefully.

No this bitch didn't just call me a hoe.

"Bitch, I'll show yo ass a hoe, come from behind that desk. Fuck you gon' talk shit behind glass? Bitch come out," I snapped as I pushed away from Blaze. "Come on bitch—"

"Peaches, go get yo ass in the truck. Tameka, shut the fuck up and watch who you talking to. Bitch, yo ass can easily be replaced, fuck wrong with you?" Blaze snapped at her.

"Whatever, Blaze. Get her ass outda here, then," she told him.

"Bitch, you come put me out. Come on, sweetheart."

"Peaches, I said shut the fuck up and get in the damn truck." That Tameka bitch was mugging mad hard.

"Fuck with me, come put me out bitch!" I snapped as Blaze pushed me toward the exit. "Stop pushing me—"

"Calm down, damn. Yo ass always tryna fight," Blaze said as he pushed me to the truck.

No he didn't just say that.

"Me?" I pointed to myself. "Yo ass should be the last one to call me out on my shit. Plus, I didn't start nothing, that's yo ass and these bitches." Getting in the truck I slammed the door.

"Don't be slamming my fuckin' door," Blaze snapped as he got in, slamming the door.

"Don't be slamming my fuckin' door!" I muffed his head to the side.

"Make me slap yo ass." He pulled off.

I rolled my eyes and sat back in my seat. Don't get me wrong, I wasn't scared of Blaze, I'd get down with his ass in a minute. But the mothafuckin' slap hurts something nasty. Hell, I still felt those hits from earlier. "Whatever you got going on with that chick, you might as well go back in there and tell her it's done. Blaze, I'm not to be played."

"Ain't shit going on with me and that bitch. I hit her ass a couple times, that's it. She know ain't shit happening." My lips twisted as I stared at him. "On G, I ain't fuckin' with her on no serious type shit." He came to a stop light. "Gimme kiss." He leaned over the seat toward me. I didn't move, just stared at him blankly. "I'm not fuckin' that damn girl no mo. Now give me a kiss." A horn blew behind us.

I glanced at the light to see it had turned green. "The light's green, go." He threw the car in park. "Blaze, go. The light turned."

"So you ain't gon' kiss me? Shid, if you want me to drive you will."

I stared at him for a long minute. My eyes soon rolled up as my façade started to break. Glancing back at him, I started laughing. "You get on my nerves." Leaning over the seat, I kissed him. "Now go." Blaze pulled off just as the light turned red. "You wrong, those people 'bout pissed off."

"That's yo fault." Glancing at me, he turned the radio off.

"Look, B, I'm trusting and believing you're not fuckin' with that chick. But if I find out otherwise, then I'm done. Blaze, I'm trusting yo word on this, so don't make me regret it."

"You not, because I ain't fuckin' her no mo." His gaze fell on me and he rubbed his chin. "While we on this shit, that little sneaky thing you was doing with Sam, dead it. His ass know what's up, now I'm letting you know. It's dead. Whatever like you might've caught for him, get rid of that shit."

"It wasn't a like with feelings, it was just head no nothing, attachment whatsoever. The moment we decided to do this it was done. So you don't have to worry about Sam and I doing anything." Blaze hummed, staring hard at me. "It was never nothing, I promise. And it was only once—"

"Shut the fuck up, I don't wanna hear that bullshit. I know how many times it was and where the shit happened at. Try to be slick though, I'ma fuck both you mothafuckas up. Like I said, Sam know what's up, I'm just letting you know. You saw what I do to mothafuckas who try to be slick." There wasn't a doubt in my mind he wasn't serious.

"Oh, so you gon' shot me in my arms and legs then make me drive myself to the hospital?"

"Damn, right I am," he spoke drily.

Nodding my head, I turned in my seat to look at him.

"You don't have to worry about it, I promise. Oh shit! Blaze, give me my phone, Kimmy ass probably going crazy right about now."

"She was, I talked to King when he called looking for you, they know where you at. Red Lobster, right?" He asked, pulling into the plaza.

"Yes, I am starving. When we leave here we're going home, right?" My black ass was tired and hungry.

"We gon' stop by mine, then I got to meet King at Magic, then to yo place." Blaze meeting up with King with us together? I was going to insist he dropped me off first.

I know my brother said he was going to step off, but he was sometimes flaky as hell when it came to me.

"What's that face about?"

"No reason." The thought of King had me staring at Blaze. "Blaze, if we're seriously doing this, I'm not to be played, whether we're officially together right now or not. I'm not going to be treated like some hoe. Just like you said, I'm trusting you not to hurt me. But if you do, I don't give second chances. Same goes for me, I won't play you. If it ever comes to the point that we feel like messing around with other people, then this wasn't for us to begin with. Be honest with me and I'll do the same," I told him, because in the end I didn't want to get hurt. And truth be told, if anyone could hurt me, it would be Blaze hands down.

"I already told you I got you. If that was the plan, I wouldn't be doing all this shit. I ain't even on that. Now let's go," he said, opening his door.

"You gon' open my door for me, daddy?" I licked my lips seductively.

"When I have that ass bent over in the backseat, don't say shit." With that, he got out the truck, coming to my side. "Come on."

I turned in my seat. Wrapped my arms around his neck.

"I don't know, daddy, that backseat thing sounding like a plan to me." I took his bottom lip into my mouth and began sucking on it before going to his top.

Blaze yanked me to the edge of the seat. He stepped between my legs. His hands slid up my dress, lifting me, he pushed my dress over my hips.

A tap on the open door had me opening my eyes to see a man standing there and I pulled away.

"You gon' quit playing with me." The man tapped on the window again. "Get the fuck away from my damn door, nigga. I hear yo ass," Blaze snapped at him.

"Blaze, chill. It ain't that serious, for real. Come on, lets go." I done seen enough of him beating some random dude ass for the day.

"I was just tryna get in my car," the man explained.

"It's cool, it was my fault. No problem." I gave him a friendly smile and closed the door. My hands slid into Blaze's large one and I led him to the entrance.

A fifteen minute wait was all it took before we were shown to our table.

Sitting down, I looked at Blaze and shook my head as I let out a soft laugh. "Somebody gon' beat yo ass one day. How you gon' get mad and snap at that man because he was tryna get in his car?"

"I ain't worried about nobody beating my ass, bet that. Yo ass bet not let nobody beat my ass with as much shit as you carry on you. I bet not ever get my ass whooped when you around," he joked.

Laughing, I rolled my eyes. "Oh, I see. Yo ass ain't tough, Booney!" I said the B in his name hard as I pursed my lips together, adding a slight pout to them.

"I'ma fuck you up, keep playing with me, Peaches."

"I like that name though. What you getting mad for, Boon—" He got out his seat. "Okay, I stop, damn. Sit down." My hands fanned toward him, motioning for him to sit. "What are you getting?" I asked, grabbing my menu, already knowing what I wanted. "I'm getting the snow crab legs, corn and red potatoes with a Mai Tai." I told Blaze.

"The Lobster tail," he was saying as the waiter came.

Chapter 29

Peaches

We were leaving Red Lobster, the food was good and our conversation was never ending. Overall, we had an amazing dinner. Even so, truth be told, I was beyond tired. Not even that damn Mai Tai could liven me up. How the hell Blaze was still going was beyond me.

"Magic's closer, so we'll stop there first. You cool? Look like you about to pass out," Blaze said, while pulling out the parking lot.

Lazily, my gaze fell on him. Comfortable in my seat, I crossed my legs, sliding down a bit more. "I'm good. They asses did not put enough Rum in that Mai Tai." My eyes were watery and I kept blinking to try and stay awake. That shit wasn't helping.

"We here, come on." He turned off the car then got out.

Damn that was fast!

Sighing, I did the same. I met Blaze in front of the truck. I came to his front, wrapped my arms around his waist, slipped my hands into the pocket of his jeans.

"What I tell you about touching my ass?"

"You said I can if I wanted to. Mmm, you have a nice ass," I finished with a nip at his chin.

Blaze moved my hands from his pockets. "I'ma knock you out, keep playing." He turned me around and pulled me into his chest so my back was to his front. "Yo ass short as hell, a nigga can't attempt to fuck you like this without having to pick you up."

"Oh, my God. Why would you say that?" I laughed, elbowing him.

"It ain't like I'm lying, my dick in middle of yo back."

"Move! Let me go." Laughing, I tried to get out his hold. "That shit ain't funny, I'm average height for a woman," I stated defensively.

"No five-eight is average."

"You a bitch, get off me. Blaze, stop!" A scream left my mouth. He suddenly picked me up. "Put me down I have on a dress—"

"Ain't nobody looking at yo short ass," he said, walking into the pool hall.

"Blaze, put me down!" Blaze placed me on my feet, then took hold of my hand. "Don't play like you ain't like that shit." *Was I gon admit that I did? Hell No.* Not after he insulted me about my height. "Don't try and act mad now," he said, leading me toward the back of the club.

"I could've waited at the bar," I told him.

"N'all, you good. I can't have you sitting at the bar alone. I'll fuck around and have to beat a mothafucka ass in here. Niggas crazy nowadays."

My head nodded in agreement.

"I know! Shid, I been with one all day, dude is stupid crazy." My voice rose dramatically.

"Make me slap yo ass." He stopped at a door, twisted the knob, but it was locked. His fist hit it loud and hard, doing a double knock three times. "Come on." We walked down the hall, to the last room. Blaze took out a pair of keys and unlocked the door to an office. A nice, big office, kind of like the one at the car lot.

"Let me guess, this your place to?" I asked, walking to the big mahogany desk while Blaze locked the door.

"Yeah, I have this one and two more," admitted Blaze.

Now I was confused.

"Can I ask you a question?" Sitting in the big black chair behind the desk, I went to open a drawer, then another and another ,but they all were locked.

"You can ask whatever you want," he said as there was a knock on his door. "Hold up." Walking to the door, he opened it and I groaned as King walked in.

"Fuck you doing back here?" He asked, not even seeing Blaze by the door. His eyes fell straight on me. "Where the fuck yo phone at?"

"Um, I'm with Blaze and he got my phone."

"And he let you back here?" King asked the dumb question.

"No shit, dumbass. How else would I have got into a locked room? And he's right there." I Pointed to Blaze who was right beside him. King looked over then jumped.

"Oh, shit! I ain't even see yo ass right there, fuck she doing back here?" He asked him.

"She with me." An older man, maybe in his early forties came to the door. "Jonas, what's up?" Blaze shook up with him. Looking down, he handed him two green bags. "Damn, both these?" Blaze asked him.

"Yeah, for two weeks. Shit leaving." Jonas' eyes finally landed on me and he glanced at Blaze.

"If another mothafucka do that I'ma beat the shit out of him, damn. She cool, talk." The man looked at King who shrugged before his eyes slid to me. "You looking too damn hard nigga, I'm over here. Talk."

I groaned as he snapped at the man, making him look at me. My hands went up before finding a paper clip, tryna break into his drawers. That didn't mean I succeeded.

"Damn, y'all niggas been pushing hard up in here. But check this, I'ma close this down for a minute. The bar and shit will still be opened, but no serving in here for a while. I'll let you know when you back up, until then the back's closed. What you got now, sell. Give 'em a little extra until its gone. Come tomorrow, it's done," he told Jonas.

"It's almost gone anyway, so that'll be good." With a nod, Jonas turned and walked, out closing the door behind him.

"Why you closing this spot?" King asked Blaze.

"Because Red—"

"Red Envy out in Marshall Town? That's yours?" Blaze stopped talking as I spoke excitedly."

"Yeah—"

"No shit? Wow, it really wasn't meant to be then. I swear me and my bitches used to sneak in there when we were like fifteen. Angel use to talk to the bouncer there. I think his name Ri—"

"Rico?" Blaze finished for me and I snapped my fingers. "Yep, that was him. We use to be in there lit. That's how Sly and I started messing around. Every other weekend when my daddy wasn't home and I was able to climb out my window. Our asses would be on the city bus going to Red Envy, drinking and playing pool. That was my spot." I boasted about the bar and a smile was plastered on my face as I thought back to the old days. Playing pool, drinking and dancing on top of the pool tables. "Yeah, we use to have fun." A laugh left my mouth before a sigh soon followed.

"No shit? Y'all hot mothafuckas. I'm 'bout to beat yo yellow ass fah that time. That's why I told you to stay away from them hot ass girls. Fifteen, Peaches?" King started snapping, making Blaze laugh.

"Yo, chill the fuck out. That was what? Nine years ago? Fifteen though, and you was at Red? Damn. And we ain't ran into each other not once. Fate, right?" Looking away from a mugging King to a wondering Blaze, I started laughing.

"Yeah, fate, with your silly ass." Shaking my head, I looked to King smiling. "Sneaking out wasn't bad, King. We didn't get into trouble, we didn't get hooked on drugs, and we finished high school without getting pregnant—me especially. No vaginal sex, drugs, or anything else. So chill, take a breather. Standing over there looking like D'mitri and the hulk." That made King laugh.

"Yo yellow ass gon' get whooped. Ebony ass too." My lips pursed at that, thinking about how Ebony was back then.

"Okay, King. Whatever you say." With that, I started back on trying to open the damn drawer with the pin.

"I'ma fuck her ass up. Now why you closing?" Biting into my bottom lip, I shook my head at King. He just couldn't let me grow up.

"Red 'bout to open back up. You know I can't have all three running at the same time, stupid shit start to happen. I done already closed The Shack yesterday," Blaze finished with a shrug before nodding his head. "You got that for me?" He finished and King reached in his back pocket, pulling out a manila envelope.

"That's the only thing that was in the box, here." Handing Blaze a key, he put the bags and envelope on the desk.

"I'ight, good looking. We'll be out in a few," he motioned toward the door and King looked at him then me.

"Nigga, you putting me out?" King asked him.

I wanted to laugh, but I didn't. I just looked around the room.

"Yep, nothing personal. You know that my nig—"

"This shit serious?" King motioned between us.

Both Blaze and I looked at him.

"Is what serious?" Ignoring me, King and Blaze shared a look.

"Hell n'all, B. Peaches I should beat yo ass." King said, looking at me.

"What I do?" I did not wanna fight with King, especially over something I didn't do. *Well, I don't know if I done it or not.*

"Man, get the fuck out here. It ain't even like that, and if it was, so what?" Blaze told him.

"Nigga, it is. You got her back here, that's serious whether you wanna believe it or not." *Oh, now I get it!* That stupid giddy feeling started to form in my stomach once again and I couldn't stop the—

"Fuck you smiling fah?" Blaze asked, cutting off my thoughts, making me laugh.

"Boy, don't start with me. I didn't say nothing." Laughing at his stare, "Whatever. Blaze,lLet me see yo keys." I

A Dangerous Love 2
Can't Let Go

didn't think he thought about what he was doing before he threw me his keys.

"Hell n'all." King just started laughing. "I can't believe this shit. Blaze, damn. I'm out man." He shook up with Blaze before coming to me, kissing my cheek. "Peaches, yo ass no what you doing, right? This ain't what I want for you, but I'ma I fall back and leave you be. Don't play no games, Peach," he said, not whispering at all. "Blaze, that's my sister. Don't fuck it up my nigga. This blood shit gets real when it comes to her."

"I got you. Nah, get the fuck out."

Shaking his head, he walked toward the door. "Just keep my sister away from yo crazy ass momma."

Blaze started laughing at that. "I told Peaches to watch her back, moms know who she is too. And Peaches hung up on her," Blaze stressed.

"You told me to!" I defended myself.

"I'm gone, Ebony calling. Peaches, stay away from his momma," he stated while taking out his ringing phone. "I'm on my way, damn," he answered saying that, then hung up. "She gon' make me beat her ass man, boss," King said, making me roll my eyes.

"I'm telling her that too." Giving me the finger, King walked out the office, closing the door. Blaze locked it behind him.

"You ready to work?" Blaze asked and I groaned, making him laugh.

"No. What you want me to do, Blaze?" I watched as he picked up one of the green bags sitting it in front of me, then took his keys, opened the bottom drawer and took out a bill counter as well as a counterfeit detector.

Staring at him, I rolled my eyes. *Not long my ass.* Grabbing the bag, I went to open it, but it was locked.

"Do this bag in fives and whatever's left sit it to the side. I'll start on the other," he said, sitting a stack of brown currency straps next to me.

J Peach

But he don't trust me, though. Blaze should slap his damn self.

"How does this work? I mean, with them selling and you, I don't get it," I asked him in disbelief as I held the last stack in my hand. This was just two much money made in a two week time.

"I don't understand yo question."

I glared at him, but then again, maybe I wasn't making sense. I just didn't get how you could make two hundred twenty thousand in a two week time period. "I mean, I know this little ass bar ain't pulling in that many costumers to make this much in two weeks." Looking at him, I pointed to the money.

"The less you know, the better," he said, putting a strap on his last stack.

"No seriously, how the hell do this little ass bar make this much money?"

Blaze laughed and shook his head. "Damn, you nosy as hell, man."

"So—"

"I don't push little shit, I only sell pounds, kilos, or eight balls. In my pool halls I only sell eight balls. If yo shit good you can sell it for two, which is what I do. So two hundred, plus five hundred fifty people a week, times that and what do you get?" he asked.

"Give me yo phone." Blaze burst out laughing. Hell yeah I was about to times that shit. If Blaze could make that much in two weeks, shid, I was in the wrong mothafuckin' business. "How you know how many people coming in?"

"I keep a list of everybody I sell to. What you have on the side?" That was smart.

"It's two hundred twenty thousand even," I told him and he handed me the bag that I'd just notice had the word Magic on it. "The bag you had is it from here too?" I asked because what I counted only include the one bag.

"N'all, it's from The Shack. I had Sam drop it off earlier," he told me.

"So, how much was in your bag?" Yes, I was nosy. I damn sho' wasn't gon' feel bad about spending the money he told me to hold earlier. I wondered if King made that much. If his ass did, why the hell was he always tripping over fifteen dollars? *Cheap ass nigga, I swear.* Looking at Blaze, he was giving me a weird look. "What?"

"Yo ass ain't heard shit I said, did you?" He was talking. "No, sorry. What you say?" I asked him.

"I said, yo ass nosy as fuck. Take thirty out that stack and put it in here," he said "Then lock it, it's the blue key."

When I was done, I sat it to the side as I watched Blaze move a big picture of a white tiger from the wall. His hands pressed into the wall then moved up. He moved the paneling wood from the wall, revealing a safe. Coming back to table, he started putting the money into the safe.

"What are you going to do with the money in the box?"

"Nosy," he said, making me roll my eyes.

"Can I have that picture?" Blaze started laughing as he closed the safe and put everything back in place. "So, is that a no?"

"Yes, that's exactly what that is."

"What are you going to do with the money on the side?" I picked up the two thousand he had sitting out.

"Nothing yet. I have to drop that box off to my moms—"

"I hope not tonight," I cut him off. I was not ready to meet his momma, especially not after I hung up on her. "Blaze?"

"We not going in, so chill. I'm just going to her garage, then running right back out." His ass ain't know the meaning of not long, so what the hell he did he know about right back out?

"So, this is the life of Blaze Carter, huh?" I thought out loud, which brought back the question I wanted to ask him earlier. "If you have all of these businesses, why do this extra?" If I had everything going on like him, I wouldn't do the drug thing.

"It's what I enjoy doing, everything else is just a cover." He shrugged, like actually shrugged.

"That's the dumbest thing I've ever heard in my life, Blaze, seriously. Your covers are making crazy money, so I don't get it."

"There's nothing to get, I like doing what I'm doing, I'm good at it. Seventeen years I've been doing this, I've adapted to it, ain't no stopping. It's an automatic reflex you can say. I like doing it and the money ain't bad either." He shrugged again.

I let it go. That wass what he wanted to do. It was him, I didn't have a say.

"If money ain't bad, let me have that picture. It would look so good in my guest room."

"Get yo ass outda here. You can't come with me no mo if you gon keep tryna take my shit."

"So, does that mean I can have it?" Cutely I asked, batting my lashes.

"Hell n'all, I got that up there for a reason."

"Go buy another one, damn. Stingy ass." I stood by the door as Blaze cleaned up.

He wiped everything down then grabbed the green bag with Magic written on it.

"Here, hold this," he handed me the money he'd set to the side.

"I'm telling you now, I'm not gon' remind you I got your money, So put it in your pocket," I held it out to him.

"Man, hold it, damn. Now, come on."

Rolling my eyes, I put the money in my purse as I followed behind him.

***

We finally made it to his place, or his big ass apartment. If he lived there, why the hell was he always at my crappy ass apartment? I would never begin to understand that man.

Taking off my shoes, I sat my purse on his dresser. I started opening all his drawers until I found his shirts.

"Why the hell you going through my shit?" Blaze questioned from across the room.

Nigga had a sitting area in his fuckin' room. His damn room was bigger than my living room.

"If you live here, why do you come to my place?" I asked while pulling out one of his shirts. I went to his King sized bed, sat the shirt down, then took off my clothes before pulling his T-shirt on.

"Why you taking off yo damn clothes fah?" This man better stop playing with me.

"I'm about to go to bed, problem?" I pulled his covers back then climbed into his bed.

"Yo ass rude as hell. How the fuck you just make yoself comfortable in my shit?" *He had his nerves.*

"Nigga, no you didn't just say that when you practically just moved in my apartment days after knowing me *and* you got a key made. Blaze, you don't wanna go there with me, baby, fo'real." Getting even more comfortable, I looked at him. "Where's your remote at?" I stared at him, awaiting his reply.

"Man, yo ass," running a hand over his face, he reached under his pillow then handed me the remote. "If you sleeping here you might as well take off that shirt."

It was my turn to laugh. "Why, so you can play with my tittie?" Finishing with a yawn, I watched as he sat his gun on the nightstand then took off his jeans and shirt.

"I'ma slap the fuck outda you, keep talking." He got in bed, moved closer to me. His hands gripped the shirt and pulled it off.

My neck stretched as he hovered over me. I gave him a simple, sweet peck.

"Go to sleep." Blaze turned off the TV as a small laugh slipped through my lips. He pulled my back to his chest and his hand quickly found my right tittie. "Boss, don't say shit." That had me laughing out before yawning.

If he only knew how much I enjoyed him doing that.

My body relaxed more with every caress to my breast. My eyes soon closed as my breathing evened out. It wasn't long after that darkness pulled me under completely.

Chapter 30

Peaches

Two Months Later...

"Bitch, you still didn't answer my question. Are y'all official or..." Kimmy trailed off, making me roll my eyes. Even doing that, I couldn't help but smile, which I seemed to be doing a lot since being with Blaze.

"We are, but we not. I don't know, Kim, I want to take that next step, but who's to say once he has me officially he won't change? I'll probably be just another bitch who fell, I don't want that." I shrugged as I stirred my Chinese rice.

Blaze and I been riding hard the past couple of months, everything had been simply amazing. For him not to be a romantic, he was nice in his own twisted way. It was actually kind of sweet. Ever since I spent the day with him, seeing his lifestyle was an eye opener in both a good and bad way.

Good in that I was the first woman he'd let into that part of his life. Even though he still didn't trust me, *as he said*, that didn't stop him from taking me to his lot or either of his pool halls to count his money.

Bad in that I knew what living that life could lead to and we weren't officially together so I couldn't bitch at him about it. Even if we were, I still wouldn't because he was smart about his shit.

Since that day we'd been practically inseparable during our free time. I was always at his apartment or he was at mine. Then there were times when we didn't see each other and he'd be out at all times of the morning. I got that he packed his money, made drops, and checked to make sure his was stuff right at that time, which took hours. That only left him with maybe an hour or two to sleep. By that time, I was up and getting ready for work or school.

"Peach, whether you fail to realize it or not, he already has you. The moment you opened up for him you established that much," Kimmy said.

"No, I did not. Sex is sex, nothing more or less," I said and she reached across the table and slapped the back of my head. "Bitch—"

"I'm trying to knock some sense into yo dumbass. Sex is sex to everyone but you. You done saved yoself for twenty-four years and after not even a whole month of knowing this nigga, you let him have it. Think about it, Peaches, as much head as you've gotten, and let's not forget about the shit you and Sly been doing for what seven, eight years, you never gave it to him. That's seven or eight years, bitch, that's a whole fuckin' relationship. But Blaze walks his sexy, caramel ass in the picture and the nigga done busted yo ass wide open. Denial won't get you anywhere," Kim finished saying while pointing her fork in my face.

"I'm not in denial. I like Blaze a lot, more than I should, but I just don't want to get played in the end."

"He's letting you in, he's showing you shit that he hasn't showed anyone else from what you tell me. I think he really likes you." She had a point, but my issue was that I didn't want to become my mom, or Ebony for that matter. I'd seen what they went through, what Ebony was still going through, with men that were in the same game as Blaze. I just wanted to be safe.

"Okay, King is the same way. He don't show me shit he does, but Ebony's ass know everything. Even so, King ass still fuck anything that walks." Ebony is King's main, but he still fuck'd bitches on the side. I honestly didn't know if Blaze was like that or not, but I wanted to be one hundred percent sure. "Anyways, enough about me. What's up with you and Mike?" She rolled her eyes at the mention of Mike's name.

"Ain't shit happening with him. He's a fuckin' child, don't nobody have time for that. I'm done trying with his ass." I didn't know what was up with my friends and those fuckin' hoods, not excluding me. Shit was just crazy.

"He's dumb, just like the rest of these niggas. You know we can always become lesbians and date each other," I told her. Kim laughed while shaking her head. "Bitch, I'm serious. I mean, I'll still be fuckin' Blaze, but besides him, I'll be faithful." I spoke truthfully. "Bitch, yo ass stupid," she laughed out. I was so serious. There was no way in hell I'd stop sleeping with him. "Bitch, you saying that because you haven't slept with him. A bitch be seeing stars when we done, girl, and that's not even including his head game. Oh, my God, bitch. I just had an orgasm just thinking about that shit. Talk about a wicked tongue, bitch, to sit on his face and ride—"

"Oh, my God, Peaches. Ugh!" She laughed. "Let the damn table go before you break it. Bitch, yo knuckles just turned white. Our relationship would be over before it even started, you damn freak. Yo ass is nasty, Peach, you be riding his face?"

Rolling my eyes, I laughed while nodding my head. "Yes, never had anything better," I stated, watching the corner of Kim's lips twist upwards. "Bitch, fuck you. I can't stand yo ass. Don't act like you don't be having all that ass on Mike's face while he tonguing that pussy."

Kim eyes went wide. "What? I didn't say anything, just thought that maybe I could have a go."

The look I gave her had Kim laughing loud and hard.

"I'ma cut yo ass, don't play with me." Shaking my head, I laughed with her. "I don't share, and even if I did, it wouldn't be Blaze's ass. That's mine alone."

"Bitches!" Missy's loud voice came from behind before she appeared at my right and sat down. Looking at me, she smiled. "Hey, boo." She winked at me.

"Yo ass crazy, it took you long enough to get here," I told her and she let out a dramatic sigh.

"Girl, arguing with Mya's triflin ass, dumb bitch. Ugh, I swear I just want to cut her ass sometimes. I hate yo sister," she told Kim who rolled her eyes.

"Bitch, right. Yo ass didn't hate her, last night bitches kept me up all fuckin' night." My brows went up at that and I looked at Missy who looked just as confused.

"Kimmy, Missy stayed at mines last night, unless she left when Blaze came home," I informed her.

Missy nodded her head and Kimmy's body went still, her mouth slightly parted.

"You lying?" Kim said dumbly, she really thought Missy was over there.

That was why I was scared to get serious with Blaze. Who's to say he wasn't like everyone else?

"I didn't know, Missy, I swear I thought it was you." Out of our small group of friends I was the only one who really knew how much Missy really cared for Mya. To be honest, it pissed me off for the simple fact that Mya cared for Missy, because if she didn't she wouldn't have stepped to me like she did.

"It's cool, we know how Mya's ass is. Plus, it ain't like we dating." She shrugged, I wanted to beat Mya's ass. *Triflin' hoe.*

"Don't sweat it, boo, you still have me." With a wink, I blew her a kiss. Missy shook her head before laughing and I couldn't help but crack a smile, but it was quickly wiped away as Kimmy suddenly slapped me. "Bitch, what the fuck wrong with you?" She smacked the shit out of me and I was two seconds from jumping on her ass. That shit hurt, had my damn cheek stinging.

"Bitch, me! After sitting here telling me we could be together, you winking and kissing at her?" She screamed at me.

That bitch was crazy, those Chinese folks were about to put us the fuck out because of Kim. She had actually stood from her seat and was yelling, drawing attention our way.

"After I told you I was pregnant with your baby!" Her voice rose higher.

I swear my mouth dropped, as did Missy's. Now I know she was playing at this point, but for Kimmy to do something like that was *unreal*. Kim hated being embarrassed, it was always Ebony and Angel who pulled stupid shit like that. Never Kimmy.

"How long have you been fucking her? Huh, Peaches? Was she good? Huh?" Kim's finger jabbed in my face.

"Wait, she fucking you, too? I can't believe this shit. But you love me though. Fo'real, Peaches? *And* you got this bitch pregnant." Missy jumped out her seat, knocking the chair back.

Oh, hell no!

Grabbing my shit, I took off toward the door. They could have those people laughing and whispering about their dumbasses, not me. A bitch was gone. I ate at that damn restaurant faithfully, I was not about to have them talking about me every time I walked in that place. Nope, not happening. Before they could blink I was running for the door.

"Peaches!" They were so embarrassing. *Why?*

"Dumb bitches, I hate them," I said out loud as I speed walked to the parking lot.

"Peaches, baby, come here. We can share you. Don't run, Peaches, I love you!" Missy yelled. I hated those hoes. "Peaches, mami, come here, baby. I'm sorry, come back!" Missy kept yelling behind me with a laughing Kimmy.

I was so busy trying to get far away from them that I passed my damn car. Turning back around, I saw Kim sitting on my hood.

"Bitch, where the hell were you going?" She laughed as I made my way back.

"Why would y'all do that knowing I'm always here for lunch? Now every time I come here they gon' be whispering that Chong shit about me. Ugh, I seriously hate y'all, for real. I'ma be late for work messing with y'all ass. Kim, get the fuck off my car before you scratch her." I grabbed her foot and yanked her hard. Kim's head hit the hood of my car. "That's for slapping me bitch and Missy—" Before I could finish my sentence, that bitch had me pressed against the driver's door with her body and her lips against mine.

235

What the fuck is she doing?
"We spoke this bitch up. Missy, here comes Mya. Oh—"
I heard Kimmy say before trailing off. See, that bitch was getting beside herself and fucking kissing me. I didn't mind helping, but she could've given me a warning before she went thrusting her tongue down my damn throat.
The fuck wrong with her? Bitch act like she ain't ever heard of a closed mouth kiss. It seriously felt like I was kissing King. Even so, I played along, but I was smacking her ass the moment Mya's ass was out of sight.
"Hey trick, who's the hoe?" Kimmy asked, but didn't get a reply as Missy was suddenly yanked from me and a fist hit hard into my face.
The punch literally knocked my ass into a state of shock.

Chapter 31

Peaches

"I told yo ass to stay the fuck away from her!" Mya yelled while jerking Missy behind her.

That bitch just punched me in the face. *Oh, hell no!* I jumped for her, but was caught from behind.

"Hell n'all, let me the fuck go! Bitch, you gon' hit me fo'real Mya!" I snapped, trying my best to get free.

"I told yo ass to stay away from her?" Myas' voice boomed as she inched closer to me.

"Bitch, we ain't together. How the fuck you gon' tell somebody to stay away from me, then you with this bitch?" Missy fussed before she flipped out and started whooping Mya's ass. Ol' girl she was with made a grab for Missy, but Kimmy snatched her up by her long weave ponytail and started pounding into her face.

"Let me go! That bitch hit me!" I did not care if Missy was beating Mya's ass, I was about to jump in for the simple fact that she put her hands on me.

"Man, calm yo ass down. You shouldn't have kissed her bitch. I should slap yo ass too fah that shit," came the voice behind.

Immediately I recognized who it was and I stopped moving.

"Blaze, let me go!" Even though I was feeling giddy as hell because he was there, that didn't change the fact that the bitch still hit me. With his hands around my waist, he moved us further away from the fight which had me thrusting around again. "Let me the fuck go, Blaze!" I snapped, but he wasn't paying me any attention as he kept walking.

"Man, calm yo ass down," he fussed.

I was so fucking mad to the point that I literally wanted to cry.

It's cool though, that bitch gon' get caught slipping and I'ma dog that hoe.
"You cool?" Blaze asked as we made it to his truck.
Pushing his hands off me, I turned around and glared as the thought to punch him crossed my mind.
"Fuck you mugging fah? You shouldn't have kissed her bitch."
I did hit him, punching him in the chest.
"She kissed me! Plus Mya's ass was with someone else so she had no right putting her fucking hands on me. Fuck that, Blaze, move!" Ooh, I wanted that bitch. I tried to push Blaze back, but his bulky ass wasn't moving.
My feet left the ground as he picked me up. He opened the back door then tossed me inside. He got in behind me and locked the doors.
"So what? You shouldn't have kissed her ass back, the fuck wrong with you? This ain't the first time I saw you kissing that bitch," Blaze sounded pissed, fussing at me.
Was he jealous?
"Really, Blaze? That's my friend, you dumbass, and she ain't gon' be too many more of your bitches. Plus, friends kiss all the time," I stated in a duh tone, which only made his mug harder. "Fuck you mugging for?"
"I ain't with that shit with yo confused ass. Fuck you kissing that bitch fah?" He asked muffing me.
"Confused? Man, you better gon'. Keep yo hands off me, Blaze." My fingers pushed his head to the side.
Taking ahold of my wrist, Blaze jerked me into his lap. "Why you wanna play, huh?"
I bit into my lower lip, looking away from him so I wouldn't smile. As corny as it sounded, I missed him. I didn't get to see him that morning, he'd left before I woke up.
"I'm not playing, that's you putting yo damn hands on me, with yo jealous ass," I said, my lips forming in a slight pout.
"Ain't nobody jealous. That bitch ain't got shit on me. We both know that, so why you playing? I still should smack yo

ass fah letting her kiss you. I don't like that shit, my bitch sucking on other bitches."

I slapped him. "I ain't none of yo bitch, so don't refer to me as one," I told him while getting comfortable in his lap.

"You is my bitch— Gon', man, damn. I ain't playing with yo little ass." Blaze laughed, grabbing my wrist as I tried to hit him.

"I do not like you. What you doing here anyway?" I asked while wrapping my arms around his neck.

"On my way to RadioShack for a cord until I saw that bright ass car, then ol' girl knock yo ass the fuck out." He laughed, making me roll my eyes.

"Mya did not knock me out. She got me though, but I'ma caught her ass." Grabbing my face, Blaze looked me over.

"She gave you a black eye," he said, scooting down on the seat with one hand holding my waist while the other laid on the back of the seat.

"Lair, she didn't even hit me in the eye, but in the jaw. No, Blaze. I got be at work." Shaking my head, I pushed his roaming hands away.

"Come here," his hands held my hips to him as he pushed his up, giving me a feel of his hardness.

Hell no, I'm not doing this with him. Hell no. Hell no. Damn, he feels good.

"No—"

"Why you playing? I missed you this morning." His eyes slanted. Tongue swiped over his lips as he moved my hips on him.

I leaned forward and licked his lips before mumbling lowly. "That's your fault you stayed out all night." Sitting up straight, I moved his hands. I needed to get my ass the fuck out of that damn truck.

"It's like that? Well, damn can I at least get a kiss?"

Why is he playing?

"No, I got to go. Blaze, fo'real. No, I can't. No."

"Fah real, Peaches, yo ain't gon' kiss me?" His hips pushed up again. "Well damn, can I get a hug? This probably the only time I'll see you until tomorrow." That had my eyes snapping toward him.

"What? Why?" That came out a bit too vulnerable, but there wasn't a way to take that back or say it differently. It wasn't a secret that I cared for and like spending time with him. "I mean—"

"I'll slap the fuck outda you if you do that. The fuck I tell yo ass about that shit?" He knew I cared way more then I should and he hated when I tried to pretend I didn't.

"I wasn't doing anything, so don't cuss at me." Moving his roaming hands from my body, he pushed me toward the door. "Man, get the fuck out." Was he seriously mad?

"Whatever, Blaze." Going for the door, I was roughly pulled back. "Dude what the—"

"Fuck you going?"

"You just told me to get out, fuck you mean?" I swear that man was going to make me go to jail for killing him. "What?" I asked as he looked up at me like I was stupid.

"So you ain't gon' give me a kiss?" He questioned, causing a small laugh to slip from my throat. "Fuck you laughing fah?" I didn't reply as I leaned over, pecked his lips. His eyes stayed locked on my mouth for a second before they jumped to mine.

Blaze bit into the corner of his and I was already shaking my head no, knowing that damn look all too well. Sucking his bottom lip then releasing it, I mentally groaned. Damn, why did that simple gesture have to be the sexiest thing ever?

"That ain't no damn kiss, quit playing, man," he complained.

A deep groan left my mouth as I gave in. My eyes slid closed and my hands went to the side of his face. My lips came back to his, giving them a slow soft peck then another.

God I love his lips.
Damn!

"Blaze I can't—"

"You ain't doing nothing," the words rolled from his mouth so smoothly.

Even knowing what that was leading to, the lust in me believed him. I wasn't doing anything, he was. My head went to the side as his tongue slid into my mouth. His hand tangled into my hair with the push of his hips.

Damn!

"Blaze, I'ma be late," I mumbled against his lips as my hands grasped the back of his neck.

"Quit." He took my bottom lip into his mouth, sucking on it then doing the same to the top. Blaze's hands held my grinding hips, moving them against him. The friction of our movement caused a moan to leave my mouth.

Damn I was weak.

"You gon' be late." With those words he pulled my shirt over my head.

"I can stop." *Lie,* I tossed his shirt to the side.

Blaze laid me on the seat, then pulled off my scrub bottoms along with my panties. Once they came off I was back up, kissing along his neck then down to his chest.

"Then stop."

Shit talking ass nigga. I chose to ignore that because if I tried to stop he'd be threatening to slap my ass if I didn't get back over to him. Plus, I was horny as hell now.

My back hit the seat and Blaze hovered over me, kissing my lips once then my neck.

Head tilted back, giving him more room as he pulled the skin into his warm mouth. He sucked and bit hard into my flesh, making me moan.

My hands made quick work with his button and zipper. I pushed his pants down his hips. My nails dug into his back as I pulled the full weight of his lower body into me.

"Baby girl, what you want from me?" Blaze asked, pulling back. I was so drunk on him right then, there was not one thing I could say.

"Everything," I whispered, trying to pull him back, but he stopped me by pinning my arms above my head. "Blaze," his name came out as a whine.

"What's everything?" I swear I was going to kill him.

"Everything that's you, inside and out, right now. I want to feel you, every inch of you." Coming back down to me, Blaze bit at my collar bone as his hands grasped my thighs.

"You're going to be late."

My back arched as he kissed his way to my breast, biting them through my bra, then kissing and licking down my stomach.

"I'll quit." Sad thing about saying that was that I was so serious at this moment.

Spreading my legs, Blaze kissed my mound then moved to my inner thigh where he kissed and sucked on the skin. He moved to my sex, running his tongue through my slit, opening me slightly, sucking on one lip then the other.

My pussy was throbbing painfully and I wanted to scream out in frustration, but that was Blaze, he hardly ever rushed, he always took his time.

Damn, right now ain't that time, though.

Blaze licked from my opening up to my clit, the tip of his tongue flicking it. His continuous toying with my pearl had me grabbing his head.

"Blaze!" I snapped at him as he pulled away, moving to my left thigh, kissing and sucking on my skin. He hardly even touched me and I was ready to cum from anticipation.

My legs were spread even wider, his mouth latched onto my clit as he pushed two fingers, knuckle deep, inside me causing a loud moan to leave my mouth. My hips grinded in tune with his fingers as my nails dug into his scalp.

"Oh, God!" I cried out. My teeth sank into my lip as my eyes rolled up in my head. "Ooh, ooh, sss," my sounds stretched as my hands pressed into the window.

His fingers continued to pump inside me, hitting my sweet spot every time.

242

"Ah, daddy. Ooh, Blaze!" My inner walls clamped tightly around his fingers, milking them. My hips jerked upwards, the muscles in my ass tightened and I began to shake. Blaze's mouth left my clit as did the hand holding my thigh. It wasn't until he pulled his fingers from my pussy that my eyes shot open, but before I could get a word out, Blaze roughly thrust inside me. He hit my cervix and I came hard on his dick.

"Oh, God, Blaze!" A scream tore from my throat as my body shook.

"Fuck!" He groaned out. Placing my leg on his shoulder, Blazes' hips slapped against mine. He pushed deeper inside me with every thrust.

His hand gripped my bra, pulled it down. Freeing my breasts, he took the little nub into his mouth.

My body still hadn't come down from the first orgasmic high and the pounding Blaze continued to give had another orgasm coming closer.

"Ah, ah, ah, ooh, Blaze!" I panted out, the sound of our bodies coming together grew louder as did our groans and moans. Letting my leg go, Blaze sat on his knees. Turned me around so I was on all fours.

"Shit, bae," Blaze groaned as he pushed inside me from behind, his hand coming down on my ass once, then twice.

The pleasurable sting had me throwing my ass back against him. My hips rolled, then grinded into him.

"Damn, Peaches, fuck!" He continued to groan out as I moved. Blaze pulled me up to his chest and I started to bounce on his dick as he turned my head sideways bringing our lips together.

His hand squeezed at my breast then rolled and pinched my nipple. "Fuck, bae," Blaze moaned against my mouth which had me bouncing faster, harder on him as my sex started tightening around him. "Ah, fuck," Blaze mumbled into my neck as I shook, bounced, grinded, and rolled my ass on him.

I loved the feel of him, it was something I would never get used to for the simple fact that sex with Blaze was always different from the last time. My orgasms were always harder than the ones before. His dick was simply magic and no matter how tired I was, I never wanted to stop. I felt so connected to him and even though I knew it was just lust, it felt like so much more.

Whether it was just sex for him or not I wanted my pussy to be the only one he thought about when he got in his mood. I intended to be the one and only person he came to when it came to sex. I was gon' make sure I was the best he ever had.

I pushed him on the seat then straddled his hips. Placed my feet on either side of him.

"You tryna ride?" He questioned, hands coming to my hips.

Without replying, I handled his dick, brought it to my soaking channel.

Blaze's hips bucked forward, his mushroom shaped tip pushed inside of me.

My head rolled back and a moan left my mouth as he filled me completely.

"Fuck, Peaches!" His eyes closed, mouth slightly parted as I bounced on him. His hands squeezed and slapped my ass as my hips rolled then grinded on him. "Ah, fuck, bae. Damn," Blaze groaned against my breast while slapping my ass harder.

My hands gripped tightly onto the back of the seat, my cries of pleasure grew louder than the ones before. "Ah, ah, ah. Baby, I'm cumming." My muscles squeezed around him, milking faster.

It wasn't long before my body started shaking violently from the intense pleasure that had built inside me.

Holding my hips, Blaze pounded into me with four powerful thrusts, sending us both to our climax.

"Ooh, God," I panted out as I leaned into Blaze. My face went into his neck as I breathed heavily, trying to catch my breath. My body hummed in satisfaction. I had never cum so hard in my life.

"Fuck," Blaze groaned. "Damn, bae, we forgot the condom!

Chapter 32

Peaches

"Fuck man, damn!" He stressed.

Whatever emotional connection we had was gone as the lustful high left, for him anyways.

Getting off his lap, I turned with a roll of my eyes so he didn't see. Stuff like that was why I questioned my reasons for liking him, ones I still didn't understand.

Grabbing the wipes I left in there for that reason, I began to wipe myself. The wet wipes against my heated skin felt amazing. It was hot as hell in that damn truck and those leather ass seats didn't make it better. I was feeling dehydrated.

"Can you turn on the air or let the windows down? It's hot." I continued to clean myself. Once I got to my sex I heard Blaze cuss, which I ignored. My body was still in a state of bliss and I wasn't about to let him ruin that because we were so caught up we forgot the condom, Especially since I'd been on birth control since we started having sex.

"The fuck that gon' do?" He referred to me cleaning myself.

"Keep me clean until I get home to take a shower." Shrugging, I balled the wipes inside a few clean ones then sat them to the side so I could get dress. "So what you got going on today that I'm not gon' be able to see you until tomorrow?" I asked. Even after that I still wanted to know.

"Why you acting so cool, like what I just said ain't shit? Boss, man, I'm slipping fuckin' with yo ass." I couldn't believe he was really acting like that over a forgotten condom.

"It ain't shit because I'm on birth control, but if it makes you feel any better we can go to Walgreens and get the morning after pill," I said, grabbing his phone from his jeans then throwing them at him.

"You're on birth control? Why the fuck you ain't say that then, with yo dumbass?"

Ugh, I fuckin' hate him.

"I'm not dumb, you should've just asked instead of whining like a fuckin' bitch. Believe me, ain't nobody tryna get pregnant by yo ass. Fuck you thinking. You get on my damn nerves," I snapped at him as I dialed Kimmy's number. "Blaze gon'. Like for real, don't touch me." He pissed me off then he gon' try touching me.

"Why the fuck you mad?"

"Hey, Kim. Aye, did one of y'all get my stuff?" I asked, referring to my purse and keys.

"Where the hell did you go? I though fah sho yo ass was gon' be swinging on some damn somebody," Kimmy said, which had the attitude from earlier coming back.

"Oh, bitch, I planned to, but Blaze ol' dumbass came grabbing me. I'm with him now, I was just tryna see if y'all got my stuff?" I told her.

"Ugh, what's wrong with you? Bitch, I ain't do it, damn." Kimmy was stupid. Her saying that brought a small smile to my lips.

"We'll talk about it later, I promise. But I don't wanna talk about Blaze in his face," I said and got an *ooh* from Kim.

"You ain't got shit to say about me," Blaze muffed my head to the side, making me hit him.

"Bitch, you dumb. Blaze, keep you fucking hands off me," I snapped at him.

"Do we need to come over there? Blaze will get the shit beat out his ass this day. Bitch, Lucy just got clean too. Do I need to bring her?" Kimmy asked, making me laugh. Lucy was her gun, Kimmy just like me and our other girls, stayed with heat and our permits. We weren't killers, but we were quick to shoot a bitch in the arm, leg, somewhere like that.

"Trick, n'all. His ass ain't that serious, nor is he worth meeting Lucy." As I laughed at her, Blaze pushed me again, making me glare at him.

"We'll, just say the word and you know we'll be there. Anyway, Missy crazy ass locked yo stuff in your car. Oh, and call King. Worrying ass if that mothafucka call me one mo time asking for you, I'ma shoot his black ass." Sighing, I ran a hand through my hair.

"I'ight, Kim. I'll call you when I get home. Bye, chick." With that, we hung up. Leaning back against the seat, I debated on calling King then realized I'd have to anyway because he was the only other person who had a spare key to my car.

"What's wrong with you?" Blaze asked, grabbing my arm and pulling me to him.

Bipolar bitch.

"So now we're cool because it's not a possibility of me being pregnant?" I pushed out his arms.

"Only reason you wasn't acting like I was is because yo black ass knew you were on birth control. I'm too young fah kids, man." *Did he really just say that?* Looking over at me, he shrugged. *And he was serious?*

"Bitch, yo ass thirty. Fuck you mean too young? Are you serious right now? Plus, whoever said something about having kids? Nigga, I'm twenty-four, believe me, I'm not rushing to pop any out no time soon which is the reason I got on birth control," I snapped at him as I pulled up a message box on his phone to text King.

"If that's the case, why the fuck you mad then?" He picked.

Sighing, I texted King, asking him to bring the spare key.

"Peaches, you don't hear me talking to you?" Again, I said nothing, and I soon heard nothing he was saying as I saw Krystal's name on a message. Before I could open it he snatched his phone from me.

He was still talking to that bitch?

I didn't say anything because I didn't know for sure, but I'd find out sooner or later. Messy bitches like that were always try to make shit known. "Blaze, don't touch me. Fo'real, gon'."

He once again pulled me to him, but this time he sat me on his lap and locked his arms around my waist.

God, I was so weak when it came to him.

"Bae, you mad at me?" He whispered, then kissed the sweet spot behind my ear. *I hated him, but I liked him more than I needed to.* "I was never mad, I know you're a natural born dick," I told him, not even trying to get out of his hold because it would be pointless.

"If you ain't mad, give me a kiss." That stupid smile crept back up to my lips at his words. He was so damned bipolar. Shaking my head, I looked out the window. "You know you gon' be the only chick that ever carry my seed, just not now though."

That had me laughing out. "Nigga, please. I would never have babies with you, especially not after you just straight acted like a bitch. My brother warned me about yo kind, Fuck no, sir, not me," I told him so seriously. I had my whole life ahead of me and having Blaze babies wasn't nowhere on that agenda no time soon.

"Peaches, you don't wanna have my babies? Huh?"

"Hell no. Blaze, stop!" Grabbing his wrist, I squeezed it tightly as he pushed his hands into my scrubs and panties.

"I'm my own nigga, so can't nobody warn you of me. Why you acting like that? You know in time you gon' be the Misses with my seed so stop actin... Shit, I can't let yo ass go after you just fuck me like that, fuck that. A nigga ain't never came that fuckin' hard, boss. I was like yo ass, I can't feel my legs."

I burst out laughing as I turned around, punching him. Then there was this side of Blaze which always seemed to outweigh the bad. Even so, no matter which side he showed, I couldn't help but like it, him. He was so different, dangerous, rude, and talked hella shit. Always pulling his gun and always threatening to slap some damn body. But that made him, him.

"Man, yo ass better stop hitting me before I slap yo ass. Gon' Peaches, man." He laughed, pushing me away from him.

"You stupid, why would you say that?" I laughed as I settled myself on his lap.

"What? I was being real. Shid, I'm starting to wonder, yo ass wasn't fuckin' like that before."

My brows rose at that and I muffed his head back. "Are you implying—"

"That you practicing with that chick you be kissing? Hell yeah, I'ma have to pop that bitch. She can't be fuckin' my shit." He was so stupid.

"We don't be fuckin', she's like my sister. Plus, I'm not gay. I'm just helping her make Mya jealous." I shrugged.

"Well, I need to slap her ass then. If ol girl can hit you, I should be able to pop her in those big ass lips of hers." I started laughing as he talked about Missy's lips.

"I'm telling her too, don't talk about my friend," I said, hitting him.

"I don't give a fuck. I ain't scared of her big lip ass, shits cover her whole damn face. I don't know why the fuck you laughing fah? I should slap yo ass fah kissing her." I playfully slapped him before leaning forward and kissing him. "Did I tell you to kiss me?" Smiling, I licked his cheek and laughed as he pushed me back. "Yo ass too fuckin' old to be doing that shit. Gon' Peaches, before I strangle yo ass."

"Whatever, you like that, so stop playing."

"Man, why the fuck we still in this damn parking lot, though? We been in this thang for damn near two hours?" He looked at the time on his phone.

"I thought you had something to do today?" I didn't want him missing anything important, it must have been if he wasn't gon' see me until tomorrow.

"Oh, shit. I forgot about that," he said nonchalantly. Then he looked me over before that sexy smile came to his lips and he pushed his hips up. "You tryna ride?"

A small laugh left my mouth. "No, sir. Miss Kitty need a break."

"Shit, I'm serious. We can go back to yours or mine."
He sucked his bottom lip into his mouth getting it wet.
"Stop that, we not having sex again. Plus, you got
something to do right?" I wasn't not about to have sex with him
again. *Nuh-uh. Nope!*
"N'all, I lied. I ain't got shit to do." He shrugged.
I looked at him like he was stupid. "Blaze, you lying?" I
said dumbly, again he shrugged and I hit him "Why would you
lie? I missed work just so you can get yo dick wet, seriously. Oh,
my God, he gon' fire my ass for real. Unlike you, some people
actually have to work. Damn!" My hand ran through my hair,
that was that shit.
"Why you mad fah?"
"Are you really asking me that, Blaze, seriously? You
think about it. After that shit that happened with you and Sly,
Teyo took over at the clinic. I don't know if he has something
against me or if Sly done told him what happened, but since that
shit happened Teyo ol' funky ass been down my neck. Nigga, I
need my damn job, that's how my bills get paid."
Teyo was Sly's older brother and he'd been running the
clinic as of late. What happened to Sly, I didn't know nor was I
going to ask. But his fuckin' brother was a dick and stayed on
my ass.
I'd been looking for another job, but hadn't found
anything yet. I'd gotten lucky with working for Sly because not
only was he my brothers associate, but the clinic was his. *Shid, I
needed my damn job.*
"Man, I'll fuckin' kill Teyo if he on that dumb shit," he
snapped, sitting up quick, almost making me fall from his sudden
movement.
"Blaze, don't okay. It ain't that serious—"
"The fuck you mean it ain't serious? Evidently it is if he
coming at you about yo job and yo dumbass still there," he
suddenly snapped at me.
"It's my fuckin' job that pays my bills. I'm not you,
baby, I got to work hard for mines. I need that job, so if I got to

keep my mouth shut toward the nigga that's writing my checks, then I'ma do that shit. I've been looking for something new, just haven't found nothing yet," I explained. I could simply do without working with the money my folks left me, but I didn't want to have to depend on that or King. I wanted to work for mines.

"You sound dumb as fuck. I can pay yo shit, the fuck yo talkin bout? I throw yo ass money every time we counting and its way more than that shit he's paying you."

"Do you not know me? I'm not looking for no handout. If I was in need of money I could easily get it from King. Even the money he do slip me, I don't use. I make my own, I don't want nobody paying shit for me. And if you think that's what I'm wanting, then you truly don't know shit about me and you fucking with the wrong one. Yo money is just that, yours. The shit you told me to hold is sitting in yo drawer under yo boxers. I don't want yo money, baby, believe that. And if I did, that shit you throwing ain't close to what I'll charge just to deal with half yo shit." Everything I just said was true, my daddy and King always told me shit wasn't free in the world nobody was giving you something for nothing. I don't work like that.

Mothafuckas always had a motive behind them and I wasn't gon' be dumb. Whether or not Blaze had a motive was unknown, but I doubted he did. Even so, I wasn't taking no handouts unless I was feeding they asses, then that was different.

"Man, shut the fuck up. Ain't nobody say yo ass was looking fah a damn handout. Boss, get yo dumbass out my shit, you just pissed me off," he snapped, pushing the truck door open, getting out then turning toward me. "Get the fuck out." Slipping on my shoes, I got out on my side slamming the door. "Don't be slamming my fuckin' door, I'll choke yo ass."

He was really mad because I didn't want his money? Shouldn't that be a good thing?

"You mad because I don't want yo fuckin' money, fo'real?" I did not understand that dude at all, but I knew one thing, I was not about to stand in that parking lot arguing with him. "Whatever, Blaze." Looking around the parking lot, I found my car and started making my way to it.

"Peaches, where the fuck you going?" He asked.

"To my car and wait for my brother," I called out as I kept walking. Sometimes it wasn't even worth fighting with his dumbass when later we were going to be hugged up and fucking like horny teenagers.

Once I got to my car, it wasn't long before Blaze was pulling into an empty spot next to me. "Blaze, ain't nobody 'bout to fight with you, so go somewhere."

"You gon' make me hurt you," he threatened.

My lips pursed together in a pouty manner as I rolled my eyes. "Daddy, I ain't worried about you," I said as he came closer, muffing my head back.

"Don't daddy me now. I still should slap yo ass." Laughing, I wrapped my arms around his waist. "Get yo hands up off me, I might see somebody. Damn, hey baby," he called to some girl walking by with a group of two girls and a guy. Two of the girls stopped, making Blaze laugh. "Man, I'm just fuckin' with y'all little asses, gone." Blaze laughed, shaking his head while waving them off. "Young ass bitches need they ass whooped. All that shit on they face," he said referring to their makeup.

"Why you wanna fight with me? Huh?" I mumbled, seeing one of the girls looking back at Blaze, making me roll my eyes.

"I want to, that's why." Laying my head against his chest, a yawn left my mouth as my hands slid into his back pockets. "You sleepy?" He placed me on the hood of my car. Tilted my head up as his came down. That was why fighting with him was pointless. "You want me to take you home? We can come back for your car," he said once he pulled back from the kiss.

"No, King's on his way," I told him. "You know how to break into cars?" I asked.

"Oh, damn, I'm offended as fuck. You asked me that shit because I'm black." Laughing, I pinched his back. "No, I don't."

"You are so stupid, I do not like you," I said biting at his chest.

"You wanna get in the truck, I can let the back seats down." That offer sounded so good.

"Are you going to try and have sex with me?" It was sounding too damn good for the simple fact he actually offered.

"Shid, probably. With the way yo ass rode me, sex is all I'm thinking about. See," he pushed into me and I felt his erection poke at my stomach, making me laugh. "Yo ass laughing, this shit is serious."

I continued to laugh at his stupid self, I was not about to have sex with him. Magic dick always had a bitch sleepy as hell afterwards. I mean, that knock out shit left my ass sleep for five hours and when I wake up, my body was still humming.

My body is still buzzing, pussy clenching together.

"Are you hungry?" Blaze asked and I was thankful for the topic change.

"I can eat, but you got to pay." He helped me off the hood then pulled me into his side.

"Shid, with that damn speech yo ass just gave, I thought you was gon' be paying fah yo own food. That's why I offered," Blaze said, looking down at me and shaking his head. "I guess yo ass ain't gon' be eating, huh?"

"Dude, fo'real, my stuff is locked in my car. Blaze, don't play with me. That's okay I don't know where yo ass sleeping at tonight."

"Shid, with you. Don't try to play that game, bae, 'cause yo ass know you can't sleep without me playing with those titties, so stop it." Blaze exclaimed, holding the door open for me.

I broke out laughing as I entered the restaurant.

I swear this fuckin' man get on my nerves.

Chapter 33

Peaches

"I'm dead ass serious, I never in my life, still to this day, seen a grow ass man, hood ass man, run around screaming like a bitch because of some damn bees. Shit was funny as fuck, ask King. Yo pops had niggas on the block crying laughing, grown mothafuckas. That shit was crazy, it was like once one got on his ass another came. Shit was funny as hell, he chewed our ass out later though. He was a cool ass dude," Blaze said, still laughing as he picked at his rice.

I laughed with him because I knew my dad and he hated bees. One sting would have his ass in the hospital.

"That's not funny, my daddy was highly allergenic to bees. One sting and he was swollen like a balloon and in the hospital," I told him while laughing.

"Yeah, I found that out later on, but yo brotha wasn't shit, that nigga stood there with us laughing." I couldn't come to King's defense because my mom and I always laughed to. It was just that my dad's reaction left no room for concern, his reaction was too funny. "Yo old dude was cool peoples though, some of everybody respected his ass. And the ones who didn't really ain't have a choice, but act like they did so they were fuck'd either way. He was a crazy, but smart man." Blaze spoke of my dad like they were the best of friends, which he seemed to have that effect on everyone he met.

"Dumb, but smart? It's a lot of those types around nowadays," I said, giving him a pointed look.

"Make me slap yo ass. I'm a smart, clever mothafucka if you ask me."

I laughed at that before pointing my folk at him. "Good thing I didn't ask yo ass. Blaze, gon' we in public." I laughed as he got out his seat. "You too old to be acting like that." Shaking my hea, I picked up a piece of shrimp and threw it at him. "I quit. So how you meet my dad?" I asked him, smiling at the smile he was giving me.

"Yo pops would probably kill my ass if he knew I was fuckin' his baby girl, let alone was her first. Damn, I can feel that hot bullet now." He emphasized with a rub to his chest. "I met yo old man when I was about thirteen. He was a hard mothafucka, but shid, in the end his ways paid off. Back in the day when it was just me and Sam, we ain't ever made as much money as we did before getting with yo pops. Smart man as I said.

"Both Sam and I was days from dropping out, shid, I had my moms and sister to feed, school wasn't important. A nigga thought he was on until I met yo pops. Dude had a nigga feeling little as fuck. Shid, I ain't even wanna slang no mo after he told us we were some dumb ass niggas that wasn't making shit. And to prove us right, nigga sent King's ass out on a run. 'Bout an hour later that nigga came back with twice as much then what we made in a month combined. Man, I ain't ever felt so disrespected or small in my life. I started to rock his ass and run," he recalled.

Blaze running from someone was a hard concept to grasp.

"You laughing, I'm serious. But I didn't, yo father was a scary mothafucka. Man, I hated being alone with that nigga, boss. From the shit I was hearing about his ass, I always just expected him to start shooting for no reason. But after we explained why we were slanging, he understood. Threw us both twenty-five each and told us we were working for 'em, which was cool with me. Shid, I had my moms and sister, but working with him came with a price. We had to finish school and make good grades, otherwise we weren't working.

"With the money we were making, shid, a nigga was making straight A's and B's'. He took us under him taught us a lot. You can't be in this game if you don't know the rules of it or the law, he use to always say. So once I graduated, I went to school for Criminal Justice. Never became a punk ass, but shid, I met hella niggas in that bitch tho. After I graduated, I went back and got my Masters in business." Everything else he was saying was tuned out after that. *Blaze went to college? Not once, but twice.* "Wait, wait, wait. I'm confused here." I would never understand this fuckin' man! "So you went to college?" I asked him dumbly and he laughed, like actually laughed. That was the first time he actually looked genuine, carefree. That was the first time he talked about his life to me period.

"Yep, IUN. Why you so surprised? A nigga can't go to school, damn?" He asked, laughing at me. I didn't expect thiat from him at all. I mean he was a crazy hood.

"No. I mean yeah. I just didn't—"

"Expect a nigga like me to be educated?"

"Yeah. Wait, no. Ugh, I hate you. That's not funny." Reaching over the table, I hit him because he was actually laughing at me. I didn't understand what was happening here.

"Damn, baby, you think that lowly of me? That's fuck'd up, I'm offended. I don't know who gon' play with those titties tonight because I ain't coming home. Fuck that," he said, biting into his bottom lip and trying not to laugh. But it was written all over his face and eyes.

"Nigga, please. Yo ass gon' be there rubbing and pinching on both these," I told him while pointing my fork from one breast too the other.

"And sucking," I started laughing as he licked his lips while staring at my breast.

"Yo ass is too much, I swear. No, but seriously though, I didn't mean to offend you. It's just shocking, I mean you're crazy, like really crazy," I tried to be serious. In a way I was, I just couldn't picture Blaze in a class room with people without actually killing someone.

"Fuck you, Peaches. Yo short ass gon' quit tryna play me."

"I'm playing, well not about the crazy part. I guess I can't call you a hood no more, huh?"

"What the fuck is a hood? You always say that shit." He took a drink from his Pepsi, his eyes still on me.

"What's a hood? Just that. A community that's never going to change or go anywhere. In turn, a hood is a person that's never going anywhere in life," I explained.

"That's some shallow ass shit, on boss. Damn. That's how you see me?" He asked, moving his drink out the way as he leaned on the table.

"You want me to lie or be honest?"

His brow rose at my question. "Never lie, always be real with me. Is that how you see me?"

"You're King's friend, so yeah I do. I don't mean it in an offensive manner. King's a hood. No matter how educated he is or how much money he has, he can't leave the hood alone. Something's always pulling him back. That hood mentality is embedded in him and no matter what, he won't leave it. Look at you for instance, your paid, but at the end of the day you're stuck in the hood, in these streets and it's by choice.

"Most people don't have an option, but the both of you do. King has money that can last him and some for a lifetime. I just don't understand it. Which is why I said I'll never date a hood, I don't want to be stuck with him, nor do I want to worry about whether he's going to come home or not." My straw swirled in my drink as I shrugged. The intensity his eyes held made me want to look away but I couldn't. The expression was so new, an emotion he was showing. I couldn't.

"Why you '*said*', past tense. Does that mean you changed your mind about dating a hood?" He asked licking his bottom lip.

I hadn't even realized the slip and for him to catch it told me he was actually listening to what I was saying.

"I don't know." Had I changed my mind about dating a hood? *No*, it was just him. He was a hood, no doubt about it. *He was changing everything*.

"That's not a no," he stated, fingering the bracelet on my wrist. Every cell in my body chilled, causing a slight shiver to run through me as I began losing myself in those light brown eyes of his.

"But it's not a yes," I breathed, out licking my suddenly dry lips. Grabbing my wrist, he gave it a slight tug. Automatically, I stood from my seat, walking to him. Blaze pulled me into his lap.

"But it's not a no," he replied, his nose tracing along my jaw as his hand roamed up my thigh until he reached the hem of my shirt and slipped his hand underneath.

My mind began to cloud as his fingers danced along my lower back, his nails dragging along the skin.

"I won't date a hood, it's just you." The truth was out and I wanted more than anything to pull it in because now I was vulnerable and I hated it, that, him. I didn't want to get hurt and he was, without a doubt, the one who could do just that.

Grasping the side of his face, my lips lightly brushed against his once, then twice, before tracing the slit with the tip of my tongue.

Blaze's lips parted before his mouth covered mine. His tongue slid into my mouth. He took hold of my waist, lifted and turned me so I was now straddling his hips. His hands grasped my thighs tightly. Our heads moved from one side to the other as we tried getting our mouths closer, which was impossible.

The clearing of a throat seemed to have made Blazes' hands tighten. We broke apart and I looked to my side as did Blaze.

"Hey, Boon," she spoke excitedly.

Damn!

Chapter 34

Peaches

A girl no more than sixteen or seventeen stood beside us. What had me groaning was that I knew her as well as the man she was with.

"Damn, what the hell y'all doing here? Please, tell me my moms ain't here?" Blaze said before I could speak? Damn, this was embarrassing.

"Hey, Peaches." Getting off of Blaze's lap, I let out a small laugh as I pushed my hair from my face, feeling even more embarrassed in front of the smiling teen.

"Hey, Brittany. Um, I haven't seen you at the clinic in a while." What was I suppose too say? I was embarrassed as hell and that was the first thing that came to mind.

"Forget that, let's talk about you getting freaky with—"

"Britt, shut up before I slap yo ass. Is ma here with y'all?"

"Nope, just me and dad. We were car shopping," she said excitedly before seating in my seat.

"Hey, Peaches, can't speak?" Marcus spoke.

"Hey, Marcus. Damn, it's been long." As embarrassing as it was, seeing an old face was always nice, especially Marcus' sexy ass.

"It has been—" Marcus started, but Blaze cut him off.

"Hold up. How the hell y'all know each other?" Suspiciously, he questioned.

I rolled my eyes at him before grabbing a chair from the table behind us and sat next to Blaze. Marcus did the same.

"Oh, we used to hook up all time," I said in a bored tone, which he apparently didn't catch. "I'm playing. King used to drop me off at his gym all the time after my mom and dad passed." I shrugged before smiling. "Which explains why I can beat yo ass," I said, laughing as did Brittany and Marcus.

"Girl, my momma thought you were a man when Boon came over all beat up. When she found out it was you, she like that little ass girl," Brittany explained.

I was offended by the little ass girl comment. I was not little, but average height.

"Britt, watch yo mouth," Marcus told her and she smacked her lips while rolling her eyes.

"So, how long you've been dating my brotha?" She asked,

I opened my mouth then closed it. I couldn't say we weren't dating because they'd just seen us.

"We're not dating, we're getting to know each other," I told her truthfully, again she rolled her eyes.

"Well, if that mark on yo neck is to indicate anything, it's that he knows you pretty well," she said with a crooked smile.

I was about to put a muzzle on that damn girl.

Blaze barked out a laugh before balling up his fist and holding it out for her to pound.

"Damn well, Britt, damn well," he stated, looking down at me, winking.

I looked at Marcus who was watching Blaze and I with a weird look.

"Anyways, Marcus, how's the gym going?" I changed the subject.

"Good, you should come by. I'm sure my guys would love seeing you again. How's your brother."

"I'll do that. And King doing good, still crazy and controlling as hell, but he's good. He was supposed to have been here, though," I said, feeling the pockets on my scrubs before remembering my phone was locked in the car. "Bae, can I see your phone?" I picked up Blaze's drink, getting some.

"Bae? But you're not dating, right?" Brittany said, I was about to slap her ass.

"Britt, shut yo ass up before I slap the shit outda you." I started choking off the pop as he spoke my thoughts.

261

"Whatever," she said, and this time I laughed.

"He be slapping you, huh?" I asked her, laughing. Shid, I knew the feeling, so I couldn't blame her for shutting up. "You do not be slapping that damn girl with yo heavy handed ass," I said, muffing his ass.

"Fuck I do, like I slap yo ass. You better keep yo hands off me," Blaze said and I muffed his ass again.

"Baby, I ain't worried about you. Brittany, I got these spiked brass knuckles, just let me know when you need them. Blaze gon'," I laughed as he pulled me out of my seat and back into his lap. "I was only playing, dang."

"Don't be influencing my sister with yo violent ass. Brass knuckles don't stop yo ass from getting slapped and it damn sho' ain't gon stop her."

"So what, but it make you think twice." My hands ran up the back of his head.

"You better stop," he said as my nails pressed into his scalp.

My tongue over my lips, getting them wet, I bit into the corner of my bottom lip, giving him a sexy little smile.

"I'm not doing anything, we just talking." Pulling his head back, my mouth went to his neck, sucking and biting at the skin.

"Aw shit. Daddy, give me yo phone."

That little girl was too much. Once Blaze's hands tighten on my waist, my right hand left his head. Digging into the cup on the table, taking a handful of ice, I quickly stuck my hand into the back of his shirt at the same time my lips covered his.

Blaze started mumbling while trying to push me away, but I held onto him tightly before I started laughing.

"Get the fuck off me," he said as I quickly got off his lap and went behind Brittany's chair.

"Blaze, gon' now. Ain't nobody playing with you, for real." Shaking his head, he glared at me as he shook the ice out his shirt.

A Dangerous Love 2
Can't Let Go

"I'm still slapping yo ass, I promise," he threatened and I laughed, knowing he wasn't going to. Then again, his ass probably was.

"I'm sorry, let's kiss and make up." I walked over to him, but he pushed me away. "Bae, stop. Blaze, you not gon' kiss me?" I mimicked him as I puckered my lips. "Blaze, fo'real, you ain't gon' kiss me?" Shaking his head he started laughing.

"Boss, yo ass, man," he said as I pressed my lips to his.

"You still gon' play with my titties tonight?" I whispered against his lips and again he laughed before pulling me into his lap.

"Aw, y'all are so cute. This going on Facebook. Peaches, what's yo name on there so I can tag you?" Brittany asked as Marcus came back with a plate full of food. "Where mine at?"

Marcus looked at her like she was crazy. "Up there, you better get up and go make one."

Blaze started laughing at his little sisters shocked face.

"Fo'real, Daddy, it's like that? You tryna show out now? Okay, remember that," she told him as he ate.

"Who are you talking to? No, you remember this when you waking me up to find a car."

Brittany's face turned serious after that. "I was just playing, why you getting serious?"

I started laughing, she reminded me so much of my younger self. Especially with the way she was talking to Marcus, the only difference with that was my dad would've hauled off and slapped my ass in the mouth.

"Blaze, let me see your phone so I can call King, he should've been here by now." It wasn't like King not to show up or call for that matter, so I was starting to get worried.

"He'll be here chill—"

"It's been like an hour, he never takes this long to come when I call him. Has he called or texted your phone back?" I asked him. King always, and I mean always showed up when I called, no matter what. Something must have happened.

263

"Calm yo ass down, I told him not to come yet. I'll call him when you ready," Blaze informed me.

I breathed out a sigh of relief. "Don't ever do something like that without telling me, God." After I snapped at him, a smile came to my lips. "So you wanted to spend time with me, huh?"

"Something like that. Don't let that shit go to yo head. Peaches, gon' with yo childish ass," Blaze complained as I kept kissing him, making his sister laugh.

"Boon, stop acting like that. You was just about to have sex with the girl in here, so stop frontin'," Brittany said.

"Yeah, stop frontin, Booney." I laughed, saying his name with a hard B. "Now gimme kiss before I slap yo ass."

"Y'all are so cute. Boon, give her a kiss," Brittany said with her phone already up. Marcus paid us no mind, he was too busy eating.

"Gimme kisses, Blaze." I puckered up my lips, pressed them to his, and heard the camera snap. "See, that wasn't hard, now was it?" I asked while rubbing my lips across his. God, I felt like one of those love struck teenagers people saw in movies.

"Hell yeah. Now get yo ass off me." He pushed me off his lap.

"Whatever, just remember this later," I stated while grabbing my cup to go refill it. Once I got there, I shook my head as his little sister appeared next to me.

"So, why you don't wanna date my brotha? I mean, he's likes you." she asked.

"I like him too, but have you met yo brother." She laughed at that as she got a cup.

"He's rough, but he's kinda nice, just in a hard way. Besides, he's different, okay maybe not. It's hard to explain, but besides with my mom and me, he doesn't joke or play as much with anyone like he does with you. So that's something, right?" I shrugged. "Look, I just want my brotha happy and apparently your making him just that. He's not the nicest, but... Forget it. There's no way in hell I can make him look good. He's crazy, always fighting… Wait, you know this yet you still like him?" She asked, looking at me with a confused look.

"Yeah, I do," I said, leaning against the railing, glancing over at the table where Blaze sat talking to Marcus. My attention was soon drawn back to Brittany as she suddenly slapped my arm hard. "Ow, what the hell wrong with you?" I was about to slap her little ass.

"You like him, really like him. Well, that's good, right? I can tell he really likes you though." That little girl was everywhere with her damn questions.

If her heavy handed ass hit me again, I was knocking her out. Shit, had my damn arm stinging.

"How you know he likes me?"

She looked me over before placing a hand on her right hip. "For one, look at you. You're wearing scrubs, that's something my mom walk around the house in. Yet you have that on and my brotha is all over you. Enough said. So does this mean you're going to be sticking around for a while?" I laughed at her and started walking away. "Peaches, I'm serious."

"If he acts right, it's a possibility," I said going back to my seat.

"Well, that's not a no." She sounded like Blaze's ass, making me laugh.

"It's not a yes, either," I stated and she rolled her eyes.

"Whatever, I know the truth. Anyway, where you get yo car from?" Shaking my head, I laughed.

"My brother got it for my birthday last year."

"Yo brother got you a car, damn he must be nice. Booney got a car lot and won't *give* me a car."

"Damn right, I ain't giving yo ass shit," Blaze told her as he stood up and I noticed immediately his mood had changed.

"You okay?" My hand brushed against his only to have him move it away.

"We 'bout to go, tell ma I'll be over there later. Come on," he ignored my question completely.

Not wanting to argue, I got up with him.

"It was nice seeing the both of you again," Brittany got out her seat coming to give me a hug.

"Boon, is you bringing her over to the house later?" She asked, letting me go.

"N'all, she got something to do," he lied, but I keep my mouth shut.

"Well, are you bringing her to mommy's barbeque Friday?" Brittany continued her questioning.

"N'all, she ain't coming," Blaze answered, his body language and tone of voice showed his irritation.

I'm ready to go now.

"Why?" She asked slowly.

"Brittany, stop asking questions. Sit down and eat," Marcus said to her in a hard voice which made her flop down in the chair.

What the hell did we miss?

"Whatever, Peaches. You got Facebook, Instagram or Twitter?" She was too much.

"No she—" Blaze started, but I cut him off.

"Yeah, I got Facebook, JuicyPeach1. Tag me when you post them pictures," I told her and she waved me off.

"Girl, I already posted them and that video, but I'll tag you though."

"Man, bring yo ass on, damn. And yo ass bet not post shit on Facebook, I'ma knock you the fuck out if you do," Blaze snapped, yanking me toward him, almost making me fall.

Righting myself, I punched him. "The hell wrong with you pulling on me like you stupid? Boy," I had to bite into my bottom lip so I wouldn't seriously cuss his ass out. I didn't know what happened with him and Marcus, but he wasn't going to be taking his anger out on me. Pushing past him, I walked toward the door then went out of it.

"Peaches!" Turning around I punched his ass hard as hell.

"Don't ever yank me like that again. I ain't done shit to you," I snapped at him. Grabbing my arm, he yanked me back before roughly pushing me into the brick like wall.

"Yo ass better quit fuckin' hitting me, I done told you. The fuck you go and give her yo Facebook shit fah?" *Is he serious?*

"You mad because I gave her my name on Facebook?" I asked dumbly.

"Yo ass shouldn't be talkin' to her, if she put that shit up there I'ma knock yo ass out," he snapped at me.

"Are you fuckin' serious? Yo dumbass heard her say she was posting that shit, I didn't tell her to do it. So why the fuck you getting mad at me?"

"This why I don't introduce bitches to my folks, y'all dumbasses start to get to fuckin' attached," he spat out harshly as he pulled me back then slammed me into the wall again.

Over some pictures, fuckin' pictures he knew she was taking. Every time it seemed like we're going somewhere, that shit happened.

"Blaze, let me go." I spoke calmly as my breathing picked up. He looked like he wanted to say something, but I jerked my arms in his hold. "Let me go, I don't give two fucks about what you got to say. I swear, I don't. Go to one of yo bitches that hadn't got attached," I told him while yanking my arms from his hold then pushing him back.

I was pissed to the point that my nails bit into the palms of my hands and my body got hot. I just want to hurt him, shoot him, or stab his ass, whichever thing I got my hands on first.

Hearing Blaze unlock his door, I went to his trunk. Opening it, I grabbed the tire iron.

"Peaches, calm yo ass the fuck down. Boss, you come at me, I'm laying you out," he threatened.

I was so tempted.

I went to my passenger side, swung the tire iron, breaking the window. After I knocked the glass out, I unlocked my door.

"The fuck yo dumbass do that fah?"

"Shut the fuck up talkin' to me!" Biting into my bottom lip, I threw the tire iron so hard toward his dumbass, hoping it hit him, but he ducked just in time.

Hurriedly, I jumped in my car and slammed the door. I got my keys out, started up and then pulled off.

I'm so done with this bipolar nigga!

Chapter 35

Peaches

"I can't believe you broke yo window, I would've busted his. Boo, you're still shaking," Ebony said, coming to sit next to me. After the whole ordeal with Blaze, I went to Ebony's. Already knowing Blaze would've gone to my apartment. I'd been here for an hour and a half, still pissed.

I had never walked away like I just had when I felt that angry. My legs bounced rapidly and my hands shook violently.

"E, I just want to kill him. God! Ugh!" Getting up out my seat, I started pacing. "He was so pissed over a fuckin' picture, like actually mad. If he ain't want her takin' the shit, his ass should've said something then, not after. Talkin' 'bout, that's why he doesn't let bitches meet his people!" I just wanted to hit something.

"Peach, calm down. Here baby, drink this." Ebony handed me a shot glass which I quickly threw back.

"Ugh, E. What the fuck is that?" My hand rubbed at my burning chest.

"Hennessey, good right?" She asked, handing me another shot.

"Hell n'all, that shit burns." I picked up the shot glass, tossed it back once again.

"You cool yet?" Ebony's fingers combed through my hair

I shook my head. "No, I still want to kill him," I told her truthfully as I took another shot.

"Okay, go shower. I'll find you something to wear then call the girls and we'll all go to Voodoo," she said and I shook my head.

"Nothing good can come if I go to Voodoo, so I'm cool. I'll shower though." After throwing back two more shots, I went into the guest room, going straight to the bathroom to shower.

***

"No, I don't love anyone but you bitches and King. I like him, I guess, and I don't like him no mo. My life is just so messed up, I feel like a bipolar psycho. I got lesbians punching me in the face, then I got you bitches that had unstable relationships, or are in unstable relationships, whatever sound better, so you bitches can't really help me. We should all just turn lesbians and date each other, well except for Missy. Her unstable girlfriend fights, that bitch hit me hard." My friends started laughing at my drunk rambling.

"Wait, Mya hit you?" Angel asked, laughing.

"Yep, bitch rocked my black ass. I was like, shid, I didn't think shit at the time, I was like frozen. My head was like, oh my God, this biatch just stole on me. That bitch was shocked though, she only hit me once then Missy just flipped. Ooh! Bitch, Blaze was talking about yo lips, girl. I was like, nuh uh, don't talk about my bitch. Ooh—"

"If yo ass 'ooh' one mo time I'ma punch you," Kimmy said, laughing.

"Nuh uh, bitch. Yo sista done already got yo hit. But you know I'ma tapping that ass when I see that bitch. And Missy, I ain't talkin' in that way either, so don't come swinging on me. Ooh— Ow, Kim."

"Bitch, I told you don't say that shit again."

"Sorry, damn. But guess what?" I said, smiling hard.

"I don't think I wanna know with that look," Ebony said, making me glare at her.

"Fuck you, bitch, but why I see Marcus today."

"Who?" They said in unison, making me roll my eyes as I got up, stumbling to the radio.

"Sexy, chocolate Marcus. The one with the gym. Pretty, hazel eyes, cocky, waves. Oh, my God, I used to be so in love with his calves and his arms. Angel used to always try rubbing up on him. Girl, I used to want to kill yo ass. Oh, this my song!" I practically yelled as Jodeci's *Come and Talk To Me* played. I was wasted and numb.

The numbness I was enjoying to the fullest. Grabbing Angel, I started singing to her like we use to do when we were sixteen, seventeen.

"Oh, Marcus. I remember him. God I use to love that man," Angel suddenly said, making us laugh. "What?"

"Yo ass dumb, like fo'real, blonde hair blue eyes all day," I said, laughing and she pushed me, making me fall on the floor.

"I hate you," she said before jumping on top of me.

"Why you do that now? I got to pee," I started saying, but trailed off as the front door opened. King walked in with like three different dudes.

"Well damn?" Was mumbled by the four of us. We all looked at each other then broke out laughing. "How I look?" I asked Angel and she started laughing harder.

"Like shit," King said, unfreezing and walking into the living room. "What the fuck y'all ass in here doing?" He looked at all of us then the table. "Y'all drunk my shit?"

"Oh, I like this song too. Angel get off me, damn. You crushing my chest, I can't breathe," I said, breathing out a sigh. "King, can you get her off me, please?"

"Y'all drank my shit?"

"Oh, my God. Boy, yes. Now get her off me." Shaking his head he walked out the room. "Bitch." Noticing the three dudes still standing there, I looked them over. All were sexy, two chocolate brothers and a caramel one with thick full lips. "Damn baby, that's too much lips for one man. Can I ride?" Wasted, but serious as hell, "I wouldn't mind sitting on his face, not at all."

"You and sitting on faces. Yo nasty ass need to stop," Kimmy laughed loudly. That bitch wasn't talkin. 'bout shit.

I rolled us over, then pushed my hands into Angel's shoulders. She grunted as I got up. I fixed my hair, then walked over to ol' dude. Once in front of him, I stuck my hand out.

"I'm Peaches," I introduced myself to the guys, taking my hand, each one shook it until dude with the lips shook and held it.

"I'm Trell, that's Donnie and Black," he said, pointing to each guy. Nodding, I waved at them before stepping closer to Trell.

"Peaches, what the fuck you doing?" Groaning, I shook my head as King came from the back.

"I ain't gon' get no head, damn. I really want to see what those felt like," I mumbled to myself. "I'm just being friendly, King." I lied.

"King, come here. let me show you something in the room real quick," Ebony winked at me, I loved that bitch.

"So, what you say, baby, can I ride?" I asked and dude laughed.

"Straight forward, I like that."

"Always. So what you say?" Holding my hand out, he took it and I started to lead him toward the guest room until the doorbell rang, making me groan. "I'll be right back." When I got closer to the door, I glanced back to see ol' dude looking at my ass. "Don't worry, you'll be tasting it real soon." I spoke to myself out loud as I opened the door. "Oh, shit." At the sight of Blaze, I cussed then quickly tried to slam the door shut. "Why are you here, man, damn. Move yo big ass out the way so I can close the damn door," I snapped while pressing my hands against the door, pushing as my feet tried dig into the tilted floors, but I was sliding.

"What the fuck is wrong with you?" Blaze asked, successfully pushing the door opened.

"Ain't nothing wrong with me," I stomped to the living room and snatched my stuff. I was not staying there with him.

"Who the fuck tasting what soon?" He boomed behind me.

I pretended like I didn't hear him until I heard a loud slap and turned around to see Trell on the floor.

"It was this nigga, right? Or was it him?" He moved to Donnie.

"Blaze, would you go some damn where. It was nobody, damn." I pushed him away from Donnie.

"Peaches, I'm 'bout to slap yo dumbass. What the fuck yo problem? Why you ain't answering yo damn phone?"

I wasn't about to deal with him. "King, come get your friend!" I was too fuck'd up to fight with his ass.

"The fuck y'all niggas in here doing? Trell, what the fuck happened to yo mouth?" King asked, looking pissed.

"Blaze dumbass hit him. You deal with him, I'm gone," I said, about to walk to the door, but Blaze grabbed me. That's when King stepped up, taking a hold of Blaze.

"Dude, I done already told yo ass what it is when it comes to her," King told him. Already knowing I was gon' have to whoop Blaze's ass, I grabbed the spike brass knuckles from my purse, putting them on.

"Get the fuck off me, this ain't got shit to do with you, my nigga." Blaze's words ran short as Trell rocked his ass. "Oh, you done fuck'd up, nigga," was all he said before he knocked Trell's ass so fuckin' hard he fell on the floor then flipped over. It looked so unreal for the simple fact that Trell was slightly bigger than Blaze. So for his big ass to flip over like he did looked like he weighed no more than a pound. Seeing that sobered a bitch up real quick. What was wrong with him?

Angel, still drunk self-stumbled as she got off the floor a few inches from where Trell fell. Out of nowhere, Donnie grabbed Blaze from behind. Before King could get to him, I jumped on his back. My arm locked around his neck as my free hands pounded into the side of his face.

Dude suddenly ran back into the wall, knocking me against it, which loosened my hold on him. Turning around, dude knocked the shit out my ass. It was nothing like King's hits, but it still hurt. He swung again and I ducked, causing him to hit the wall. Then I came back up, sending an uppercut to his chin, then punching him in the jaw hard. The spikes pierced into his flesh. Once he fell, I started stomping him, my bare feet slamming hard into his face.

"Fuck ass nigga!" I spat out as I kept kicking until I was grabbed from behind with my arms locked to my side.

"Peach, he's out, baby girl, calm down," King said, holding on to me as he walked away from the unconscious man on the floor. "You cool, man?"

"Yeah, my damn hand hurt though," I said, shaking my right hand. He placed me on my feet and I grabbed my purse from the floor.

"B, let that nigga up, man, he done." No sooner than King said that, two shots went off and I quickly pulled my nine, pointing it, turning toward Blaze, as did King. "B, what the fuck nigga?" King snapped at him whereas I just stood there, frozen, gun still pointed his way, watching the blood seep from Trell's head into the carpet.

Black, dude King knocked out, was back up, gun in his hand pointing it toward Blaze. King was too busy focusing on Trell's dead body to see. Black pulled the hammer on his desert eagle.

"Don't!"

Chapter 36

Peaches

I screamed as my finger pulled the trigger.
I shot.
I kept pulling the trigger. I watched the jerking of his chest as he stumbled back into the wall. He fell against, it then slide to the floor, eyes wide.
The clank signaled the emptiness of the gun. Even so, I continued to pull the trigger. His eyes were blank, void of emotions, lifeless.
"Damn," the word came out regretfully as a hand covered the gun I held, still shooting. Pushing the gun down, it was soon pried from my fingers, pulling me out my dazed state. I looked at Blaze.
"I… I had to. He was—" I was mumbling until Blaze cut me off.
"I know." That was my first body and I didn't know how to react. I wasn't a heartless killer so I couldn't say I felt nothing. A life was a life and I just took somebody's. I'd shot at a few people, but I never killed anyone.
I felt a certain kind a way, but I didn't know the feeling. The main thought in my head was what if he had kids. I just took someone's father away from them. Even so, I had to. He was going shoot Blaze and I couldn't let him do it.
Two more shots sounded, making me jump as I quickly turned toward the sound. King stood over Donnie with his gun pointed at him, putting two holes in his head.
"Fuck, man. Ebony, go to my house, take them with you. Blaze, call the twins," King instructed.
"I already did, they're on the way," Blaze said. Besides him and King, no one else moved. The girls stood frozen in the hall's entranceway just as shocked as I was.
"Why the fuck y'all just standing there? Get y'all dumbass in the room and get yo shit. Hurry the fuck up," King

snapped at Ebony, which pulled her out of the shocked state she was in.

"Don't yell at me."

"Ebony, it ain't the time. You know what? Just get the fuck out," King said in a calm voice.

"I'll be at Kimmy's, y'all lets go." Ebony grabbed her purse and headed for the door. She bumped past King, but he grabbed her pushing her roughly into the wall.

"When I get home, yo ass better be there, otherwise I'ma beat yo ass," he told Ebony before kissing her. "Go." He nodded toward the door as he let her go. Once the door closed behind them. King turned our way, walking straight up to Blaze and throwing his fist into his face. "This is why I ain't want her fuckin' with you. Nigga, she just got a body when this shit could've been fuckin' avoided. Damn!" King snapped at him.

Walking over to the couch, I sat down. My hand ran through my hair before rubbing my forehead.

"Who were they?" I asked King.

"Nobody important, just some block niggas that ran errands for me. Don't worry about this."

Easy for him to say.

But I was going to try and do just that. I did what I had to and would do it again if need be.

"I did what I had to." It wasn't a shrugging matter, but I shrugged. Sighing, I got off the couch, grabbing my purse and keys. "I'm going home. I'll see you later." Kissing King on the cheek I walked toward the door. "Keep the gun, I don't want it." Closing the door behind me, I went to my car.

"Peaches, hold up," Blaze called, but I ignored him as I started up my car. "Peaches!" He yelled as I pulled off.

***

My skin was red, my hands felt raw from how hard I scrubbed them to get the blood off. But no matter how hard I did,

I still saw blood as well as Black's lifeless eyes staring into my mine.

My eyes closed and I stuck my head under the shower spray. The steamy hot water pounded against my body, rinsing off soap that covered me. I washed my skin over and over again until the water turned cold.

I wrapped the towel around my body then walked into my room.

"What are you doing here?" I stared at Blaze who sat on the edge of my bed with his head in his hands.

When he heard me, his head came up, his eyes locked with mine.

"About earlier—" He started to explain, but I didn't want to hear it.

My head moved from one side to the other.

"It doesn't even matter, you said what you had to. Honestly, I don't care no more. I'm done, I just can't do this with you. Just go." I couldn't do that with him.

"The shit coming out yo mouth is just that. You care, if you hadn't yo ass would've let dude shoot my ass. So kill that bullshit you spitting." He came toward me and I moved back.

"Don't touch me. I didn't let him shoot you because your King's friend. Blaze, move, don't touch me." Pushing him back, I walked to my dresser and felt him follow. My eyes shut tight as I let out a shaky breathe. I was falling, no I fell hard for him and there was no coming back from it if tonight was anything to go by.

"Why you lying? You knew this was me from the beginning, but now you wanna be done? N'all, man, fuck that. We rockin', ain't no backing out with me unless I say so and I ain't said shit." He turned me around then placed me on the dresser.

How was that fair? It wasn't.

"Just let me go, be done with me. That's what I want, I don't want this no more, I don't want you so let me go." I couldn't do this.

"N'all." Blaze yanked the front of my towel as he forced himself between my legs, his pants already undone and down his hips.

That wasn't right.

"Blaze, don't. Please don't," I pleaded desperately. I couldn't fight him even though I wanted to so bad. But I was too far in. In too deep. My body had already given in, surrendering to him. "I hate you so much."

"No you don't." With that he thrust inside me and I cried out. "I can't let this go, you go. Mmm, fuck." He groaned into my ear as I panted heavily. Blaze held my pelvis tightly to him as he dug into me.

He rolled his hips before he started to drive roughly into my wet core. Blaze's mouth soon went to my right breast. He sucked on the little pebble.

My head fell against the mirror on the dresser as Blaze pulled my legs over his shoulders. Gripping my thighs, he lifted me off the dresser. His pounding became furious.

My cries grew louder from the pleasurable pain he caused. My nails bit into his forearms, holding onto him, hating it but not wanting it to stop. And that had my nails digging deeper into his flesh, wanting to hurt him.

Blaze moved to the bed, laying me on my side as he settled himself behind me holding my left leg up. I moaned out from the sensation.

Hands fisted the sheets, forehead pressed against the mattress as I cried louder. Blaze kissed and sucked at my shoulder as he kept up his rough thrust, making the wet sound of our body's grow louder. Within seconds I was cumming and screaming his name like a banshee.

He flipped me on my back, his hands held my shoulder. Blaze pulled out then rammed his monstrous dick back into my contracting channel.

I couldn't move up the bed or away from him. My nails raked along his back before going to his ass, tryna pull him in deeper. Blaze bit into the side of my breast, grunting. Lifting his head, he covered his mouth with mine as I rolled us over. His hands squeezed my ass while I moved back and forth. Thrusting his hips up as I rolled, bounced and rocked on him. The sensation was so intense I didn't know how I wanted to move ,I just knew I wanted to get to that heavenly ending. Then again I didn't want that, I wanted to feel him, feel that he needed me, wanted me.

I hated that it had to come to sex for me to feel that, but it was a feeling, his feelings. All I needed was to know he felt something.

And I guess that was the only way.

***

My head lay on Blaze's chest. Fingers slowly moved alongside his waist, drawing invisible circles as my leg nested comfortably between his. We just lay in bed, not saying a word. I honestly didn't know what to say or how to feel at that moment. I was becoming weak because of him, I was too attached. And the fact that he wouldn't let me go had a blank hope settling inside me. Everyone I said I didn't want to be like, I felt I was slowly becoming. And I hated it. Hated him.

"I didn't mean that shit I said earlier, I don't even know why the fuck I blew up like that," Blaze said, letting out a breath as the hand on my ass began trace invisible patterns.

"It doesn't even matter—"

"Peaches, don't do that shit, man, damn. A nigga tryna apologize," he snapped, making me roll my eyes.

"Do you really think it's that easy? Spit that stupid shit you say then apologize?" I asked while looking up at him.

"Yeah." Bad thing about that, he was serious.

"Are you really this cold or is it just a defense mechanism?"

"Defense mechanism? I ain't got no type of anxieties. Man, yo ass can take the damn apology or don't. I ain't gon' give a fuck whether you do or not. I done apologized and I ain't gon' keep doin' the shit."

"This what I'm talking about, Blaze—"

"Man, I ain't tryna hear that shit. Damn, yo ass always got to be whining about some shit. Shut the fuck up, boss," he snapped as he removed my body from his.

"I don't whine about anything, but it ain't cool the way you talk to me either. I should've let that mothafucka shoot yo dumbass." Even though I didn't mean it, I wanted to hurt him like he had hurt me so I snapped, spat those words out harshly. Only out of anger.

His hand shot out so fast. Successfully, Blaze slapped the hell outda me.

"The fuck you just say? Bitch, don't ever speak no bullshit like that." He looked so mad, Blaze got out the bed and started pulling on his clothes.

I watched him silently, until he had everything on before I started talking shit again.

"Yeah, get yo ass the fuck out you trifling—"

"I ain't too triflin', yo hoe ass just fuck'd me you stupid bitch," he spat harshly.

"I fuckin' hate yo ass."

"But you love my dick. And yo ass wanna call somebody triflin' when yo hoe ass open yo legs fah any nigga with a mouth," his voice boomed.

Grabbing the lamp off the nightstand, I threw it at his head. When he ducked, I jumped off the bed and ran up on him, swinging.

"You a disrespectful ass nigga. I fuckin' hate you!" I yelled at him as I punched harder. Grabbing me by my neck, Blaze slapped me once, then twice before throwing me on the bed.

"I don't give a fuck! Bitch, you ain't special. Yo ass ain't shit but a quick nut. Another piece of pussy, that's all yo ass gon' ever be to me." The harsh reality of his words had a lump forming in my throat and my eyes burning as they began to water.

Licking my lips, a laugh left my mouth as my eyes locked with his.

"I hate you and I wish I hadn't stopped him." At that moment I wished I didn't stop him from getting shot.

"You say that now, but you just like every other dumb bitch I fuck. Desperate and thirsty for a nigga to lie to you that good shit then fuck you like he mean it." He spat on my floor as he looked at me like I wasn't nothing,

I bit hard into my bottom lip as I nodded my head, but that didn't stop the tears from falling and rolling down my cheeks.

"Get out," my voice was calm, but I was anything but. Without another word he turned around and walked out of my room, seconds later I heard the front door slam shut. I wasn't gon' break down, I was better than that.

My shoulders shook violently as my chest heaved up and down. Tears silently rolled down my cheeks non-stop. I curled into my covers without a sound, just letting water fall from my eyes.

Blaze wasn't worth it.
I was done with him.

To Be Continued...

A Dangerous Love III

Coming Soon

Coming Soon From Lock Down Publications

BLOOD OF A BOSS

By **Askari**

BONDS OF DECEPTION

By **Lady Stiletto**

DON'T FU#K WITH MY HEART **II**

By **Linnea**

BOSS'N UP **II**

By **Royal Nicole**

LYING LIPS **II**

By **Mahaughani Fiyah**

SLEEPING IN HEAVEN, WAKING IN HELL **III**

By **Forever Redd**

THE KING CARTEL **II**

By **Frank Gresham**

RICH MAN'S WOMAN, POOR MAN'S DREAM

By **Kanari Diamond**

THE DEVIL WEARS TIMBS **III**

A Dangerous Love 2
Can't Let Go

By Tranay Adams

LOVE KNOWS NO BOUNDARIES **III**

By Coffee

Available Now

LOVE KNOWS NO BOUNDARIES **I & II**

By **Coffee**

SLEEPING IN HEAVEN, WAKING IN HELL **I & II**

By **Forever Redd**

THE DEVIL WEARS TIMBS **I & II**

By **Tranay Adams**

DON'T FU#K WITH MY HEART

By **Linnea**

BOSS'N UP

By **Royal Nicole**

A DANGEROUS LOVE

By **J Peach**

CUM FOR ME

An **LDP Erotica Collaboration**

THE KING CARTEL

By **Frank Gresham**

LYING LIPS

By **Mahughani Fiyah**

BOOKS BY LDP'S CEO, CA$H

TRUST NO MAN

TRUST NO MAN 2

TRUST NO MAN 3

BONDED BY BLOOD

SHORTY GOT A THUG

A DIRTY SOUTH LOVE

THUGS CRY

THUGS CRY 2

TRUST NO BITCH

TRUST NO BITCH 2

TRUST NO BITCH 3

TIL MY CASKET DROPS

Coming Soon

TRUST NO BITCH (EYEZ' STORY)

THUGS CRY 3

BONDED BY BLOOD 2

Made in the USA
San Bernardino, CA
20 February 2016